THE MAN FROM BARBAROSSA

Nobody could have foreseen that the abduction of an old man in   jersey would be the prelude to a drama played out on the world's stage. Or that it was the first step in a plot so ingenious and skilful that the stability of nations would rock wildly to its adroit tune. Or that around the world a name now indelibly associated with the horror of genocide—Babi Yar—would once again be headline news. Or that soon an unlikely alliance would take place between the KGB, the Israeli Mossad, and the French and British Secret Intelligence Services. And all because of an organisation, hitherto unknown, the *Scales of Justice*. For James Bond it meant a twist that no-one could have invented in their wildest dreams before the era of *glasnost* and *perestroika*—for this new assignment James Bond would be operating under KGB control!

JAMES BOND
in

John Gardner's
THE MAN
FROM
BARBAROSSA

CHIVERS PRESS

Library of Congress Cataloging-in-Publication Data

Gardner, John E.
    The man from Barbarossa / John Gardner.
        p.   cm.—(Eagle large print)
    ISBN 0–7927–1350–8 (softcover)
    1. Large type books.   I. Title.   II. Series.
[PS3557.A712M36   1992]
823′.914—dc20
                                                             92–7448
                                                             CIP

British Library Cataloguing in Publication Data available

This Large Print edition is published by Chivers Press, England, and Curley Publishing, Inc, U.S.A. 1993.

Published in the U.S.A. by arrangement with The Putnam Berkley Group and in the British Commonwealth by arrangement with Hodder and Stoughton Ltd.

U.K. Softback ISBN 0 7451 3410 6
U.S.A. Softback ISBN 0 7927 1350 8

Photoset, printed and bound in Great Britain by
REDWOOD PRESS LIMITED, Melksham, Wiltshire

For Ed & Gretchen
who both know the realities of
living double lives for their country

CONTENTS

No gravestone stands on Babi Yar;
Only coarse earth heaped roughly on the gash:
Such Dread comes over me.

Yevgeni Yevtushenko: *Babi Yar*

THE MAN FROM BARBAROSSA

BABI YAR

They came in an orderly fashion, the Jews of Kiev. They came anxiously though not really afraid—not yet, for the notices posted around the city had simply said they were to be relocated. They came with what they could carry. They came in their hundreds, men, women and children. They came with hope. They came at peace with God. They came unprepared. They came, rightly as it turned out, with fear. They came to the corner of Melnik and Dekhtyarev Streets, just as they had been told.

Hitler's invasion of Soviet Russia, code-named Operation Barbarossa, had begun only three months, seven days earlier, on June 22nd 1941, for it was now September 29th of that same year—the year Stalin had disregarded all warnings of a Nazi invasion, believing it to be a trap set by England to promote bad feeling between Russia and Germany.

Ten days previously, the Twenty-Ninth Corps and the Sixth German Army had overrun the proud city of Kiev, capital of the Ukraine, known before the Revolution as Holy Kiev, for the city stood on the site of the first Russian Christian church.

Now the Jews came as they were bidden, allowed themselves to be organised into ordered rows and marched slowly along Melnik Street out towards the old Jewish cemetery and the bleak forbidding Babi Yar ravine.

The men who surrounded them were from Sonderkommando 4a, comprising men of the SD and Sipo—the Security Service and Security Police—together with the third company of the Special Duties Waffen-SS battalion and a platoon of No. 9 Police Battalion, reinforced by Police Battalion No. 305 and units of the Ukrainian Auxiliary Police.

When they drew near to the ravine, the hordes of Jewish people were funnelled through barbed wire. They were made to hand over their valuables, then strip naked and advance towards the edge of the ravine in groups of ten.

Once there, they were gunned down by the SD, Sipo and SS units. There were cries of terror once the shooting began, but those detailed to send the people forward showed no mercy. They closed their ears to the hysterical screaming of the women and children, closed their eyes to the awful sights, closed their minds to everything except their duty. Like men who work in an abattoir, they dragged the children, mothers with babies, old men, weeping and praying stark naked towards the edge of the ravine.

When the day ended the bodies were covered with a thin layer of soil and the death squads went back to their barracks and extra rations of vodka.

For two days there was nothing but blood, shattered bone, riven flesh and the eternal yattering of the machine guns and when those two days were over, thirty-three thousand, seven hundred and seventy-one Jewish people had been murdered in that wild, desolate and horrible place. Those who visit the awful site today will swear they can hear the screams and pleading which, for forty-eight hours, filled the air, punctuated only by the rip of bullets.

The instigator of this fearful crime against humanity, SS-Standartenführer Paul Blobel, was sentenced to death in 1948. He was hanged at the Landsberg prison on June 8th, 1951. During the trial, much was said of Blobel's deputy, SS-Unterscharführer Josif Vorontsov. He was the one, they said, who drove the men, women and children on towards their deaths, herding them in groups of ten to the ravine at Babi Yar.

What made Vorontsov's crime more heinous was that he was a Ukrainian who, in 1941, during the early stages of Operation Barbarossa, surrendered to the SS and became one of the many 'foreign recruits' serving with the Waffen-SS Special Duties Brigade. Once the war ended, many organisations and individuals searched for traces of the man, but found little. It was known that he had, at one point, sometime in the summer of 1942, served under the infamous SS Commandant Franz Reichsleinter at the Polish extermination camp near the town of Sobibór, where many hundreds of thousands of Jews were sent to the gas chambers.

When the Polish underground finally brought about an insurrection at Sobibór, Josif Vorontsov evaded capture. Years later, in 1965, during the investigation of eleven SS officers who had served at the camp, more information came to light concerning the Ukrainian turncoat. There were even hints that he had escaped to North America with the help of Spinne or Odessa, the groups that proved so adept at transforming former SS officers into blameless citizens. There were, however, no hard facts.

His name went on to the lists of wanted war criminals, but he was never found. Nothing more

3

was heard of Josif Vorontsov until December 1990.

CHAPTER ONE

HAWTHORNE

The town of Hawthorne, New Jersey, is less than one hour's drive from the centre of Manhattan, yet a stranger, dropped there by some magic, could be forgiven for imagining that he was in a small English North Country town.

True, the main road is wider than any you will find in Lancashire, Yorkshire, or Tyne and Wear, but the terraced brick houses have that same look you see in some of the hardy uncompromising communities around, say, Bolton or Blackburn. The overhead power lines and traffic lights signal that you are in America, but the feel of the place is strangely similar to the English North.

One of Hawthorne's favourite eating places is a single-storey Italian restaurant called Ossie's, named after its proprietor. On most nights it is full, and the tall dark figure of Ossie threads his way through the tables, taking orders, engaging in banter with his regulars and providing what he, and his clients, believe to be the best Italian food in the whole of the United States.

On Wednesday December 26, 1990, he greeted one of his most stalwart customers with a sympathetic, almost compassionate smile, for old Joel Penderek ate at Ossie's on at least four nights of the week. Before the previous September, Joe, as he was generally known, had only been a weekly

4

visitor together with his wife Anna. But Anna, who was never known to have had a day's illness, had died with a suddenness which shattered old Joe's happy and ordered life, on the previous Labor Day. There, baking and chattering one minute, and dead the next. The doctor said it was a massive heart attack and that he had already warned Anna several times that she carried too much weight and her cholesterol level was way above the acceptable norm.

This helped old Joe Penderek not a jot. He had met, and fallen in love with Anna, on the boat in 1946, and had married her as soon as they both knew they had been accepted by the immigration authorities.

Joe was twenty-nine years old when he came to America, Anna was twenty-seven and they both acknowledged that they were among the lucky ones. They seldom talked about their experiences in Europe, but those who spent any time with them knew they were Russian Jews who had been saved from one of the Nazi extermination camps, spending several months in one of the Allied DP centres before being passed on, via a compassionate American major, and swallowed by a group of assorted survivors earmarked for the USA. Anna had told her neighbour, Debbie Mansell, that all her family who had escaped death had been sent back to Russia where they disappeared. Joel's relatives had all died in the camps. It was wicked and cruel, but who said life would be fair?

Within a year of their marriage, Joe, who until then, had kept them both by taking casual labour, landed a good job with a local construction company, and, as the years passed, so he had risen,

5

from labourer to foreman, from foreman to site manager, and from site manager to retirement with a healthy pension. Now he had become a sad, lost figure who preferred his own company, as though some inner pride dictated that a man should be able to exist alone, and in his own private environment, once his life's partner had gone for ever.

So he kept to himself, nodded a half-hearted thanks-but-no-thanks to those who tried to befriend him, going about some routine which became almost ritualistic and included dining alone at Ossie's on four nights of the week. People stopped at his table, passed a few words with him, but seldom stayed long, for the old man seemed positively to resent old friendships. For the first time, people noticed that the tall, once muscular man had acquired a haunted look, there, deep in his eyes. It was a look which said, 'Have care; do not come too close, for I am a man estranged from the world. I am a man born to sorrows.' The craggy face seemed to have been affected by the eyes which appeared to have grown larger than folk recalled. The leathery skin was cracked, as though some plastic surgeon's work had gone awry, the skin itself taut against the cheekbones, while the lips were afflicted with a perpetual tremble. People said he was not at all like the old Joel Penderek they had known and loved all their lives. This was a shadow of that man.

Nobody had seen Joel over the holidays—which in the United States, unlike the splurge in the UK, last only for Christmas Day—but on the night of Wednesday 26, Penderek ate well, drank a small carafe of his favourite red wine, paid his bill, and left around nine in the evening by the side door. It

6

was the last time anyone saw him, though nobody reported him missing until the following night when Debbie Mansell became alarmed, having heard no sound from her neighbour's house and noting that the blinds remained drawn. This was odd, for she usually heard the old man's radio every day.

When the local police broke in they fully expected to find a body. Instead, Joel Penderek's home was almost abnormally tidy, with little out of place, the bed made up and not slept in, the kitchen clean and neat without a pot or pan out of place and a scattering of junk mail uncollected in the box.

Nobody had seen anything strange, and that was the way it had been planned. What happened on the Wednesday night was never fully explained, but in reality the facts were simple. The old man had walked out into the car park alongside Ossie's, turning up his greatcoat collar against the cold and pulling his woolly hat down over his ears: a blue and white knitted concoction he wore like a badge of office—for nobody saw him without it in the winter.

Being slightly hard of hearing, Joe shut out sound completely with the thick hat, so he only became aware of the car pulling out from the other parked vehicles when it came abreast of him. The driver's window was down and the man at the wheel shouted, 'Hey, buddy. You tell us the way to Parmelee Avenue?' He brandished a map, and Joe pulled the hat from his right ear, took two steps towards the car and muttered something which sounded like, 'You want what?'

Then another man jumped him from behind, the rear door of the car sprang open and, in less than

7

thirty seconds, the vehicle was just another set of taillights heading back towards Manhattan, but with Joel Penderek already unconscious in the rear, where a former medical orderly had plunged a hypo needle through three layers of clothing and into his right arm.

Nobody could possibly have foreseen that the abduction of an old man in New Jersey would be the prelude to a drama played out on the world's stage. Or that it was the first step in a plot, so ingenious and skilful, that the stability of nations would rock wildly to its adroit tune. One missing old man, and the fate of the free world would be at stake.

Even when they knew he was missing, none of his acquaintances in Hawthorne connected him with the big news story that broke on the Friday morning.

It came in over the wire services and was picked up by most of the national newspapers, while the major TV networks ran it as a third lead. If the Russian government had wanted to keep it quiet, they could not have done it, for the *Scales of Justice*, as they called themselves, made certain all the wire services had the text at exactly the same time as the Kremlin. The message was short and very much to the point.

Communiqué Number One: Fifty years ago, in June, the Jewish population of Kiev was brutally disposed of at Babi Yar. The chief executioner has long since been brought to book, but his assistant, Josif Vorontsov, a man of Russian origin, was never taken into custody. We now have the criminal Vorontsov who has been

8

masquerading as a citizen of the United States of America. We hold him safe in Eastern Europe and we are prepared to hand him over to the authorities. The new spirit which is abroad in our beloved land promises true and complete justice. We require the government to commit itself to a complete and unbiased trial of Vorontsov. The government must prove that it is willing to right wrongs suffered in the past and we will hand the criminal over once we are assured that he will be given a full trial open to the world's press corps. The government has one week to comply.

It was signed simply *Scales of Justice*, in Russian *Chushi Pravosudia*.

Nobody seemed to have heard of the *Scales of Justice*, but the world's media were able to run and rerun the facts concerning Babi Yar. They also pointed to this new event as an opportunity for the true spirit of *perestroika* and *glasnost* to be fully active. Trials in the old Russian Empire had often been for show, or remained secret. Now, with *glasnost*, the government could demonstrate their impartiality by bringing to book the assistant murderer of so many Russian Jews.

The media also took note that the communiqué appeared to contain an unspecified threat, by giving a time limit for the judicial authorities to declare themselves willing and able to prosecute a mass murderer.

The Kremlin announced they were reviewing the entire matter, and would give an answer before the deadline set by the *Scales of Justice*, whoever *they* were.

It was not a huge, headline-grabbing story, but

9

there was plenty of interest to keep it alive.

Nobody, not even the media, knew of the dilemmas which existed behind the political scenes. There was no way in which they could be aware of the controlled panic the *Scales of Justice* had brought about within the KGB, or the secret and alarming interest suddenly expressed by the Israeli Mossad, or even the slew of signals that passed between Dzerzhinsky Square, Moscow, and the British Intelligence Service in London.

If the media had caught a minute whiff of the confusion, the story would have quickly knocked most other subjects off the front pages, and the in-depth investigators would have been burrowing into those secret covens which still exist in all countries.

In London, the complete facts were not handed on until January 2nd, six days after the first *Scales of Justice* communiqué. But once the ball began to roll, *Fallen Timbers*, as it became known, took on a momentum of its own.

CHAPTER TWO

FALLEN TIMBERS

James Bond preferred the old ways, particularly when it came to the Registry files. There was something firm and honest, he felt, about going to Registry with his docket, exchanging the docket for a file encased in a buff folder, signing the file out, reading it and then passing the thick wedge of paper back to one of the nice young women who used to see to it that Registry ran smoothly.

All this had disappeared when the Service 'went decimal', as the jargon described the computerisation of its filing system. The nice young women were history, and though he was familiar, and literate, with computer systems, Bond never felt so positive about files which came seemingly from nowhere at the command of a series of keystrokes. It was, he considered, like a cheap magician's trick. He liked magicians, because sleight of hand and body was part of his stock-in-trade, but he did not care for the down-market, cheap variety. Their tricks, he thought, could usually be bought for a few pounds sterling, and that was no way to run a railway let alone the Secret Intelligence Service.

He felt all this now as he sat on the vile, white and hygienic cubicles off the main Registry work stations.

Bond had only been back on active duty since the beginning of December, following recovery from serious injuries received in the United States of America during his last operation, and things had changed greatly since then. Now, at the start of a new year, he had no desire to go out into his old European haunts until the game of nations had returned to some form of status quo. He believed in the changes that were taking place, but not that the world had seen the death of Communism. He even seemed content to sit shuffling documents or following paperchases from his desk, though he suspected this initial sense of satisfaction would last only a short time.

He arrived at Registry's work stations via M's anteroom. Moneypenny, the Chief's personal

11

assistant whose security clearance bordered on the stratospheric, called down to say that their mutual lord and master had something he wished 007 to read. He did not even have his customary chat with M. Moneypenny, after giving him the usual cow-eyed look, handed over a small blue slip—blue being the Registry colour for Most Secret and Above—on which had been typed two words: *Fallen Timbers*.

'We're on battles this month,' Moneypenny gave him a glittering smile. 'Lucknow, Marne, the Somme, Arnhem, Blenheim. Fallen Timbers. You've probably never heard of it, but it *is* a battle. Plenty of belligerence.'

Bond raised an eyebrow, a smile turning up one corner of his mouth. 'Not for me I hope, Penny?'

She gave a mock sigh and reached out to retrieve the blue slip which she popped into a small desktop shredder with a terrible finality. 'Fighting with you could be rewarding, I should think.' She followed the sigh with a little moue, and Bond leaned across the desk to kiss her lightly on the forehead.

'You're like a sister to me, Penny,' he smiled, knowing her remark about cryptos being battles was to let him know the file was secret. New. Not some old case taken out to play with while Moscow and the old Eastern Bloc went through its varied agonies.

'I don't feel sisterly.' Moneypenny never even bothered to hide the deep passion she nursed for Bond.

'Oh, come on, Penny, I don't want to add incest to injury,' and with a broad wink, he left the office.

At the Registry work station, Bond typed in his pass number, followed by the words *Fallen Timbers*.

12

The impersonal screen told him to wait, then informed him that he was cleared for the file. Seconds later the printer started to spit out sheets of paper. There were seventy in all and the cover page bore the usual Most Secret ciphers and the subject heading *Scales of Justice*; Cross ref Josif Vorontsov, this file.

Most of the facts contained within the three score and ten pages were background: detail concerning Vorontsov's past and the recent abduction of the man called Joel Penderek from some obscure New Jersey town to, it was thought, a nameless point in Eastern Europe. (There were photographs attached, which meant that either someone had been doing his homework or the pix had already been in Registry for some time.) Then came some scant details regarding the organisation which called itself the *Scales of Justice*. These last were, if anything, sketchy, even conflicting. But finally, the meat within the file lay, not in the middle, but at the end. It was contained in two separate reports. One from the KGB, which appeared a tad muddled and indecisive, the second from the Israeli Service, the Mossad, which was terse, to the point, factual and not discomposed in any way. Bond was left wondering which report was more accurate, for distracted indecision could in the covert world be a cloak for clarity.

It took an hour to read and digest the file, after which the flimsy printed sheets were consigned to the large shredder by the door. The pieces rolled through into the burn bag which, he knew, would be removed within the next half-hour. Now, with much on his mind, Bond returned to his desk and informed Moneypenny that she could report to the

13

Chief that he had followed instructions.

There was no waiting, and within ten minutes Bond sat on one of the straight-backed chrome skeletal chairs that M had recently installed during a refurbishing of his inner sanctum. He had noticed the changes to his Chief's office when reporting back to work. He had wondered then if the new decor was a reflection of the massive shifts taking place in the world beyond the surreal existence they all shared in the anonymous, and ugly, tower block overlooking Regent's Park which was the headquarters of the Service.

The room had lost its old nautical flavour; even the paintings of great naval battles had disappeared from the walls, replaced by uncharacteristically insipid watercolours. M's desk was now a large steel and glass affair, tidy with heavy transparent In and Out trays, three different-coloured telephones, one of which looked as though it had been a prop in some Hollywood sci-fi epic, and a huge glass ashtray the size of a bird bath in which the Admiral had rested his evil-smelling pipe.

'Chairs're damned uncomfortable,' the Chief growled without looking up from the papers upon which he was working. 'Ministry of Works tell me they're more labour-intensive, if that's a real expression or more assassination of the English language. Suppose it means you're so damned ill at ease in 'em that you want to get up and out, back to the grind, in double-quick time. Won't keep you a minute, 007. Pictures are interesting.'

Bond took this as a hint so he left the chair and walked over to one of the watercolours. It was of a flat landscape that could have been Germany or some view of the Fens. Then he gave a little gasp

14

when he spotted the artist's signature, *R Abel*.

'Nice, eh?' M grunted, his head still down as his gold fountain pen raced along lines of word-processed text.

'*The* Colonel Abel?' Bond asked, for Rudolph Abel had been one of the most successful Russian spies of the fifties, the man whom the Americans had eventually swapped for Gary Powers, the famous U-2 spy plane pilot shot down over the Soviet Union causing great distress to the Western Alliance.

M finally put down his pen. 'Oh, yes. Yes indeed. Bought 'em from Walter in Washington. Drove a hard bargain, but they're there to remind me of how things used to be, and how things are, if you follow my drift. Sit down 007.' Walter was a legendary former archivist of the American Service, and it was rumoured that his apartment was papered with rare, very collectable memorabilia of the Cold War. 'What d'you think of *Fallen Timbers*?' M glared.

'I gather it was a battle.' Bond returned to the discomfort of the labour-intensive chair.

M grunted again. 'Yanks. After the Revolution. Battle with Maumee Indians in Ohio. Don't learn that kind of thing in English schools these days.'

'Never did.' Bond adjusted his posture, realising the chair was more endurable if you sat to attention, which, presumably, was one of its design features.

'Anyway, *Fallen Timbers*. What d'you think?'

'Moscow Centre appears to be getting very concerned over a relatively straightforward matter. Old war criminal. Old history. Is it really this man, Penderek?'

'Appears to be. Just as it appears *not* to be, if

15

we're to believe the Israelis.'

'They're usually right when it comes to war criminals. The Israelis have long memories, sir.'

'Quite. They've sent one of their best people over to brief us. He's *very* good, and we've let him into the inner circle. Y'see, I've had a request from Moscow. Quite extraordinary, when you consider the past history. They say they need two men. Russian speakers. I think you and the Israeli might fit the bill; do the trick for them. Your Russian still up to snuff, 007?'

'It was the last time I looked, sir.'

'Good. There's a possibility that you might have to go in and take a peep with the Israeli. Could be interesting, working for Moscow Centre after all these years of labouring in an opposing vineyard, so to speak.'

'Distillery, rather than vineyard, I would have thought.' Bond gave a quick smile, but saw that M was not amused. 'Can you expand on the Israeli theory?' He realised that he was asking questions just for the hell of it. The idea of being sent on attachment, as it were, to the KGB, together with a Mossad agent, was quite alien to Bond.

'Not really. Only what's in the file.' M was scraping out his pipe with a metal reamer which seemed to have more tools attached to it than a Swiss Army knife. 'They're convinced, as you know. If they're telling the truth, the Israelis have had Vorontsov under surveillance for the best part of three years, and he's holed up in Florida. Again, if this is so, then these *Scales of Justice* people've picked the wrong man. The question is did they snaffle the wrong horse on purpose?'

'Why would they do that, sir?'

16

M frowned and raised his hands in an untypically Gallic shrug. 'How the hell would I know? Don't have a crystal ball, don't read the runes, don't sort through the entrails, don't dabble in ESP. Know as much as you do. Possibly the Mossad Johnny can tell us, but my gut feeling is that the people who really know are stewing in Moscow Centre. You'll probably be able to get it out of them if you have a mind to. After all, they appear to know something about the *Scales of Justice*, which is more than we do.'

'And our man from Mossad?'

'Peter. Likes to be called Pete. Pete Natkowitz. Incidentally, don't you think it's a shade strange that KGB hasn't brought the Yanks in? After all, this suspect, Penderek, was lifted right out of their bailiwick.'

'Perhaps Moscow Centre prefer to play with us . . .'

'Us and the Israelis. Strange bedfellows, what? Would've thought the US of A would've been called upon at some level.'

'You can never be sure with KGB, sir. Never could. What about the Mossad man, Natkowitz? When do I get to see him?'

M was now reloading his pipe, lost in some obscure ritual. 'Natkowitz? Any time you like. He's been here for the past twenty-four hours. Chief of Staff's been lookin' after him. Babysitting him, as they used to say. Actually he's had him down on the Helford estuary showing him how we operate in shallow waters.' The Service still retained a small facility on the Helford estuary where trainees went through the rigours of scuba diving, clandestine water landings and all things connected with that

17

kind of work. They had been there since the dark days of World War II and nobody had thought to close the place down.

'Getting his feet wet?'

'Who, Tanner?'

'No, the Israeli. Tanner already has webbed feet. We did the course together more years ago than I like to recall.'

M nodded. 'Yes, I think Chief of Staff said something about giving Mr Natkowitz the odd mouthful of seawater. Let's see if they're back.' He began to operate the sci-fi telephone console as though he had read and understood the copious manual that obviously came with it. Leisurely M pressed a button, then spoke as though into an answering machine. 'Chief of Staff,' he said.

From the built-in speaker there came the ringing of an internal phone followed by a click and Bill Tanner's voice saying a calm 'Chief of Staff.'

M gave one of his rare smiles, 'Tanner. M. Would you care to bring our friend up?'

'Aye-aye, sir.' Tanner was always inclined to use naval expressions around M. He had even been heard to refer to the Chief's office as 'the day cabin', and the shrewd old Admiral was, as often as not, amused by what he considered to be Tanner's peculiarities.

M continued to look at the phone. 'Don't like gadgets as a rule, but this is damned clever. You just say the name of the fella you want to talk with and the machine works it all out, dials the number and all that sort of thing. Clever as a performing monkey, eh?'

A few minutes later, Tanner himself stood in the doorway, ushering in a short, stocky man with

18

sandy hair and bright eyes who, for some reason, reminded Bond of Rat in *The Wind in the Willows*.

'Pete Natkowitz. James Bond.' Tanner flapped a hand as he effected the introduction. Bond stuck his own hand out and received an unexpectedly firm shake that all but made him wince. There was nothing ratlike about Natkowitz close to. Just as there was nothing distinctly Israeli about the man's demeanour or characteristics. His complexion was that of a ruddy gentleman farmer, as were his clothes—cavalry twill slacks, soft, small-checked shirt with a frayed tie which looked regimental and a Harris tweed jacket complete with double vents and a flapped side pocket. He would have passed for the genuine article in an English country pub, and Bond thought to himself that there is nothing so deceptive as cover which matches a man's natural physical characteristics.

'So, the famous Captain Bond. I've read a lot about you.' His voice was soft with undertones of the drawl one associates with the British stockbroker belt—the kind of accent that is stuck halfway between East London and Oxbridge, a shade shy of the slur which pronounces 'house' as 'hice'. The smile was warm, almost 100 degrees in the shade, with teeth as white as fake Christmas snow. After all the physical come-on, he added, 'Mainly in top secret documents I admit, but it's all been good. Delighted to meet you.'

Bond controlled the urge to play games and say something about access to the Mossad's files already. Instead he merely smiled and asked if Natkowitz had enjoyed Helford.

'Oh, there's absolutely nothing like messing about in boats.' Natkowitz gave Bill Tanner a

19

sideways glance and Bond went straight for the million-dollar prize. 'So, they want us to work for the Russians, I gather, Mr Natkowitz.'

'Pete,' he said, his face lighting up like Guy Fawkes night, or the Fourth of July, depending on which side of the Atlantic you are standing. 'Everyone calls me Pete; and, yes. Yes, I'm told we're going into the old badlands. That should be interesting.'

Bill Tanner coughed and gave M a quick look which said, 'Have you told them the bad news yet?'

M made one of his harrumphing noises which were often the advent of unpleasant tidings. 'Mr Natkowitz,' he began, 'I have no control over your decisions, but, for the sake of James, I must advise you both of the dangers, and your rights, in the matter we now call *Fallen Timbers*.'

The pause was long enough for Bond to register the fact that his old Chief had used his first name, always a prelude to fatherly advice, and usually a signal for him to beware of dragons.

'James,' M continued, looking down at his desk, 'I have to say that this operation *must* be undertaken on a voluntary basis. You can step down and walk away at any point before we begin and nobody'll think any the worse of you. Just hear me out on a couple of points, then give me your decision.' He looked up, clamping his eyes directly on Bond. 'It is our opinion that what we are going to ask of the pair of you could be damned dangerous. Also, Moscow is in an unconscionable hurry. Too quick off the mark if you ask me. But then, everyone has a right to be jittery. They've got the Baltic States. America and ourselves have the Iraqis—as indeed do you, Mr Natkowitz.'

Bond opened his mouth, frowning and puzzled, but M held up a hand. 'Hear me out first.' He made a grim little movement of the lips, half smile and half grimace. 'We'll tell you what we know, and Mr Natkowitz here, will tell you what *he* knows. It's not a lot, and it leaves huge blank spaces. Dead ground, as it were.' Another pause, during which the only sound came from outside the building. An aircraft on approach to Heathrow. Bond's mind suddenly filled, unbidden, with pictures of disaster, wrecks and bodies overlapped and floated vividly in his head. These near nightmarish images were so clear that he had to make an effort to pull his mind back to what M was saying.

'The disappearance of an elderly man in New Jersey, followed by that puzzling communiqué from these people who call themselves the *Scales of Justice*, seem to have caused unnatural concern in Moscow. They are asking for the pair of officers to sniff out the *Scales of Justice* and bring in this fellow Penderek. Specifically they've asked for two members of our Service with good Russian. The cover will be fully provided *in situ*. If this goes forward, I've agreed that we will not tell them that Mr Natkowitz has been made an honorary member of the SIS, which is fair enough because I have to admit that I'm leery of letting anyone go. Old habits die hard, and I cannot feel wholly happy about my people talking to their people, as they seem to say in business circles these days.

'Finally, and here's the rub, to do this properly, Moscow says you'll have to operate under *their* control, as it is a job none of their people can do. What's more they want you in Moscow yesterday, or more realistically, by tonight. It's all too fast and

21

too iffy, but it might, just might, be of great importance to the continued freedom and stability of the world. You follow me?'

'Not really, sir.' Bond had already heard the warning bells ringing behind the technicolor pictures of disaster which he could not exorcise from his mind.

CHAPTER THREE

FIRST LONDON BRIEFING

Holiday Avenue is, perhaps, the most exclusive street in the small community of Holiday which lies off Route 19, a few miles north of Tampa, Florida. It is a side road, flanked by luxury single-storey dwellings, set back from well-manicured lawns, shaded by palms and foliage.

Most of these houses show outward signs of protection. The windows are tastefully barred, and telltale red boxes, or stickers, let the casual and not so casual passer-by know that they are shielded by such and such a security firm or system.

In this pleasant, affluent little cul-de-sac, the homes are owned by retired doctors, lawyers or former financial Indian chiefs from the East coast. These good people live out the September of their years in the mild climate, shielded from the sun by a well-ordered rearrangement of nature's bounty, from poverty by their own good sense and careful management and from the would-be criminal by electronic devices which alert the nearest police headquarters in seconds.

They live quiet, though rich, lives these people of Holiday Avenue. They attend the same cocktail parties, meet at the same nearby 'country' club—an excusable misnomer in this part of Florida—and they lounge by their secluded pools, exercising with a daily swim most of the year round, though this turning of the year had been one of the coldest on record, with the citrus fruit hanging encased with ice, an indicator of hardships yet to come.

On this particular afternoon, while most of the good senior citizens of Holiday Avenue were having a light lunch or taking their afternoon nap, a Federal Express van pulled up in front of 4188, a white stucco, red-roofed, Spanish-style place, almost hidden from sight by judiciously placed fronds and trees.

The Federal Express man got out of his van with a long parcel, checked his clipboard and walked up the path to the stout oak, metal-studded door. He rang the bell and, as he did so, another smaller van pulled up almost silently to park behind the FedEx vehicle. As he stood waiting, the FedEx man was conscious of the lawn sprinklers, of the spick-and-span nature of the property and the heavy wrought-iron grilles—again Spanish style—which protected the windows. He rang the bell for a second time and heard a grumbling from behind the door.

Finally the door was opened by a tall, elderly man, grey-haired but with a figure not yet run to fat, and a back ramrod straight suggesting a former military career and a mind conscious of health and physical fitness. His eyes were hidden by dark prescription sunglasses and he wore expensive designer jeans and a leisure shirt which could not have left much change out of two hundred dollars. He remained in the shade of the doorway, his body braced between the door and the jamb, as though uneasy and ready to slam the port in his visitor's face.

'Package for Leibermann,' the FedEx man smiled. 'Has to be signed for, sir.' He balanced the package under his left arm as he proffered his clipboard and a pen.

The older man nodded, his face turned, looking curiously towards the package as if trying to see who it was from. He reached out for the pen and as he did so two men in dark slacks, sneakers and black turtleneck sweaters slid from the rear of the FedEx van and began to run soundlessly towards the house, keeping well out of the sightlines from the door.

At the same moment, just as Mr Leibermann held the clipboard in one hand and the pen in the other, the FedEx man shifted the parcel slightly under his left arm. It was an oblong package, around eighteen inches in length and some two inches square. His right hand moved beneath the package which he raised like a weapon.

There was a 'plop'. No more than this. Not a bang nor even a pop. Simply a plop. If heard it would raise no alarms nor cause dismay.

The plop came from a small air pistol within the package, the barrel held firmly in place by a snugly fitting wooden jig, the butt and trigger accessible through a hole cut neatly in the rear underside. Leibermann dropped the pen and the clipboard, his right hand clutching at his shoulder where the dart had penetrated with the sting of a bee.

He said nothing and did not even cry out as the

24

strong, carefully measured anaesthetic moved rapidly into his bloodstream, paralysing him for a second, then plunging him into total unconsciousness. By the time he crumpled, the two men from the back of the FedEx van had caught him. The FedEx man swept up his pen and the clipboard then closed the door firmly. By the time he reached his van, the other pair had carried Mr Leibermann from the house and bundled him into the back.

The FedEx van drove away in no haste and the smaller vehicle remained, its occupants scanning the street for any sign that this small act of violence might have been spotted by an inquisitive neighbour. But the good people of Holiday Avenue did not stir. The only observer appeared to be a tired dog who dozed under a tree bordering 4188 and 4190. The dog opened one eye, then closed it, stretched its body lazily and returned to sleep.

Yet somebody else did see the entire drama. Across the street at 4187, the elderly couple called Lichtman viewed the whole thing and took frantic action. Nobody knew the Lichtmans well. They were the kind of couple who kept themselves to themselves, and in the two years since they bought the house there had been much neighbourhood talk about the good-looking young men who visited them and stayed, sometimes for a week. Mrs Goldfarb, who knew everything, was one of the few people who had managed to get the Lichtmans into her home, for lunch, and she told other people that the Lichtmans had seven sons and fifteen grandchildren who visited all the time.

Asher Lichtman was on the telephone at this very moment talking to one of his 'sons', describing what had taken place, giving the licence number of the FedEx van and the smaller vehicle still outside 4188.

They had used 4187 as a surveillance post for two years. In fact, everyone was keyed up, expecting the order to snatch Leibermann any day. Now, under their very noses, the target had been grabbed, disappearing almost into thin air.

After waiting for five minutes, the other van drove away, the figure in its passenger seat talking rapidly into a microphone.

Markus Leibermann was due to be at a small dinner party that evening, given by the Rubensteins at 4172, so that a few of their friends could meet their son, the psychiatrist, Adam, on a short visit to his parents. Adam did not get to meet Mr Leibermann, and though he was not to know it, he did not miss much.

* * *

Natkowitz did his stuff with the assistance of two slide projectors and a large computer screen, the kind software manufacturers use at trade shows. They had all trooped down to one of the secure briefing areas shielded from external directional mikes and bugproof, forty feet below ground in the huge basement, half of which was car park, the rest being rooms like this, or debriefing facilities.

The room was not unlike a film company's screening theatre. There were no distracting pictures on the bare walls and it was furnished with soft, comfortable chairs which were bolted to the floor. A little console of coloured telephones was built into an enlarged armrest in the seat reserved

26

for M. Apart from Bond and Natkowitz, M and Bill Tanner were joined by the man they all referred to as the Scrivener, Brian Cogger, an officer of great skill when it came to the preparation of documents, mainly passports and assorted pocket litter which made up the outward and visible signs of many an agent's inward and spiritual cover. It was a hint that M had already made up his mind about the operation into Moscow. The Scrivener's art was a dying trade, yet he was a busy man and his presence suggested that his talents would be required.

Bond wondered if they were taking precautions out of habit or whether there was yet cause to believe the old Eastern Bloc and Soviet intelligence communities were still at it and could pose security problems. Eventually he decided that, whatever the politicians said out loud, tolling the tocsin for Communism and the Cold War, the secret world would go on playing by its own rules. It was safer that way.

The hearty dilettante farmer image Natkowitz had presented in M's office seemed to slide away once he started to brief them on the Mossad's side of things. It was like watching a snake shed its skin but in reverse, for Bond felt the man had put on his true nature once he began. Here was the real Pete Natkowitz—able, steeped in the arcane ways and the secret language and with his subject at his fingertips.

First he dealt with the question of identity using great blow-ups of Joel Penderek side by side with existing pictures of SS-Unterscharführer Josif Vorontsov as he was in 1941 when he served with the Waffen-SS Special Duties Brigade.

Natkowitz flicked between the two side-by-side

27

photos and a copy of Vorontsov's recorded details filched from the SS files.

'As you can see, the height's about right,' he said, his accent changing from the drawl to a more clipped, authoritative tone. 'Around six one in 1941 according to the SS; and Joel Penderek about the same in '46 if US Immigration is to be believed. The age is also nearly correct. Vorontsov was born January 19th, 1917, while Immigration says Penderek's birthday is November 19th, 1916, which makes him a Scorpio if anyone should be interested in that kind of thing. It also makes him a couple of months older than Vorontsov, which is okay, or as near as damn it.

'If, as we suspect in Tel Aviv, the *Scales of Justice* have gone out of their way to find a ringer, they've done a lot of homework.' He took his wooden pointer and started to tap first one of the photographs and then the other. 'You see, even in relatively old age, there is a resemblance. Look particularly at the nose, the eyes, chin and forehead. Distinct similarities. On the surface Joel Penderek could be taken for Josif Vorontsov.' He gave them a knowing smile and gestured with his right hand—a quick tipping motion, fingers splayed. 'Someone wishes us to believe they are the same person. But, on close examination, this is not so.'

He started to enumerate the obvious features. Vorontsov had a tiny scar below his lip and above the chin, the result of a childhood accident involving sharp little milk teeth and a tumble in his father's Ukrainian home. There were blow-ups of the area on both sets of pictures. The scar was there for young Vorontsov while it was missing from old

28

Penderek.

Again he turned to the details from the SS files on one hand and US Immigration's profile on the other. A scar on Vorontsov's right thigh was not mentioned in Penderek's distinguishing marks listed in 1946. There was also the matter of an appendicitis operation performed in the Gorky University Hospital, Kharkov in 1939. 'Vorontsov's father was a medical practitioner who taught anaesthesiology at the university, and, it seems, was a favourite of Stalin. Certainly he escaped Stalin's Great Terror, and our psychological profile of Josif suggests that he was both anti-Semitic and ambivalent about the way things were being run in the USSR at the time of the Nazi invasion— *Barbarossa*. This made him an ideal candidate for the SS recruitment, or so our tame shrinks tell us.

'The US INS, the Immigration and Naturalisation Service, seems either to have missed the appendix scar or it just wasn't there. No prizes for guessing which.'

Natkowitz continued with further contradictions, this time in a more detailed manner, using a computer programme which converted the photographs into three-dimensional heads. Someone had entered what measurement details existed on the two men, and the result showed likely bone structure which in turn drew attention to large discrepancies.

'The pretty pix?' Bond queried.

'What about them?' Nobody but Pete Natkowitz attempted to answer.

'Obviously we've all got Vorontsov's stuff on file, but what about Penderek? He on file as well? Does the Mossad know something we don't?'

29

'James, you're a doubting Thomas. No, nobody had Penderek on file, except INS, passport control, and the FBI who found a large box of snaps in the poor old guy's bedroom. FBI kindly circulated them for us. We *all* got them, including those wonderful people who gave us the camps on the Gulag, the mental hospitals for those who held different views, the quick bullet in the back of the neck in the Dzerzhinsky dungeons and encouragement to families to betray one another while they tickled every would-be traitor as a poacher tickles trout.'

'Come on, Pete,' Bond interrupted, 'we've all done our fair share of tickling, most certainly your Service...'

'Not to the extent KGB did it,' Natkowitz snapped. So Bond kept his thoughts to himself as the Israeli continued. 'We *did* have a large file on the real Vorontsov.' Natkowitz ran his splayed fingers through his fireball of hair. 'And don't accuse us of fomenting family feuds when I say it's common knowledge that we in the Mossad use a large number of part-time agents all over the world. One of those led us to Vorontsov. An accident, like so many others. An old lady, whose name I'll keep to myself, was doing some grocery shopping at a Winn Dixie in Tampa, Florida, about four years ago. She turned a corner, from the canned goods to frozen foods, and there he was, his back towards her, selecting a TV dinner.

'Identified by his back? Don't even think of asking, James. This particular old lady had been on intimate terms with Josif Vorontsov. She made it through Sobibór, and at that camp Vorontsov was her personal torturer. She swears she would know

30

him anywhere. You see he raped her, not once but around one hundred times in an eight-month period. It would appear that these rapes were what kept our informant alive. He liked the way she fought back, and all those years later she knew him, by the way he stood, by the set of his shoulders and the manner in which he held his head.

'Eventually he turned around and she saw his face. It was undoubtedly her torturer, so she followed him, got an address and alerted us. We sent some people in.' He gave a little amused gesture using his body, hunching his right shoulder forward and turning his head in what would have been in another person a coy expression. 'I have to be discreet. These people shouldn't really have been there, but they took a ride up to Tampa and did a short surveillance. *Son et lumière.* Everything. Now look.' He flashed a new photograph on to the screen so that it sat alongside the official SS black and white.

The Israelis had cropped the clandestine picture to match the earlier uniformed version. They had also chosen it because of the angle of the old man's head and the way his eyes looked straight into the camera. It was the perfect before-and-after-match. Age had not altogether wearied the Ukrainian, nor had the years completely condemned him. It was unmistakable, even before Natkowitz showed the computer-enhanced shots and the stats of the INS forms, plus a very private medical report. The scars were all there and nobody could doubt they had the real man.

'Your Service did nothing?' It was M who, though he knew the answer, put everyone's question square on the table.

31

Natkowitz made another gesture, this time a one-handed business, the hand moving upwards as though he were tossing some invisible object into the air. 'It is difficult,' he said quietly. 'You know how difficult it can be. He calls himself Leibermann now. When he entered the United States, he came as an Austrian of Jewish parentage. We had sight of all the documents which were not altogether forgeries. Markus Leibermann was certainly an Austrian. Son of a bank clerk. The entire family perished in the Polish camp of Chelmno. It was the way the SS used everything, even dead men's shoes and papers. Josif Vorontsov became Markus Leibermann by courtesy of Spinne, that organisation which was so successful in getting its murderers out of Europe to safety. You know how many war criminals came to shelter using the papers, and the lives, of those they had killed? I tell you, many more than we have ever caught. I often wonder when I'm in New York, or Florida, if that nice old couple you see in a restaurant or at the beach in fact hold nightmares in their heads and laugh quietly to themselves about how gullible the Americans have been.'

'So you knew about this man, yet nobody did anything?' Bond rammed home the question.

'We took photographs. We prepared a case. Our American friends lobbied the authorities. You see, we like to be sure that we'll win when we identify someone like this. So many have slipped through the net and there are young men in power who cannot be made to understand. They say, "Sure. Sure it was a bad time, the Holocaust. Six million Jews murdered, but that was then. Now is now, we must forgive and forget. We're all friends now.

32

Look at the Japanese and the Germans. What's the point in prosecuting an old man or an old woman who were only obeying orders in youth?" These people really do not understand.'

'You couldn't make a good enough case against Mr Leibermann?' from Bill Tanner.

'Let's say we were quietly told that it was unlikely that Leibermann would be extradited. Unlikely that he would ever be expelled.'

'So you let it drop?' Bond again.

'Not altogether. There are ways, and we have the means which are not unlike the methods the *Scales of Justice* used on poor innocent Penderek.'

As if on cue, the small red telephone buzzed at M's elbow. He answered in a low, cautious voice, the looked up quickly at Natkowitz. 'A man who calls himself Michael appears to know you're here, Mr Natkowitz. Would that make sense?'

The Israeli nodded. 'Only three people know, sir. Michael is one. He wishes to speak with me?'

'No, gave me a message for you.' M slowly replaced the receiver.

'Well?'

'He says you'll understand if I tell you Rachel is missing.'

Pete Natkowitz stood unnaturally still for a second or two, his face frozen as he drew a sharp audible breath. Then he relaxed. Unsmiling, he said, 'Markus Leibermann has disappeared, gentlemen. Something has gone very wrong. I should speak with Tel Aviv, but this worrying news should be something kept between *us*. I don't think anyone else will be officially informed just yet. In view of what you're proposing, sir,' he looked hard

33

at M, 'I think we might well have some unfortunate problems.'

CHAPTER FOUR

FROGS IN THE OINTMENT

It was just before six thirty in the evening that Nigsy Meadows took the call from his junior. It was the simple code they altered once a week—more recently since the Gulf crisis—sometimes as often as three times a week.

'Mr Meadows, sir, could you drop into the office sometime this evening,' Williamson said as though it could not matter less. 'Sylvia has a couple more letters for you to sign. They want them in the bag for London tomorrow.'

'Can't it wait till Thursday?' Nigsy hoped he sounded bored. Shabak, the Israeli Security Service, had all the embassy and consular buildings in Tel Aviv bugged and monitored out of existence.

''Fraid not, sir. They're part of the stuff the FS's yelling for.'

'All right, okay, I'll be in later on, but don't hang by your nails.'

Translation: there is a top secret flash from London unbutton personally. Fine, I'll be in within the hour.

Nigsy had been looking forward to a quiet evening watching a video of a concert, taped by his wife in London and broadcast the previous week on BBC2. The 'eyes only' signal, he figured, could be anything from a run-and-hide, to some panic-button crash meeting with the one man he

34

still ran in Arafat's shop.

He had only been on station for six weeks and knew it was temporary because his real forte was Eastern Bloc and the Soviets. Now the Service was behaving like the old army days when they used to make a cook into a gunner and an all-round athlete into an education officer.

Good old Nigsy, they had said. Got a bit of the Moscow twitch. Been over there too long. Bring him in and let him rest up in Tel Aviv for a while. 'Only a few months,' M said when he last saw the old man. 'Change of scene. Do you good.'

Silly old devil, Meadows had thought. Shoving me out into the Middle East where I don't know my arm from my elbow, and at a moment of historical crisis as well. But he *did* like the climate though he missed his wife because it really was not worth her while coming over if this was really going to be a short-term posting.

He listened to the radio for half-an-hour—the end of Swan Lake, followed by a Chopin Prelude—(the one Barry Manilow pinched for *Could it be magic?*) The time was up and he went out into the chilly night, checked the Range Rover and drove from his end of the compound to the embassy building.

Williamson, one of life's perpetual juniors who must have been five years Meadow's senior, unlocked the cipher room and they both used their keys to prime the machine. The flimsy was in the safe and it took Meadows fifteen minutes to work the magic.

Flash from M to Head of Tel Aviv Station. Alert all assets to possible abduction of a Markus

35

Leibermann aka Josif Vorontsov from Tampa, Florida, to some Max Sec Town Hall Stop Be prepared to return Oxford direct within forty-eight hours Stop Relief briefing already on finals Stop Greetings M Stop

Town Hall was a catch-all for Tel Aviv, Haifa or Jerusalem. Oxford was Moscow and the rest meant that M had him marked up to whizz straight back to Moscow when his relief arrived in the next forty-eight hours, not even calling in at London on the way.

Nigsy Meadows hoped M had sent winter clothing with his relief. In Moscow at this time of the year it could get down to −44F, cold enough, as they say, to freeze the medals off a brass general.

*　　*　　*

M had sent the flash signal to Tel Aviv and recalled Flossie Farmer from leave during a short break in the briefing. Allowing for normal signal traffic delays, he knew Meadows was unlikely to receive the instructions much before six or seven Tel Aviv time. Whatever Natkowitz had said, M was not convinced that the Mossad had no hand in Leibermann's sudden disappearance. Just to be on the safe side, he also sent flash signals to Oxford, Banbury, Reading, Colchester, Basingstoke, Frome and Bicester (Moscow, Berlin, Prague, Paris, Bonn, Budapest and Warsaw). Later he would deal with the remainder of the old Eastern Bloc countries.

Moneypenny had grabbed him to sign the day's mail and to draw his attention to a couple of signals which seemed to require action now. One was a

'Confidential' from MI5—the Security Service—concerning something that might just have repercussions on the main matter in hand. M worried at it in the back of his mind as he returned to the briefing room, this time to deal with the small amount of intelligence they had on the *Scales of Justice*.

They had given up any pretence of special briefing, sitting together for a general discussion, first listening to Pete Natkowitz who related every scrap of information he had supposedly wrung from Tel Aviv. In the end it boiled down to the unpalatable fact that the Mossad surveillance and snatch teams had been left-footed and had no idea who had spirited Leibermann/Vorontsov from Florida, let alone where the man had been taken.

After these troublesome tidings, M asked Natkowitz to state the Israeli position regarding the *Scales of Justice*.

'I want to make this absolutely clear,' the Israeli began. 'The *Scales* have nothing to do with the Mossad, nor do we support them in any way. The Israeli government has no lines into them and they have *never* sought succour from my country, though it would seem they would like people to believe we have very firm links with them.

'Our first knowledge, like that of most people, came from GSG-9. Alert 1042/90. You've all seen it?' He looked up in query.

The German Counterterrorist Unit's Alert had indeed been among the many documents Bond had looked through when he came back from sick leave. These days, he considered, they had more terrorist Alert signals than anything else. In fact, it was no secret that the old 00 Section, which had officially

37

ceased to exist, had become his own Service's élite counterterrorist unit.

Just to refresh everyone's minds, Bill Tanner thumbed through a heavy bound loose-leaf file of European Alerts until he came to the one dated October 10, 1990.

'On three occasions in the past month, according to the GSG-9 circular, we have had evidence of a new quasi-terrorist organisation which appears to be ill-defined and with blurred, uncertain aims. The sources come from a raid, following an informant's tip, on a house in the Sankt Georg district of Hamburg. Two men were arrested and later admitted to belonging to a unit of the Red Army Faction. Among various pieces of the usual literature seized were two leaflets, one in German, the other in Russian. They purport to come from a group calling itself the *Scales of Justice* which claims to have a universal membership of six hundred spread throughout Russia, Eastern Europe, the United States of America, Germany, France and the United Kingdom. Its aims are not apparent from these leaflets, but similar items, found after the arrest of two women at Frankfurt airport on September 15th, indicate that the SoJ is a group organised from within the Soviet Union. Its aims are set out in a document called Dossier Number 4 which was seized, together with a handful of names and addresses, from a known member of the so-called Grey Wolves group. It would appear that the SoJ is a tyro organisation which seems to be dedicated to the spread of pro-Israeli and pro-Semite feelings and freedoms within the frontiers of Russia and her former satellite countries. Also it appears to have some unusually close attachments within groups diametrically opposed to its aims—People like the RAF and the Grey Wolves.' Tanner looked round as though asking if they could all understand that.

'And what else have we, Chief of Staff?' M jollying things along, knowing well enough what evidence was to hand.

'The addresses, circulated by GSG-9, were in Paris and London. The French GIGN, [*GIGN. Groupement D'Intervention de la Gendarmerie Nationale—the low-key, efficient, élite anti-terrorist unit.*] in tandem with the DST, [*DST. French security service.*] invited two people, a man and a woman, to help them, sir.' Tanner's tongue was not stuck in his cheek, but he looked firmly at the ceiling.

'As I recall, they were no help.'

'None whatsoever, sir. The French people named in the list recovered from the Grey Wolves were very respectable. As, indeed, were the five our own Special Branch pulled in. Almost a stink about it as one of them had friends in very high places. Fact of the matter is that the *Scales of Justice* "phoney list", as it became known, drew a blank.'

'And your people, Pete?' M asked, his face unreadable.

'Until now we had come to believe that the SoJ was an empty shell.' Natkowitz's face was equally expressionless, the pause held just a shade too long before he added, 'However, something *did* happen in early November that made some of our analysts wonder.'

'General Brasilov?' M spoke placidly.

'The assassination of Leonid Brasilov, yes. Shot in the classic terrorist manner as his car waited at

39

traffic lights less than a mile from Red Square, in broad daylight. Ride-by. Two motorcycles and a pair of Uzis. There is evidence that the Kremlin wanted to hush things up but too many people saw it happen.'

Bond stirred. 'And General Brasilov was well-known for his anti-Semitic views?'

'And actions. You know what the Russians have been like over the years. The anti-Semitism; the examples that were made; the difficulty Russian Jewish people have had just living in their own country. Yes, things have eased, they have flooded into Israel, but—Well, I'll not be coy. *More* are still in Russia wanting to get out. *More* are still being denied exit visas. The Russians will not own up to this, naturally, but the late General Brasilov was one of the largest thorns in that crown worn by so many Soviet Jews.'

'And the day after the assassination ...' Bond began.

'The day after, there were posters all over Moscow. "The *Scales of Justice* accepts responsibility for the death of L. L. Brasilov." Some of the posters rendered the name not as *Chushi Pravosudia*, but as *Moshch Pravosudia*—the *Weight of Justice* which, in Russian, is a little more sinister. Yes, I've no doubt that the KGB are somewhat anxious, for, since then, there have been reports of one attempted bomb outrage in Leningrad and a failed assassination attempt within the Kremlin itself. Both attributable to the SoJ.' Natkowitz gave a thin smile, looking round the room. 'You know how my Service felt about getting me involved with you British ...' he paused, a silence of carefully premeditated effect, for they all

40

knew it had taken some swallowing for the Mossad to agree to an operation hand in glove with the British Service. Mistrust between the two intelligence services had been spawned long ago, and it was an unsavoury truth that the Savaret Matkal, the formidable Israeli anti-terrorist military unit, would not speak directly with the British SAS. All communications went through Germany's GSG-9.

'We can guess how they felt,' M said quickly. 'In a manner of speaking, we're making a little history here, yes?'

'I hope so.' Natkowitz spoke with some feeling. 'Yes, sincerely I hope so.'

There was an uncomfortable silence, broken by Bill Tanner.

'We've established that the SoJ cannot be easily pinned down. We suspect that they operate from within the troubled borders of the Soviet Union. We must also suspect they have some kind of reasonable organisation.'

'It is conceivable that they are freedom fighters of a kind,' Natkowitz said flatly, as though that was the end of it.

M cleared his throat, 'But, if there is a real connection between the SoJ and the abduction of the man Penderek, mistakenly instead of the real target . . .'

'You *really* believe mistakenly?' Natkowitz laughed, one note, pitched high, his head thrown back.

'Pete?' Bond's head slowly came round towards the Mossad officer. 'Pete, you're telling us that the Penderek abduction was no mistake?'

'I think whoever did it wanted us to believe it *was*

41

a mistake.'

'Any reason? Logic?'

'Just a nasty, sneaky feeling. Gut reaction. Intuition. Maybe we in the Mossad have become cynical, or even paranoid. But I cannot believe in coincidence. The error in snatching Penderek is so obvious. I also have to admit I find the new development—the disappearance of the real Vorontsov—very disturbing. I suppose I'm really waiting to hear what KGB are after. Maybe that will give us a lead towards the truth. Perhaps you are ready to tell us now, sir.' This last to M.

The Chief gave the impression of a man waking from a doze. 'Yes, why not?' He looked towards Natkowitz. 'You know, I presume, KGB appear to be aware of your Service's theory that the *Chushi Pravosudia* have lifted the wrong man?'

'It doesn't surprise me, sir.' Natkowitz gave a little smile which Bond translated to mean that the Mossad had almost certainly dropped the information into Moscow Centre via some handy go-between. He also found it odd to hear M using the Russian term for the *Scales of Justice*.

'The Kremlin,' M pursed his lips as though he still found it difficult to believe they were on speaking terms with his Service's old enemies, 'are of a mind to turn down any idea of bringing Penderek to Russia, and trial. They haven't announced it yet, but almost certainly will do so the minute you're both in Moscow. Their reasons are going to be based on the information you have just given us. That it is the wrong man.'

Natkowitz nodded, once more signifying that this would be the sensible thing for them to do.

'They feel that a refusal might well bring the
42

Chushi Pravosudia into the open, and this is really where you come in. Moscow claim to have two members of the *Chushi Pravosudia* in custody. They are both male and both of British origin. They say the pair have been sweated and the sweat has produced interesting results.'

'Do we know any more about these two?' Bond's brow creased.

'Not a thing. The Foreign Office has not been informed of any British subjects missing, or detained, in Moscow or anywhere else. It's under wraps, as our American cousins would say. The interesting thing is that Moscow believes the SoJ to be organised in non-intercognisant cells. The interrogation appears to have brought out a method of getting into the main Russian cell who are expecting a visit from two British members known only by cryptos.'

'And they're suggesting that Pete and I take the trip?' Bond's right eyebrow shot upwards.

M nodded like a wise old Buddha. 'Mmmm,' he said.

'But somebody, with all due respect, sir, somebody within the main Russian cell will be able to make a physical identification, surely?'

'Mmmmm.' M again made the sound of a happy bee on a sunny afternoon. He seemed oblivious to the unspoken peril. Then, 'I *did* warn you, 007. I *did* say that this was a mite dangerous. If you want out, you only have to say.'

'I'd personally like to know the chances of success.' Bond rarely minded putting his life or career on the line, but he preferred to know the odds.

M spread his hands. 'If KGB are telling me the

truth, and I have no real reason either to believe or disbelieve them, you'll be monitored all the way. The idea appears to be that you'll become stalking-horses. They will, I am promised, keep you under surveillance every inch of the journey.'

'I've been known to throw KGB surveillance in the past.'

'That you have, 007. But this time the trick will be to keep them with you.' He turned to Natkowitz. 'Are you willing to do this?'

'I have little choice.' Natkowitz did not look unhappy. 'I volunteered in Tel Aviv. Once you do that in the Mossad, it is not wise to back down.'

'James?' M asked.

'I have no choice either. Not really, sir, as you well know.'

'Mmmmm.' M again made his all purpose yes-no-maybe sound.

'Is there a full briefing, sir? You said they wanted us quickly. Tonight?'

M took his time answering. Then, 'I think we might have to keep them waiting a little longer.' His head bowed towards the Scrivener. 'Brian, here, has to make up some new idents for you. Can't have you going into Russia on the Boldman identity; you've used it too often. Also, we've taken on the chore of providing papers for Mr Natkowitz ...' He frowned, catching his breath, the words left unsaid.

'Something else, sir?' Bond could see it in the Old Man's eyes.

M nodded slowly. 'As a matter of fact, yes. A minor something came up when we broke for Mr Natkowitz to call Tel Aviv. Could be nothing, on the other hand, it might just be an opportunity for the pair of you to begin working together. One

44

evening should do it. That give you enough time, Scrivener?'

Cogger did not talk much. It was said he believed words entrapped people. He had done it so many times on, and with, paper that he seemed to have lost the art of conversation. He nodded and added a handful of words which indicated he would need a half-hour with Pete Natkowitz. 'Photographs, that kind of thing.'

'Right.' M rubbed his hands together vigorously, like someone going out into a cold morning. 'Now to something completely different, as they say. It appears that we have visitors in town, or so Five tell me. Usually when our brothers-in-arms from other counterterrorist agencies come into the country, they tell us first, that is with the exception of your boys, Mr Natkowitz, no offence meant.'

'None taken, sir.'

'Well, this one's very odd. Two French officers arrived in London this morning. One is a fairly senior member of GIGN; the other, a woman, is a field officer attached to DGSE.' [*DGSE. Direction Général de Securité Extérieur, the equivalent of the British Secret Intelligence Service and the American CIA.*]

'We know both of them,' M continued. 'Henri Rampart, a major, and part of their quick deployment team, is a tough bird by any standard, a Russian speaker and no stranger to that country. The young woman, and she *is* young, 007, turns out to be Stephanie Adoré.' He gave another of his tight-lipped smiles. 'That's also her real name, not some crypto thought up by whoever runs PR for DGSE. She spent two years as head of the French Moscow station. Also served in the Middle East,

45

I . . .'

'Not a couple getting away for a little fling, sir?' Bond asked with an innocent deadpan face.

'Contrary to the rumours spread abroad by novelists, and possibly yourself, 007, most intelligence and security services do not encourage interservice affairs. No, Rampart is happily married, and Ms Adoré, though attractive, has an exceptional record.'

'Visit to their embassy, perhaps?' Bond tried again.

'No. There's a strange connection. Neither of them have been in touch with the embassy. They arrived on different flights. Ms Adoré using a field identity, Charlotte Hironde, Rampart, the name Henri Rideaux. They are both staying, in separate rooms, 007, at the Hampshire, very expensive, off Leicester Square.'

'So what's the supposition, sir? Has it anything to do with *Fallen Timbers*?'

'We have no idea, but it would give you and Mr Natkowitz an opportunity to work together. Get to know each other's handwriting as it were. Ms Adoré visited the GIGN compound outside Paris for two days last week. It looked to our people like some kind of briefing. From another source we have information that their files on the *Scales of Justice* travelled up to the GIGN compound for that briefing. This very firm intelligence, coupled with these officers' particular skills and their knowledge of Russia indicates that they might just be thinking of hopping over to Moscow on a jaunt.'

'A jaunt?' Both Bond and Natkowitz spoke simultaneously.

'For jaunt, read operation,' M snapped. 'I don't

46

think either of you would be happy about these people snooping around Dzerzhinsky Square while you're there. They could be a real pair of flies in the ointment.'

'Or Frogs in the ointment, sir.'

M gave Bond a withering look. 'That is a racist comment, Captain Bond, and you know how I feel about such remarks. Now, would you like to take a look? Get close to them this evening? I hear the food's awfully good at the Hampshire's Celebrities Restaurant.' M wrinkled his nose with disgust at the name. 'You know it, 007?'

'In a vague sort of way, yes, sir.'

'Well, perhaps when the Scrivener's finished with Mr Natkowitz, you might wander over. Prise them from their rooms, give them a bite...'

'Eat them alive, if you like, sir.' The corner of Bond's mouth turned up in one of his more sinister smiles.

M nodded. 'I'll let you see the files. I'll also clear it with Five who're almost certainly going to be touchy if you just go barging in.' Bond's Service had, at one time, run a long and sometimes unpleasant feud with MI5. Nowadays things were better, but M never took chances.

After the Scrivener had taken Natkowitz away to do the necessary photographs, the meeting broke up, but Bond lingered behind.

'You going to feel happy about this, 007?' M asked.

'When we've had the full and final briefing, I expect to sleep easier, sir.'

'Wouldn't if I were you. You trust friend Natkowitz?'

'Do *you*, sir?'

M locked his cold grey eyes on to Bond. 'I trust none of them. I don't trust Natkowitz or his service; I don't trust KGB; I don't trust what we've been told about the *Scales of Justice*. I do, however, trust you, James.' He laid an almost fatherly hand on Bond's sleeve. 'On the day John F Kennedy was assassinated in Dallas, he said to Mrs Kennedy, "We're going into crazy country." That's what you're about to do, James. You're going into crazy country, so you would do well to trust nobody but yourself. Now, sort these French people out, get to know Mr Natkowitz as well as you can and we'll go over the essentials in the morning. Meanwhile, remember it's crazy country over there.'

Bond was about to leave when M spoke again, very quietly, as though he was afraid of ears at the door. 'One other point, 007.' He motioned his agent back to his chair.

'There is one piece of information I don't intend to use in the final briefing, but I think you should know of it.'

Bond waited for M to continue. 'You know of General Yuskovich, I presume?'

'Naturally, sir.' General Yevgeny Yuskovich was one of the most powerful senior officers in the Red Army. He had close ties with KGB and was known to be an old-time hardliner. He was also the most senior officer concerned with the Soviet nuclear deterrent and a man constantly at odds with the Kremlin throughout the slow and unsteady march of *perestroika* and *glasnost*.

'We came across this during our routine check of the files on Vorontsov.' His eyes broke contact with Bond's. 'It seems that Yuskovich and Vorontsov are related—something the general would certainly not

48

wish to have paraded in public. The family tree goes like this ...' M continued to talk for ten minutes, and it was a more anxious Bond who left the office to do battle with the French.

CHAPTER FIVE

PERADVENTURE

Stephanie Adoré looked like a professional woman—a banker or corporate lawyer—and her dress sense was so in keeping with the image of a power-woman that men, though attracted by her undoubted beauty, were often intimidated by her, closing their minds before she even opened her mouth.

Mlle Adoré's hair was the colour of well-preserved copper. When she let it down, women in crowded rooms often gazed at her with jealousy, for it was the kind of hair that could go through a hurricane and yet, after the event, fall neatly into place without assistance. Usually she wore it in a somewhat mannish style, pulled straight back and tied in a great knot at the nape of her neck. When her mood was frivolous she decorated the knot with a velvet bow which always matched the tailored suits she wore with elegance.

At six thirty that evening she was at her most vulnerable. Almost naked, she stood in front of the closet in the dressing room of her suite at the Hampshire.

As she pondered the question of what she should wear, she looked at herself in the full-length mirror.

49

What she saw almost pleased her. The copper hair tumbled over her bare shoulders, and the rest of her body, which was nearly entirely visible, looked good even to her exacting eye.

Her skin was marble-smooth, the stomach flat, breasts full but not overripe, with large pink-aureoled nipples. She did not need to tighten the muscles to keep her buttocks firm, and her legs were long and slender.

She adjusted the fastening of her right dark silk stocking, gave the lace suspender belt a minute adjustment and went back to choosing tonight's outer shell.

She had put on a white silk shirt with a simple wrap-over tie prior to stepping into the full skirt, of a slightly military navy two-piece by Geiger, when the telephone rang. Hurriedly pulling at the waistband of the skirt, which was rucked and drawn off centre, she moved in stockinged feet to the drawing room and picked up the telephone.

'Yes,' she answered in a calm snap, designed to put anyone off.

'Mlle Hironde?' James Bond spoke into the house phone in the foyer.

'Who is this?' Just the merest hint of an accent. There for a second, then gone like a whiff of Gauloise, Bond thought.

'You won't know me. James Boldman. I have to speak with you. It's official, I'm afraid.'

'Why are you official? What are you afraid about?' Her voice retained just enough of Paris, but with a certain stiffness. No smiles.

'Perhaps you could come down. I'm in the foyer.'

'What sort of official business?'

'I suggest you come down, Mlle Adoré.'

50

At the use of her real name, Stephanie's lips pursed. 'Who are you?' she spoke very quietly.

'My job has a certain affinity with your own. I'll be waiting by the elevators.'

'Give me five minutes,' she said a little throatily.

Bond put down the phone, glancing to his left where Natkowitz was hunched over a similar instrument, having dialled M. Henri Rideaux's room. Finally the Israeli replaced the instrument and shook his head. 'No reply,' he said.

'Could be taking a shower.' Bond gave a small frown. There was one lonely watcher from MI5 on duty at the front of the hotel. When they had checked with him, the man swore that neither of his targets had left. He was prepared for Bond and Natkowitz, he had been friendly, even amicable, for the pair of officers from the SIS had authority to follow either of the targets. The watcher from MI5 was happy about that because it made his life a little easier.

'Try him later,' Bond suggested. 'Just keep out of the way for now, the adorable one's coming down.'

'I'll keep my eyes open.' Natkowitz gave him a curt nod and retreated to a seat with a good view of the entire foyer and opened a copy of the *Standard*.

Upstairs, in her suite, Stephanie Adoré raised an eyebrow. 'They're on to me.' She spoke French to the tall, balding man who sat like a statue on the settee.

'Who?'

'I gather it's MI5, their Security Service.'

'Stephanie, I know what MI5 is. They're here? They want to see you?'

'I think only one of them. It was always a

possibility. I said that coming here under a pseudo wasn't wise. It never is with the Brits. They've been jumping at shadows for years. Give them a pseudonym and they'll reply with a probe.'

Henri Rampart gave a thin smile and rose. He walked towards the window and pulled back the curtain to make a tiny peep-hole. He held the thick material delicately between thumb and forefinger, the other fingers outstretched. It was an odd gesture, dainty and out of character, for the man looked exactly what he was, a soldier—tall, broad and carrying himself with that confidence which comes only from men who have endured not only the hardships of special forces training, but also the nightmare of action. His face also showed these things. There was nothing benign or genial about him. At first sight, his features seemed to be all angles—nose, cheekbones, even the sharpness of his jaw and the mouth which looked purpose-built for issuing orders, while the granite eyes had that hard, flinty look born of suspicion and a warrior's caution.

He let the curtain drop and turned back into the room. The movement was precise with no unnecessary action of any part of his body. Major Henri Rampart was a strangely still person.

'If they're on to you, they could be watching for me also. How will you deal with this spook?'

A smile danced across her face. 'It depends. If he is the usual dull, government servant, I will be at my most charming. If he has anything attractive about him, then I shall be even more charming. What d'you think I'll do? I'll give him the arranged story, and maybe, just possibly, I will have a small, how do the Brits say it? A small frivol.' This last in

English.

Rampart's shrug was a tiny lifting of the shoulders, not the usual heavy Gallic movement using hands, arms and shoulders in a dramatic piece of body language. 'Well, you have until midnight.'

'That is plenty of time.' As the dialogue had progressed, so Mlle Adoré had moved between the drawing room and dressing room, putting on her shoes and the short jacket, decorated with gold trim and buttons. At the door she gave a tinkling giggle. 'If he is in the least bit attractive, I shall tell him that I turn into a pumpkin at midnight.'

'Be there,' was Major Rampart's only response.

*　　　*　　　*

Bond's first reaction was that she appeared more attractive than her photograph. She was instantly recognisable coming out of the elevator, a raincoat, which could only be French, over her arm, and with the skirt of her suit flowing around her legs and thighs in a provocatively sensual movement. It was all liquid, drawing attention to the lower half of her body and what might lie beneath the skirt.

'Mlle Adoré?' He took two steps towards her.

She gently took his hand, a simple touching, not a handshake. 'Mr Bold ... er ...'

'Boldman,' Bond smiled, his eyes hardly leaving hers, yet taking in the whole picture, his brain developing it in Kodachrome with a soft filter. She was enough to cure impotence and make a happy man very old.

'And are you?' She smiled, the accent not quite coquettish, but full of the ruffled 'rs' and throatiness of an English-speaking Parisienne.

'Am I what?' Bond asked, pretending to be dense.

'A *bold* man.' The tinkling giggle forced a shade as though through muslin.

'It depends.'

He could be very cruel, this one, she reflected. He had a way with his mouth, a barbarous smile. 'Well, I'm here,' she went on quickly. 'What was it . . . ?'

Bond looked around. Natkowitz still sat reading his *Standard*. Touring Japanese and Germans prepared to go off to the National, or to catch *Phantom* or *Cats*. The groups were drifting out into the Leicester Square traffic, while the few people entering the hotel were being checked by the terrorist-conscious security men stationed close to the door. Women turned out their handbags, men opened briefcases, all with the resigned patience which came from the knowledge that death now stalked the world invisibly in the disguise of toothpaste tubes or pens which could spew death in seconds.

'A drink?' Bond suggested, gesturing lightly towards the bar, glancing around the panelled foyer and thinking it must be like living in a cigar box to be here for any length of time.

She said she would have champagne. 'What else is there for a single girl these days?' Bond gave the bartender explicit instructions for a champagne cocktail for himself. 'Easy on the brandy, no orange and only show the Angostura to the glass, no sugar.' As the bartender busied himself, he recalled one espionage novelist dictum: 'Once you have made a champagne cocktail, you should give it to somebody else.'

54

'So,' she said brightly when they were at last seated, a little close to one another, 'your health, Mr Boldman,' raising her glass.

'James, Mlle Adoré. James, please.'

'Your health then, James.'

'*A votre santé.*'

'Oh, how quaint, you speak a little French.' She gave her trademark giggle, and Bond tamped down any slight rise of irritation he might have felt.

'Now,' she hardly paused for breath, 'you wanted to talk to me. Official you said it was, yes.'

'I have to ask you what your business is in London.'

Her eyebrows arched just for a millisecond, a blink of a twitch. 'I thought we were all in it together now, James. The EEC against the rest of the world. The frontiers all but disposed of.'

'In our world, as you well know, Mlle Adoré, no frontiers have been set aside.'

'Stephanie.' She looked at him over the wide champagne glass which was quickly dissipating the bubbles. 'Please, Stephanie.'

'Okay. Stephanie. Frontiers have *not* been set aside for people such as ourselves.'

'And what is our business, James?'

'Yours is intelligence outside the not insignificant borders of France. Mine is the defence of the realm; the security of Great Britain.'

'Can you prove that?'

'Certainly.' He reached into his jacket and produced the excellent piece of work provided by the Scrivener which said he was a security officer attached to the Home Office.

'And me? Can you prove it about me?' She played with him, dividing the two short questions

55

by dipping her mouth to the glass and sliding her delicious pink tongue into the liquid.

'Yes, if you insist, I can prove it, though it wouldn't make a very interesting evening. You would have to sit in an uncomfortable waiting room while some disinterested duty officer goes through the files. Personally, I prefer dinner, but...'

'You know any nice little French places?'

'Maybe.'

'Perhaps after we've seen my file.'

Bond shook his head. 'Don't even think about it. There wouldn't be time. Not even if you were aiming for lunch tomorrow. Let me tell *you* what I know. Your real name is Stephanie Annie Adoré; you are an officer of Direction Général de Securité Extérieur. You've seen active duty in Moscow and Beirut; you are, at present, on attachment to the Soviet section at La Piscine. You are thirty-three years of age and have your own apartment above a bar-tabac on rue de Buci. You live alone and, last year, June through October, you had a lover who worked at the German Embassy—we suspect that was work, but I'm not even going to ask. Enough?'

'Very good, and between us, no, it wasn't work. It was fun, and very sad when it ended.' She poked her tongue into her champagne again, then sipped it. 'Your people are very good. We were most discreet. I don't think my own office knew about it.'

'We had someone in the embassy. Your friend had a motormouth. He talked.' Bond thought he sounded a shade smug and almost instantly regretted it as he caught, for one tiny moment, a hint of pain in her eyes.

'You've convinced me.' She did not look at him.

56

'You want to know why I'm here? What I'm doing in your ugly city? London is so foreign to a Parisian, did you know that?'

'It's not hard to guess it. So, Stephanie, why are you here?'

'Because *you're* here.'

'Meaning?'

'Meaning the powers that be asked me to come into London under a pseudo, stay for one night and see if anybody caught on. It is like a small test. Here.' She opened her handbag, extracting a four-by-three card which she placed on the table next to his glass.

It carried the DGSE logo at the top and a short legend in French and English to the effect that Mlle Stephanie Adoré held the rank of major in the above service and was travelling, without any forward clearance, under the name of Charlotte Hironde. At the bottom there were two questions to be asked and signed by a member of the British Intelligence or Security Services. First, had Mlle Adoré been detected as a member of another EEC country's intelligence service immediately on arrival in that country. Second, had she been approached by any member of that country's intelligence or security service. Under the line which demanded a date and signature there was a small note which said, in effect, that this was part of a routine training exercise being carried out by DGSE in all other member countries of the European Community.

Bond tried not to look either angry or shocked. Inside he boiled at the presumption of the French in testing another country's service in this manner. His fury would go back to M, and from thence, he

57

would bet on it, to the Prime Minister who would, in turn, raise merry hell in Paris, or maybe Brussels.

He smiled and answered the questions, then excused himself, walking out into the panelled foyer in search of a duty manager and the use of one of the hotel's photocopy machines.

Mlle Adoré was looking startled when he returned and handed back the card. The copy was folded and inside his breast pocket. 'It isn't your fault, Stephanie, that your superiors are stupid enough to waste the time of well-trained agents on both sides of the Channel.' Then he whisked her up, helped her into her raincoat and led her outside. Flagging down a taxi he asked for the Café Royal.

They ate very simply: a *potage Longchamps*, followed by mounds of smoked salmon, the meal topped off with a very good chocolate mousse laced with brandy on Bond's special pleading. They talked constantly, discussing mutually interesting topics which ranged from the current status of known terrorist groups in Europe to the latest best-selling fiction, to the fact that Communism was alive and well and flourishing in the Kremlin in spite of rumours to the contrary. They touched on matters of grave importance, in particular the developing crisis in the Persian Gulf. Following Saddam Hussein's invasion of Kuwait and the massive United States' arms deployment, together with her allies, all eyes were on Iraq. The United Nations Security Council had given the coalition of countries, siding with the US, a mandate to liberate Kuwait by force at any time after January 15th. There were now only thirteen days to go and the world waited, knowing what might follow.

Stephanie was vociferous about possible Arab terrorism which would be a major fall-out if war broke out. Bond noted that she spoke with a complete and clear understanding of the situation.

It was eleven thirty by the time he got her back to the hotel and walked her to the elevators.

'James, this has been wonderful. We must do it again sometime. I'll give you my phone number. If you're ever in Paris...'

'The night's young, Stephanie...'

'Maybe, but I, my dear James, turn into a large *marron glacé* at midnight.' She scribbled an eight digit number on a business card, kissed him lightly on the cheek and waved as she walked into the waiting elevator.

*   *   *

'A real night on the town, eh?' Natkowitz was behind the wheel of a souped-up London taxicab which had remained last in the small rank near the hotel all evening. He had covered his red hair with a cloth cap and looked quite the part.

'Paid a damned great bill and got her phone number. What about the boyfriend?'

'Henri hasn't stirred all night. Not a peep.'

'Well, hang around, Pete, I still don't trust them.' He was not going to say anything about the DGSE running a test on British security. In any case he did not altogether go along with the delicious Mlle Adoré's story. Too pat, too devious and too unlikely.

They exchanged a couple of words before Bond crossed the street to where the battered grey van was illegally parked. Any passing policeman or

59

traffic warden was supposed to leave it alone because of the official sticker just below the licence disc, but it was not always so. Bond recalled one occasion when a vehicle from the motor pool had been towed away by an overzealous beat policeman, endangering a highly important surveillance. But that was in the Cold War which was now officially over. James Bond thought about this for a while, pondering the reasons for still monitoring the Soviet Embassy and running people in the former Eastern Bloc countries. A bellicose M had recently said, 'The Kraken of Communism sleeps, but it will awake again, stronger and more rarefied from the succour we in the West have given it.'

Bond sat quietly in the van with the engine idling, his eyes moving the whole time while his hand loosely held the microphone of a two-way radio tuned to a scrambled channel. He saw the young man from MI5 trying to look either like a lamppost or a man waiting for a bus, though there was no bus stop.

At exactly five minutes to midnight Stephanie Adoré came out of the hotel. She now wore a dark greatcoat and her hair was tucked up under a fur hat. The doorman waved at the three taxis standing idle and waiting. One came to life, its For Hire sign extinguished as it stopped for the doorman to see the young woman into the squat, black vehicle.

'Here we go.' Bond waited until the girl was in the cab before pulling out and overtaking it. He allowed Adoré's cab to overtake him just as they reached the bottleneck of traffic in Cranbourne Street, turning into the Charing Cross Road. Glancing in the mirror, he saw no activity behind him. If friend Rampart appeared, it was

60

Natkowitz's job to follow him in the cab. In the meantime, Bond clicked the switch on his hand mike and muttered, 'Predator. We're off and running.' Every few seconds he continued to give their position, hoping that at least one back-up team from the office was on the way.

Stephanie Adoré's cabbie was good, showing courtesy to other members of the fraternity and cutting up 'civilian' drivers unmercifully. Bond had the feeling that he was taking instructions from his fare, which was good tradecraft—give the cabbie a rough destination, then change your mind and navigate for him. The cabbie must have been very happy if that was what she was doing, for the cabbies of London pride themselves on being the best worldwide, and they do not like directions from the paying customer. Bond could almost hear the conversation, 'Wake up darling, either you know where you want me to go or you don't. Just give me an address. I'm like a bloody homing pigeon once you give me an address.'

Mlle Adoré certainly knew London if she indeed was navigating, for she ran all the possible back doubles, eventually setting a course for Knightsbridge.

Bond continued to monitor the radio and watch his mirror. No sign of Natkowitz, though a little black VW seemed to latch on to them for about half a mile as they negotiated Kensington Road. But it had gone by the time they swept past the Albert Hall, with Prince Albert to their right, standing under his Gothic canopy, uninspired by the open book in his hands.

He had put some three to four cars between him and Stephanie's cab and, though the traffic was

61

light, there was enough of it to give reasonable protection. The VW appeared again halfway up Kensington High Street and overtook him just west of the library. Two minutes later, Bond saw Adoré's cab turn left into the Earl's Court Road with the VW close behind.

He shot the lights amidst a blare of illegal and furious motor horns and just caught sight of the VW making a turn into Scarsdale Villas, once a late-Victorian bastion of the upper-middle classes, now a road of tall elegant houses gone to seed, given over to bed-sitter land, doctors' surgeries and pre-school kindergartens.

Glancing left as he overshot the turn, Bond saw the cab and the little car had both pulled up about sixty yards into the street, in front of one of the big terraced houses which run all the way through to Marloes Road at the far end.

He pulled over, parked and leaped from the van, walking quickly back to the Scarsdale junction just in time to see Stephanie Adoré finish paying off the cab, then turn and hurry towards the house. Above her, on the steps, a tall figure was already fumbling with the lock, and for a moment as he turned the key, his face was illuminated by the street lights. At fifty yards Bond had no difficulty recognising him. He continued to walk, but two paces on, both of the targets had disappeared through the door, while the VW remained parked, oblivious to the operational ground rules of the trade, left in an almost arrogant manner for all to see.

It had started to drizzle, and a sharp cold wind suddenly choreographed the detritus of the gutters into tiny ritual flurries. Bond felt the cold and dampness, turned, hunched his shoulders and headed back to the van to radio in.

Ahead were the comparative bustle and street lights of the Earl's Court Road. To his left the big old houses that made up Scarsdale Villas stood back from the pavement. About forty yards from the junction the houses gave way, putting him against a wall.

He had been conscious of the headlights of a car coming from the far Marloes Road end of Scarsdale Villas, but now, a few paces from the turn into the Earl's Court Road, the sound of its engine was all but blotted out by a tall red bus passing the T-junction ahead of him.

He sensed the danger, swivelling back towards it, and saw the headlights bearing down on him, the wheels of a big old Rover mounting the pavement, aiming to crush him against the wall.

There were other noises—a shout, the scream of brakes from the Earl's Court Road end behind him—but his concentration was on the car barrelling towards him. Seconds before it hit, Bond launched himself towards the bonnet, rolling it like a movie stunt man, then breaking his fall into the road on the far side by going down, his right arm flung flat and his shoulder taking the full force of the fall, just as they had taught him long ago.

As he rolled past the driver, he glimpsed a hand and the dull metal of a weapon, but when the shots came, they were far away. The road leaped up and he felt the jar of pain down his right side as he continued to roll. Then there was the sound of the car crunching against the wall, the crackle of bodywork being mashed against brick and the revving of the motor.

In the final seconds of the roll, he lost control.

The momentum of the car and the force of his own spring across the bonnet had made for a clumsy landing, for he was travelling very fast. His head snapped back and hit the road. A million stars were flung bright and exploding against the darkness and the world seemed to spin.

Far away, he heard Natkowitz's voice shouting, asking if he was okay. Then the word 'Peradventure' scuttled through his mind and in the wink between consciousness and oblivion he laughed, for the memory was of an old joke—the elderly lady who always refused to say 'Peradventure' because of the quotation from the Book of Common Prayer—'If I say, Peradventure the darkness shall cover me.'

The darkness covered him, lifted him up and spat him out over two hours later.

CHAPTER SIX

FINAL BRIEFING

He came back to consciousness for a brief moment and saw Natkowitz's face floating over him, the Israeli's head circled by a halo from the street lighting. There were police all over the place and a lot of noise. 'I'm okay, give me a minute.' He recognised the kneeling figure who was pushing up his sleeve. He felt the slight sting, then the calm darkness washed over him again.

When next Bond opened his eyes, he knew exactly where he was, even though he had only set foot in the place a couple of times in his entire career. As his eyelids fluttered and he got his first slanted view of three walls and part of a ceiling, a picture of the safe house's exterior flashed into the back of his mind, as vivid as if he had been standing outside. Essex Villas, he thought, knowing the exact location of the place, tucked among the affluent houses north of Kensington High Street.

'All right, James?' It was one of the Service doctors. A Harley Street man who was on the P4 list of professional men and women, doctors, lawyers, accountants and the like on call for use by both MI5 and the SIS. His was the last face Bond had seen near him in the street. He thought to himself that the doctor had got there damned quickly.

He sat up, rubbed his right shoulder which was sore but not uncomfortable. Then he blinked, doing his own damage assessment. He felt bruised, a little nauseous, slightly giddy. As the doctor made a careful examination, concentrating on eyes and ears, the giddiness and sickness passed off, leaving him feeling much more in control.

'Twenty-four hours,' the doctor pronounced. 'No concussion as far as I can see, but you were out for a little while.'

'And you finished the job, eh?' Bond's mouth and throat were very dry and he recognised the effects of some anaesthetic.

The doctor looked at his watch. 'For about two hours. Trust me, James. It was necessary.' He turned to Bill Tanner who sat quietly in an armchair on the far side of the room. 'Can you do without him running around for twenty-four hours?'

Tanner gave a grim smile, and Bond noticed that

65

he cut his eyes away from the doctor. 'Not really, Doc. But if it has to be a day ... well.' He made a gesture of capitulation.

'What the hell happened?' Bond asked, now sitting on the edge of the bed once the doctor had left. 'And why the hell did he put me out?'

Tanner took a deep breath. 'Someone used common sense for a change. When things started to roll, they sent the doc and one of the private ambulances in that direction—the doc was on duty. He was briefed to make sure that, if either you or Pete were injured, you were to be taken out of it for a while. As it turned out, the initiative was correct. A lot of cops and civilians were about. You just might have said something we didn't want broadcast.'

Bond thought for a minute. 'Okay. So what actually happened before I went down?'

'Hope you can fill in some of the blanks, James. M's waiting for me to talk with you. How much did you see?'

He told his story, leaving nothing out. When he got to the Scarsdale Villas incident, he shook his head as though blaming himself for what had happened. 'I recognised the Volks from the plates. It wasn't difficult because I've been bringing myself up to scratch on most things. It was on a list of secondary vehicles tied to embassy staffs and I'd seen it only a couple of days ago. It belonged to Krysim—Oleg Ivanovich, if I remember correctly. Second Secretary Soviet Embassy. Moscow Centre's third man in London. It was him. After all he's been here for three years and I've come across him a number of times.'

'You're certain he was there?'

66

'Absolutely. Positive. Saw him quite clearly going into the house with the Adoré woman. I was going straight back to the van to radio in. I know a car tried to swat me, but ...'

'You did some little tricks,' Tanner supplied. 'Proper stuntman games. Could've broken your neck...'

'Better than being smashed to bits against that wall. Who was it? Rampart?'

'The same. Major Henri Rampart. He was out to shut you up. Made a mess of the Rover he was driving...'

'There was shooting,' Bond recalled.

'There was indeed. Causing us no end of a panic. Pete Natkowitz was behind Henri. We didn't even know he was carrying. He put three rounds into the rear tyres of the Rover.'

'So you got them all?'

Tanner shrugged, a rather hopeless gesture. 'Not one. Henri slewed the car away from the wall and took off on the rims of his rear wheels. Made it into Lexham Gardens which is what? Couple of blocks south? Quite a long way, and nobody on his tail, though there were plenty of witnesses. The local law are still questioning people, and we've got the Branch to do some PR—gangland violence, that kind of thing. In fact, M was still working on them a few minutes ago when I checked. The law have Natkowitz in the local nick.' He paused, his eyes making a God-imploring movement which suggested they had been through an all-time cock-up of Olympic standards. 'But, with luck, we'll have him out quickly. Also, with luck, the morning papers'll carry a story about rival criminals shooting it out in Kensington. No terrorists

67

connections, no questions.' He wrinkled his nose, then again added, 'With luck.'

'That'll please the local residents of snooty W8.' Bond frowned. 'You didn't get anybody?'

Bill Tanner gave another sigh. His eyes lost contact with Bond's and he shook his head.

'You lost them? You lost the adorable Adoré and the Russian as well?'

'I'm afraid so. We had people there, with the law, pretty fast. Birds had all flown by the look of things. They'd also cleared out their hotel rooms. Bills paid, all that kind of thing.'

Bond cursed. Then, 'Make any sense of it, Bill?'

'None at all; and we have the problem of what to do about the Soviet Embassy. A senior French lady spook and a notable member of their counter-terrorist unit slide into the country waving false flags, then set up a meet with the Russians' number three legal. What *do* we make of it? Even with the prevailing goodwill, O.I. Krysim will swear he sold the VW weeks ago and his suffering brothers'll say he was at home all night playing billiards. I should imagine M'll have something to say to his opposite number in Paris, but . . .'

'Maybe I can give him a cause.' Bond got to his feet and took a couple of exploratory steps, like a man testing the water on a sea shore, but it seemed the giddiness and nausea had gone altogether. His jacket was slung over the back of a chair and he reached inside for the stat of Mlle Adoré's official, and impertinent, card. Explaining the story about a French test of British security, he handed the paper to Tanner.

The Chief of Staff grunted and shook his head. 'Never seen anything like this before, and I'll bet

68

my pension that's rubbish, but we can try. How y'feeling, James?'

'I'll live. Shoulder's bruised. That's my own stupid fault, but there wasn't much of an option.' He blinked and moved his head around. 'Don't think there's any concussion. Bit annoyed at the doc putting me out. I'd have kept quiet, and you should all have known that.' Then, as though the thought had just come into his head, 'I suppose the Old Man's pretty furious. He wanted us to be up and away tomorrow.'

Tanner nodded. 'You might still be off tomorrow night. He considers it important. Even sent you some private reading. I'm to sit here until you've done with this.' He had reached into his briefcase on the floor beside him and pulled out a slim buff-coloured file. 'You read, James, and I then destroy. M's playing whatever this is very close to his chest.'

Bond opened the folder. It was headed *General Yevgeny Andreavich Yuskovich: Profile*. Below the heading was a photograph of a man who looked more like a stereotype scientist than a Red Army general. A slim, almost ascetic, certainly scholarly, face. Clear eyes looked into the camera from behind heavy-rimmed spectacles. Below the picture was a physical description.

Bond frowned then remembered how M had cautioned him. General Yuskovich was a direct first cousin to Josif Vorontsov through the latter's mother. The lineage was detailed on the next page where a small note had been added, dated that day, January 2nd 1991.

To all subscribers, reference Operation Fallen

Timbers. Given the initial claims that the Chushi Pravosudia *(Scales of Justice) have snatched Josif Vorontsov and are insisting the Soviet government accept him as a war criminal, the knowledge of Vorontsov's blood relationship with General Yuskovich must be taken into account. Bearing in mind that Yuskovich is a very powerful military leader, who has shown himself to be highly critical of the current leadership and its aims and objects, we cannot rule out attempts by this officer to undermine any positive action taken by the Kremlin. It should be noted that he has retained his place within the military hierarchy because of his undoubted expertise in his field: namely, nuclear ordnance and delivery systems.*

The note was written in M's familiar hand and the green ink he invariably used. Bond turned the page to read the brief, but succinct details of Yuskovich's career, which was impressive.

Born in 1924, Yuskovich had joined the Red Army in 1942 where he passed the short junior commander's course and went straight to the front as an artillery battery commander. Following the Great Patriotic War, as the Soviets refer to World War II, he attended the famed Frunze Military Academy, graduating in 1950. From there his career had been meteoric. First, as a major, he commanded a rocket battery becoming Chief of Staff only a decade later, when the Soviets had begun to make significant strides in delivery systems and rocketry in general.

From 1963 to 1965, Yuskovich attended the General Staff Academy, graduating with the coveted Gold Medal and obtaining the rank of major general serving in Turkestan, at the Ministry of Defence, and, later, as Commander-in-Chief, Southern Theatre Forces. He became C-in-C Rocket Forces in 1985 and had remained in that command ever since.

His military writings included learned papers on strategic matters, ranging from titles such as 'The Mighty Guard over the achievements of Socialism' to his most recent paper, published in the autumn of 1989, 'In Constant Combat Readiness.'

There were further notes which made it clear that, while he had clashed with the Kremlin leadership on many occasions, he remained the most experienced officer on rocketry, missiles, nuclear weapons and a whole range of delivery systems.

An unidentified Kremlin-watcher had added a note to the effect that the general was probably the most powerful hardline officer within the Central Committee of the Communist Party to which he had been elected as late as 1986. Yuskovich, in spite of his obvious anti-*perestroika* and *glasnost* views, had retained his position within the CC CPSU because he was simply the best military mind on his chosen subject. The man, the author maintained, still posed a real threat to the current leadership and the section ended on a sombre note. 'Yuskovich is an officer to be watched with great caution. During the ideological transition he has consistently and vociferously opposed the people at the top yet remained in power—a feat unshared by any other political or military figure.'

'The Chief said you were simply to assimilate that stuff for background.' Tanner watched Bond close the file. 'In fact he was most insistent about it. Kept

71

repeating "background".'

Bond nodded his understanding. 'So what's the score now?'

'You heard the doctor. He says twenty-four hours...'

'I don't need twenty-four hours. If we're going to do this, we should move fast.' He sat on the edge of the bed again. 'Look, Bill, I've been down this road too many times of late. Last year, for instance, I went into a situation in the US posing as a member of another group, and look what happened. I don't relish the idea of doing it in co-operation with KGB. But, if there's no other way...'

'I'm sure that if there was another operational course, M would take it. This simply appears to be the best Sunday punch.'

'Tell him I want to do it now then.' He looked steadily at his old friend. 'I'd like to get myself cleaned up and organised. Can I go back to my place? He can get me there any time he wants.'

Half-an-hour later, Bond was back in his ground-floor flat off Chelsea's King's Road. Before even beginning to clean up, he packed a lightweight flight bag with things he regarded as necessary for a trip to Moscow at this time of the year. The gear was more utilitarian than modish—thermal socks, underwear and gloves, together with thick rollnecks and cold weather outer clothing—though he did include a couple of suits and several normal shirts. Who knew where he might find himself?

He made careful choices of ancillary equipment which included the ASP 9mm automatic and several clips of ammunition. Though the ASP was no longer being made, Bond had retained it as his weapon of choice. After all, he knew that similar pistols were in great demand, changing hands at between $3—4,000 a time. The new, bulky 10mm automatic, now being used by the American law enforcement and counterintelligence agencies was certainly a man-stopper of the highest order, though he considered it too bulky for him to carry in his kind of work.

He rechecked everything, then headed for the bathroom where he stood for a long time under a scalding hot shower, trying to ease the bruising from his shoulders. He followed this with a stingingly cold shower, then towelled himself down vigorously.

He was about to climb between the sheets when the secure, direct line from headquarters rang.

'007?' It was M's gravel voice.

'Sir?'

'We're sending a car for you at eight thirty in the morning. Chief of Staff tells me you're anxious to get going. You feel fit enough?'

'Perfectly, sir.'

'Good man. Bring anything you might require. We plan to get you off sometime tomorrow evening. I'll give you all necessary updates in the morning.'

The Old Man had cradled the telephone at his end before Bond even had time to reply. He arranged an alarm call for seven, then turned out the light. He was asleep within five minutes.

★   ★   ★

Though all exit points from the United Kingdom were being watched by members of the Security Service and the police, nobody paid much attention to the tall girl with long jet black hair who boarded

73

the first British Airways flight, BA 446, out of Gatwick airport to Amsterdam. That is, they did not pay any attention to her in the sense of security. Certainly, on this bitter morning, many a young officer's blood was stirred, for she wore a pair of jeans designed, it appeared, as a second skin, and a very tight turtleneck sweater. She had a heavy camel-hair coat over one arm and carried only a small flight bag. Her British passport showed that she was Harriet Goode, thirty years of age and a senior executive of a small firm which dealt in precious stones, mainly diamonds, in Hatton Garden. She was polite and even flirted a little with the passport control officer who checked her through on to the air side.

The flight took off shortly after seven thirty, only ten minutes late. Mlle Stephanie Adoré ate the complimentary breakfast with obvious enjoyment—after all, it was the first food she had taken since the meal with Mr Boldman at the Café Royal. As she looked out across the grey desert of cloud, she thought it would be good to get into Amsterdam. For one thing she would be able to rid herself of the wig which was uncomfortable and hot. She would vanish as Harriet Goode, and that would be a relief. She also wondered how Henri Rampart was faring.

He was, in fact, surviving very well. Just as the British Airways Boeing 737 Stretch was starting its approach to Amsterdam's Schipol Airport, Major Henri Rampart was calling a great deal of attention to himself as he boarded the 310 Airbus that was KLM Flight 118 at Heathrow. It was not the overtly sexual attention which had been afforded to Mlle Adoré at Gatwick, but rather the consideration reserved for the crippled or maimed.

74

Rampart had transformed himself into an elderly man requiring assistance from the airport authorities in order to board the flight. His height was camouflaged by the fact that he was in a wheelchair and by the more sophisticated magic of present-day disguise, his almost bald head had become a straggle of grey hair. On paper he was Robert Brace, a British citizen resident in Amsterdam who was returning, following a brief business trip to London, during which he had damaged his right leg in a fall. The leg was in plaster and Mr Brace was not in the best of moods. In fact he was downright bad-tempered and the personnel who had taken him down the jetway and on to the aircraft were relieved to see the back of him. They had also made certain that a message would go ahead to Schipol that he required some delicate and diplomatic handling.

It was, perhaps, significant that Mr Brace became charm itself once they were airborne, and nobody would need to be concerned about the arrival at Schipol for he mentioned that his daughter would be meeting him.

★　　　★　　　★

'I wanted a word with you alone, before Mr Natkowitz joins us.' M sat behind the big glass desk, looking tired and all of his years. He had greeted Bond warmly, enquiring about his health and again reassuring himself that his agent was quite prepared to undertake this mission. 'The Chief of Staff tells me you want to get it over with, though you did mention to him that you've been used in this stalking-horse capacity maybe a little

75

too often of late. Eh?'

Bond said he was merely making an observation to Bill Tanner. 'I did say something about not being ecstatic about working with KGB.'

M grunted. 'Well, we have no other option. You read the stuff about General Yuskovich?'

'All of it, sir. You think he's going to be involved?'

'No idea, 007. No idea at all. But I wanted you to see all we had on him, if only to alert you to possibilities. If we know he is the war criminal, Josif Vorontsov's cousin, then we can take it for granted that he is also aware, and that he'll fight to keep Vorontsov, or anyone who is fingered as Vorontsov, out of the USSR. If he's had any influence, he has already succeeded. You seen the papers this morning?'

Bond shook his head.

'Well, I'll talk about that when Mr Natkowitz joins us in a few minutes. What I wanted to say to you is that it is our object to settle this matter, one way or another, as quickly as we're able. The business with Iraq might blow any time. I don't for a moment believe that Saddam Hussein is going to blink, as they say. The American Secretary of State can make overtures, as can anyone, but I would stake everything on the unpalatable fact that this wretched dictator's going to require a sharp lesson by force before the politicos can get down to real talking. I have no sides, because my job precludes me from being a political animal. I wouldn't even want to suggest to you what I think *should* be done. But I am pretty certain I know what is going to be forced upon the coalition countries in the Middle East, and, when that happens, I'm going to need

76

every experienced field agent I can lay my hands on. Understand?'

'Only too well, sir.'

'Good. This is a small sideshow. A small and undesirable sideshow, and the very fact we have the Mossad involved means you have to clean it up as soon as possible. I would prefer to have Mr Natkowitz back in Tel Aviv long before anything blows up in Iraq.' He seemed about to carry on, when the buzzer sounded on the control panel and Moneypenny's voice came through the speaker, saying that the Chief of Staff was there with Mr Natkowitz.

Natkowitz came in full of apologies, as though blaming himself first for Bond's predicament—what he called the 'argument with Rampart's car'—and the second for the problems his own arrest had caused.

He was even oversolicitous regarding Bond's physical health, until M closed him down with a rather harsh suggestion that they get on with the business in hand.

'I want to draw your attention to small reports which appeared in most of the London morning papers,' he began. Bill Tanner was passing photocopied sheets to both men. 'You'll note that the news appeared on the front pages of only two papers—the *Express* and the *Mail*. Everyone else carried it on page two. This should tell us that it is not being treated as a high-class priority in this country.'

Bond scanned the sheets Tanner had given to him. Most of the papers had simply reprinted a Foreign Office press report. The Kremlin had announced that they had now deliberated on the ultimatum given to them by the *Scales of Justice* regarding the so-called war criminal, Josif Vorontsov, and had decided that they respectfully reserved the right to deny this man's extradition into the Soviet Union. The grounds were plain and straightforward. 'Bearing in mind our own intelligence on Josif Vorontsov, we are not convinced that the so-called *Scales of Justice* has, in fact, apprehended the correct man. The State Organs, meaning KGB, have irrefutable evidence as to the condition and whereabouts of the real Josif Vorontsov.'

'I need to tell you,' M said, looking at Bond and then Natkowitz in turn, 'the Kremlin has no information from us, and I presume, Mr Natkowitz, your people have been even less forthcoming.'

'I spoke with Tel Aviv an hour ago, sir. They remain alert and are still searching for the man we *know* is Vorontsov.'

'Good.' M sat back. 'The information you are reading was released at midnight, London time. That is, three a.m. Moscow time. There have been developments.' He nodded to Tanner, who passed a typewritten sheet to each agent. 'The paper you hold in your hands contains the response by the *Scales of Justice*. We don't know what to believe, or whether they will attempt to carry out their threat. I want you to read and digest because it'll bring you up to date. You will see the deadline is six o'clock, Moscow time. That's three this afternoon over here, and by that time I hope to have the pair of you en route to Moscow.'

Bond felt a distinct nudge of concern as he read the terse print-out which was the *Scales of Justice*'s

78

last message to the Kremlin.

Communiqué Number Two: We have received the negative response to our justified demands that the Kremlin take into custody the traitor and war criminal, Josif Vorontsov, who we hold against his trial in the Soviet Union for the reprehensible offences committed by this man on Russian soil during the Great Patriotic War. We ask the Kremlin to reconsider. At the same time, we are taking steps to make video recordings, which will be made available to many concerned countries, proving the case against Vorontsov. However, while we do this, we hope for a change of heart by the leaders of the homeland. To show that we mean what we say, if the authorities do not respond in a more positive fashion by six o'clock this evening, a member of the so-called State Organs, known also as KGB, will pay the penalty. So if we hear nothing of a change of attitude by six p.m. today, January 3rd, 1991, a senior member of KGB will be publicly executed.

As before, the communiqué was signed *Chushi Pravosudia*.

'They mean it,' Bond said flatly.

'Course they mean it, 007,' M grunted, as though he were addressing an imbecile. 'Sometime after fifteen hundred hours, London time, they're going to take out a visible KGB target. Agreed, Mr Natkowitz?'

'I should imagine they have some kind of capability, sir, yes. They've done it once on the streets of Moscow; tried it within the Kremlin. Yes, I think they mean it. I also suspect that their next

79

step will be to ask the Kremlin to prove their own theory by showing them the man *they* say is Vorontsov.'

'And continue with the terrorist attacks until they do,' Bond interjected.

M gave a sage nod. 'I would guess that, in the new spirit of freedom, they will approach your Service, Mr Natkowitz.'

'It'll be gall and wormwood in their mouths.' Pete Natkowitz did not smile. 'But they'll probably swallow their pride and ask Tel Aviv.'

'And Tel Aviv'll have to tell them what?' M's face held the vaguest hint of a smile.

'Tel Aviv will either lie to give us more time or tell them we've lost him.' Natkowitz did not come a thousand miles near to a smile. 'Personally, I think they will lie.'

'And KGB officers, or members of the Central Committee, will go on being executed,' M began to play with his pipe.

Bond nodded. 'If *Chushi Pravosudia* have the means, or until KGB can get a handle on them.'

'Well, gentlemen,' M leaned back, 'I suggest we get you into Moscow in double-quick time. The sooner you're there, the quicker KGB will be able to explain matters to you.' He held up one hand, palm facing outwards as though warding off a blow. 'Here, I must give you a definite instruction, and, Mr Natkowitz, it's an instruction I've cleared with your Chief also. If, once you've listened to KGB's briefing, you conclude that what they suggest is no-go, then you are to decline and ask to be pulled out with no fuss.' He paused for effect. 'I have made this clear to KGB. Now, let me tell you what we've arranged. You leave London at fifteen hundred hours from Northolt in a Royal Air Force transport which has been cleared into the military airport outside Moscow. After you've landed . . .' In all, M talked for the best part of an hour. There was another hour of questions from both Bond and Natkowitz, then another briefing by specialist officers.

On the stroke of three that afternoon, a Royal Air Force VC10, brought down from Lyneham, lifted off from the RAF base at Northolt, west of London. Bond and Natkowitz were on board.

*　　*　　*

Colonel General Victor Gregor'evitch Mechaev, one of the three most senior officers attached to KGB's First Chief Directorate, was on his way into Moscow from the FCD's modern Finnish-designed Foreign Intelligence HQ building at Yasenevo, just off the Moscow ring road. It was exactly six thirty in the evening, Moscow time.

He was in civilian clothes and bundled up against the harsh weather. As the car bowled along the road towards Moscow, Mechaev worked on the papers he would soon be delivering to KGB Chairman at Dzerzhinsky Square.

They were in traffic now as they drew near the exit, and it was with surprise that the colonel general heard his cellular phone start chirping beside him. He picked it up and answered.

'Mechaev.'

'Comrade Colonel General,' the voice was low and urgent, 'there have been some disturbing events regarding the documents you are taking to the Chairman. This is Riuchev.' Colonel Riuchev was one of the colonel general's aides. 'We are on the way, following you from Yesenevo now and I would respectfully ask you to pull over before the exit so that we can catch up with you.'

'Must I?' The colonel general looked at the traffic which, while not heavy by Western standards, was moderately thick.

'I think it would be best, comrade, if we are not to look a little stupid.'

'Very well. How far are you behind me?'

'About five minutes, comrade Colonel General.'

'I'll pull over now.' He leaned forward and tapped his driver on the shoulder, ordering him to get into the slow lane, then off the road altogether. 'Pull off before the Babushkin exit. Another car will join us,' he said.

The driver nodded, signalled and started to move over. A couple of minutes later he stopped and glanced round. The colonel general did not even notice the battered old Zil which had drawn up behind him, but the driver saw it and smiled.

'What are you smiling at?' the colonel general snapped, seeing the round smooth face of the driver grinning at him.

As he glimpsed the pistol pointing over the driver's seat, Mechaev realised he had been too busy to notice this was not his usual driver, but he hardly ever paid attention to the lower ranks who drove him, guarded him or saw to his necessary minor needs. As he threw an arm across his face as if to ward off a blow, he also thought to himself that it was not Riuchev's voice on the phone.

Mechaev's face was completely blown apart by the two heavy-calibre bullets with hollow points.

Later, when the investigation began, nobody

82

came forward to report a uniformed KGB driver leaving an official car and entering a very dented, limping and ancient Zil.

At seven fifteen, the duty officer at Number Two Dzerzhinsky Square took a telephone call which was later traced to the Kosmos Hotel on Mira Prospekt. The unidentified voice simply gave him the location of Colonel General Mechaev's car, then said, '*Chushi Pravosudia* have carried out the execution.'

CHAPTER SEVEN

FOUR WALLS

Their aircraft landed a few minutes before eight forty-five local time at Moscow's central military airport. The Scrivener had provided both of them with British papers. Bond was James Betteridge, the managing director of a firm which dealt in farming machinery, while Pete Natkowitz, with a stroke of the pen, had become Peter Newman, an accountant.

As soon as they were parked with engines stopped in a far corner of the facility, away from the executive buildings, two cars drove out accompanied by the maintenance van, halting near the steps which had been manhandled into place by a Russian ground crew. One of the cars was a long black Lincoln with tinted windows and big snow tyres.

Two plain-clothes men came on to the aircraft first, smiling and nodding, approaching Natkowitz and Bond with reassuring gestures.

In English they asked for passports in which they quickly stamped entry visas. 'When you are ready, please come straight down to the Lincoln,' one of the men nodded to Bond. 'He's waiting for you. Oh, and wear your gloves and parkas. Don't leave your skin uncovered. This is very much Russian winter.' Another broad smile and a cheery nod.

They went down the steps and walked, bundled in heavy parkas, to the long, comfortable looking Lincoln, ice crystals crunching under their mukluks.

In the darkness, snow seemed to surround them, sparkling in the lights from the cars or humped in high dirty banks on either side of cuttings gouged out to make roads and runways accessible. A driver, padded and fur-hatted, descended from the front of the car as they approached, slung their two flight bags into the boot and made hurrying gestures towards the rear passenger door like a sheepdog rounding up and penning a pair of strays.

The heat in the back of the car hit them like a humid front coming in suddenly in the wake of some unusual winter weather pattern.

'So, you have come. Good. Pleasure! Pleasure to meet you!' His accent was almost Oxbridge, but came out in a great boom, the sound of a merrymaker, a man of constant good humour. Bond had a clear view of him for the best part of a minute while the interior lights stayed on.

His first impression was of a large, powerful man, the face long and broad with oddly clownish Slavic features, thin light-coloured hair, one wayward lock falling on to his forehead. The man was alive with goodwill, twinkling eyes and a mobile mouth.

84

Instinctively Bond knew he would be a good mimic and an excellent teller of tales, the kind of person who would do all the accents.

'Stepakov,' he said, drawing out the second syllable Step-paaaa-kov, and clutching Bond's hand with a paw of very large dimensions. Then again, 'Stepakov,' to Natkowitz. 'Friends call me Bory—Boris—but they call me Bory. Please you also call me this, yes?'

'Delighted,' Bond felt there was need to put on a kind of silly-ass accent, though it was uncharacteristic, and he could not have said why he did it. 'James Betteridge. Friends call me James.'

'Good, so, James. And you must be Pete. London said to call you Pete.'

Natkowitz nodded in the gloom. 'Newman,' he said aloud.

'*Da*, very good. As in feeling like a new man, eh?' A gust of laughter, and the car began to pull away from the aircraft around which the ground crew was swarming. The pilot had said they would be on their way back within half-an-hour.

'New man, as in feeling like a, yes? You wish for something hot? Brandy? Stoly? Coffee?' Stepakov's face was occasionally lit as they drove past overhead lights.

They chose coffee, and the Russian proudly opened a built-in bar which contained, among a number of bottles, large flasks of coffee, black and scalding hot.

'You have used the, how do you say it, the facilities on the aircraft, yes? You have had pee?'

They both nodded.

'Good. If you want to pee again, let me know in good time and we will arrange something. It will

85

have to be at some service stop. No way you can do it in the open unless you wish to have your genders decapitated, so to speak. Frostbite is no respecter of person or personal effects.'

His laughter was infectious and he moved around a lot in the seat, taking up a great deal of room. The Lincoln had obviously been customised. Bond sat next to the Russian, while Pete Natkowitz faced them on one of a pair of jump seats flanking the cocktail bar.

'You see, we go quite a long way.' They could feel the man's smile.

'Not just into Moscow?' Bond asked.

'Oh, no. Definitely not into Moscow. You think we're going to give you guided tour of Centre?'

'We had hoped . . .' Bond began, and the Russian laughed again.

'You wanted to see the famous Memory Room where we keep pictures of our most famous spies, yes?'

It was Bond's turn to smile. 'It might be useful.'

'Sure,' Stepakov rumbled. 'When I come to London you take me to Special Forces Club, eh? Hans Crescent, Knightsbridge. I see some of the pictures there. Then VIP trip around your Century House. Good for a big laugh.'

'Welcome you with open arms, Bory.' Natkowitz nodded in the darkness. 'Where we going, Bory? Just so that we know.' His voice was even, but with an undertow of something that bordered on threat.

For a few seconds it was silent in the car. When Stepakov spoke again, all traces of the natural good humour had gone. 'Okay, I put you straight. Is necessary. Tonight the *Chushi Pravosudia* did what they promised. The body of a senior First Chief

86

Directorate officer was found, near Exit 95 on the ring road. They discovered his regular driver, drugged and unconscious, right inside the Yasenevo headquarters, and even the legendary Houdini couldn't get in there. So,' he seemed to take a long, sad, deep breath, 'so, is very secret all of this. We don't wish for it to be known, except for a very select number of trusted people, that you are in the country. These *Chushi Pravosudia* are serious. We're certain they have a very sophisticated organisation with people inside KGB and maybe even the Central Committee. They are not just hooligan elements. This is very critical business. Maybe affect the entire leadership, actually. So we have to be circumspect. Secret. We must move like ghosts from the enchanter fleeing—this is your poet Shelley, yes?'

'Possibly.' Bond frowned in the dark.

'Definitely. "Thou, from whose unseen presence the leaves dead/ Are driven, like ghosts from an enchanter fleeing." This is definitely Shelley. I read many of your great poets when I first learned English. Wordsworth, Longfellow, Shelley and your last poet of the people, Betjeman. Now him I really enjoyed. Our poets are full of gloom.'

'Not really up on Shelley, Bory.' Bond had never been a great one for poetry, unless you counted Homer.

Pete asked again, 'Where we going, Bory? Or is that *too* secret even to tell us?'

'Where do you think? Safe house, of course. Or really a safe dacha.'

'Ah, we would be talking about something around twenty-five miles west of Moscow then?'

'About that, yes.' They were on a main road now,

87

passing through a built-up area and Stepakov's face was lit up in a strobe effect from the overhead lights. He was smiling and nodding. 'I think you know the place, James. More coffee?'

Bond was now certain they were heading for either Nikolina Gora, Zhukovka or one of the other communities near them. In the bad old days, these places, west-south-west of the Kremlin, had been the luxury communities, the dachas for favoured writers and artists and the special so-called villages where the Party leaders lived in style. These areas used to be referred to by those in the know as Sovmin or Academic Khukovka. Sovmin was a well-guarded complex in which Cabinet ministers had their dachas hidden among beautiful woodland below the gentle hills outside Moscow. Bond had no reason to believe that anything had changed in that direction. Maybe the ideology had altered but the leadership would still have its privileges.

'Just sit back, James, and enjoy the journey.' Stepakov's voice took on a soothing tone. 'You will soon be asked to look at the harder side of life in this winter of discontent we appear to be suffering in Russia. Which means when we turn you loose, you will also suffer a little. Enjoy while you have the chance.'

Bond nodded, sipped his coffee and put his mind into idle. Pete Natkowitz appeared to have fallen asleep.

'He's called Boris Stepakov,' M had said. 'Boris Ivanovich Stepakov. Forty-five years of age. A career KGB officer with a lot of experience of terrorist groups throughout the world and an expert on dissidents within the Soviet Union. He's a product of the Andropov Institute also and he knows his stuff.'

Stepakov's experience ranged from service with the twentieth department of the First Chief Directorate—dealing with emergent, developing countries—to the investigation department of the Second Chief Directorate, which, in the main, oversees internal security and counterintelligence.

Tanner had said Stepakov was 'a man of awesome knowledge; in some ways, he wrote the book, literally. A KGB internal publication he called *The Stray Dogs*, an obvious reference to Qaddafi's infamous 1985 speech when he ranted about "hunting down stray dogs".' 'We have a right,' Qaddafi had said, 'to take a legitimate and sacred action—an entire people liquidating its opponents at home and abroad in broad daylight.'

The book dealt in great detail with such incidents as the 1969 attempt on Brezhnev's life, the many unreported hijackings of the seventies and the bombing of the Moscow subway in 1977. Tanner had claimed Stepakov to have been very honest throughout the book, advising his senior officers that KGB should take care when having dealings with terrorist organisations, particularly the PLO and others in the Middle East. He had even chided the KGB hierarchy and the Central Committee for having had dangerous affairs with Arafat and people like Ilich Ramîrez Sánchez, *The Jackal*.

'You will find him exceptional,' the Chief of Staff had said. 'Personally, I believe he had a great deal to do with the Soviet change of policy towards international terrorism in the 1980s.'

Now, in the back of the Lincoln, rocking its way through the frozen dark towards God knew where, they had come face to face with Boris Stepakov who was to be their case officer, their control in whatever the Russians needed to do in flushing out the *Scales of Justice*, the *Chushi Pravosudia*.

'You wrote a book, Bory. We've been told you wrote an excellent book,' Bond said after they had covered another mile.

The Russian laughed as though this was a joke. 'Sure, I wrote a book, but it didn't get into the best-seller lists, except inside KGB. I was young and foolish—well, maybe not so young, and for "foolish" you should read "honest". For a time, I thought I'd end up counting the trees.' He repeated the phrase in Russian, '*Schitayet derev'ya*.' It meant, in the old Russian argot, being sent to the Gulag.

'Our people think most highly of it.'

'They do? Well, it eventually had some success here. I would very much like to be able to write a great novel, but I have been confined to one unpleasant area of life. I am a specialist, so to speak. I was the one who asked for two people from your Service to help us out. There were some here who thought this a very daring move.' The light caught his face again, for a moment, and Bond thought he saw concern dance across the big Russian's eyes.

'We also thought it daring.' Bond tried to make light of the remark. 'Some of us thought it insane.'

There was a rumbling chuckle which seemed to come from deep inside Stepakov's stomach. 'Perhaps it *is* insane. Who knows? Personally, I think it's obvious. We have two English members of this *Scales of Justice*. Two men who are expected by these people. They are here to do a particular job and we have nobody who could pass themselves off as English. So we come to you.'

'These two ...' Bond began, but Stepakov cut him off.

'Wait, James. Wait until we can talk in complete security. No, that is not good English. You cannot talk in silence. I mean in absolute security.' He seemed to glance up and Bond saw that he was looking towards the broad back of the driver who concentrated on the road ahead. 'He's silent as a tomb. Been my driver for years. But...'

They were in open country now. No lights, just the impression of snow in tall banks, blown from the road to allow free passage of vehicles. Beyond the snowbanks the countryside remained blotted out by darkness. No moon or stars, just a blanket of black like a solid wall. They passed no other vehicles, only the occasional sign of life—a lonely single outpost or a huddle of houses and wooden shacks which made up some village, a small desolate community.

Bond remembered the first time he had driven in the American Midwest. He pictured the vastness, of great fields of grain in the Midwest, rippling to the far skyline, knowing that the corn or wheat went on for miles, further than the eye could see. As one who had been born into an island society, he had not been prepared then for the sense of space, and here it was again, even in the darkness—the realisation of being in a country so huge that it could even swallow the vastness of the United States and tuck it away into one corner.

At last they started to slow down and there were signs of life. Buildings and pavements at the sides of the road. Lights, then darkness again. More lights and a sudden turn to the right, taking them on to a broad unmade path where trees suddenly swallowed them up. A security post of some kind and a stunning blast of freezing air as the driver operated his window, threw out a hand and passed a document to a uniformed figure with a sub-machine gun slung over one shoulder and his face masked against the weather.

They were waved on, and a pair of great metal gates opened ahead of them, leading to a well-made road twisting between trees heavy with snow and ice. The roadway, Bond noticed, was clear and free of ice. Just inside the gates he saw a dark, thick horizontal line signifying the presence of a hidden barrier, probably a tall steel wall which would leap up from the road to stop any attempt at further progress by unauthorised persons.

They drove slowly, the tall firs thick on either side, and through them an occasional wink of light. About a mile further on, another turn to the right, then, suddenly, they burst from the trees, the house appearing as though by some illusion.

It was large—a two-storey structure mainly of wood with a low overhanging roof and windows set well back. Broad steps led up to what appeared to be the main door, though the entire structure was surrounded by a wooden platform, the roof supported by carved wooden pillars, a porch on which to laze during summer.

The thick dark circle of trees, the ice and the snow painted a raw picture. Whenever they tried to capture a scene like this in films, even on a real location, Bond considered, they failed utterly. The reality was always harsher, for in spite of the beauty of this house in the large clearing of firs, the impact upon the eyes, and then the mind, was bleak.

To the right of the house three cars were already

parked—two saloons and one that looked like a Range Rover, all with broad, studded winter tyres. The place was bathed in light from the windows and from hidden exterior bulbs, and Bond had to admire the way in which the dacha had been shielded from view until almost the final moment.

Natkowitz stirred and Stepakov shifted his bulk with a sigh. 'We're here. Wake up, Mr Pete, Mr New Man,' he split the name in two.

'Ah!' Pete gave an imitation of a hibernating animal making its first stir after the winter. 'This is it? We came all this way just to visit a ski lodge?'

Two men came down the broad wooden steps, opening the doors, taking their luggage from the boot, assisting them out and motioning them towards the door.

They walked from the freezing air into warmth from hidden heating and a large wood-burning stove in the great hallway. There was a smell of polish, wood and strong cigarette smoke. Bond's first thought was of descriptions he had read as a boy, descriptions of hunting lodges in *The Prisoner of Zenda*, or books of adventure by Dornford Yates. It was all there, from the polished floor, the rugs, the trophies on the walls, to the deep leather chairs and the feeling of height and space. A wide uncarpeted staircase curved down from a gallery which traversed the entire hallway and great carved beams angled up to the steep roof.

The door closed behind them and for the first time they saw Stepakov clearly—a tall, big man, smiling happily as he unzipped his long padded coat. He nodded to the pair of men who had come down to the car.

'These are my assistants.' His voice boomed like

93

a man with slight hearing loss who compensated by speaking too loudly. It was as though he were breaking some accepted behaviour, a boorish tourist talking stridently in a cathedral where people were worshipping. 'Alex and Nicki.' He introduced them, the two men coming forward and shaking hands without a hint of deference.

Alex was short and plump with a face straight from the Tenniel illustrations of Tweedledum and Tweedledee in *Through the Looking Glass*. Nicki was slim, dark, good-looking and muscular. He moved like a street fighter, and the same arrogance showed in his eyes. They were both dressed casually, and Bond instinctively tagged them as highly trained muscle, not knuckle-draggers but men with sharp IQs. They certainly worked as a pair, for their movements complemented one another and they seemed to hang on Stepakov's words in unspoken loyalty.

'Come, you'll be hungry.' Stepakov was now revealed to be dressed as casually as his assistants, in slacks, heavy sweater and a checkered shirt, unbuttoned at the neck. The slacks were baggy and crumpled as though he had slept in them—a man dressed for comfort, or action. The butt of an automatic pistol, tucked firmly into the small of his back, protruded from his waistband. He carried it as though the weapon was part of his body, a sign instantly recognisable to Bond. Now Stepakov led the way past the staircase to double doors which he flung open to reveal a long and wide room dominated by a table piled high with food.

Natkowitz's eyes slewed towards Bond and he raised one eyebrow, for the spread laid out for them was enough to feed all five men for about a

94

week—plates of *pirogi*, the glorious pies and pasties famous for their myriad fillings of egg, cabbage, sour cream, cucumber; large assorted plates of *zakuski*, salmon, herring, caviar, cold meats, salads, great loaves of black bread and salvers of *blinis* to eat with the smoked fish and caviar.

'Come, eat and drink. This is the best way we can get to know one another.' Stepakov strode to a separate table at the far end of the room, where serried ranks of bottles were ranged with military precision—wines from Moldavia to Armenia. 'We prefer sweet wines, James and Pete. You, from my studies, seem to like a drier variety...'

'I'll take whatever you have.' Natkowitz stuck his head forward. With his red hair and gentleman farmer's face, he looked for a moment like an expectant dog who has heard his master rattle a feeding bowl.

'This is good. A wine from Fetjaska. Dry. A fresh dry white.' The Russian showed no finesse, simply sloshing wine into two glasses and handing them to Bond and Natkowitz, while Alex and Nicki began to fill plates for them.

Here, Bond thought, one has to be careful. The notorious drinking habits of the Russians could rebound. M had said, 'Beware socialising, 007. I don't have to tell you no matter what favours we're doing in a spirit of co-operation, those people are still an intelligence-gathering organisation.' He did not really have to be reminded as he sipped the wine and began to dig into the plate overflowing with fish and meats.

'We were obviously badly informed,' Natkowitz took a large swallow of wine. 'In the West we're told that Russia is suffering from a dreadful food

95

shortage this winter.'

Stepakov's face split into a grin. 'Yes, you will see that soon enough, but you are guests of the Party. As our President has rightly said, there is only one true way to *perestroika*, and that is through the Communist Party.' He paused for a second, his eyes glistening with humour. 'There is not so much difference between the ideologies of capitalism and Communism, you know. The difference is simple. Capitalism is the exploitation of man by man,' a further pause, 'and Communism is the reverse.'

Alex and Nicki did not laugh as hard as their boss. They had undoubtedly heard the joke many times before.

As they ate and chatted, Alex and Nicki stood apart, one at each end of the room, like bodyguards. Finally Bond asked, 'Shouldn't we start work, Bory? We're here to do a job after all. I'd like to get at it.'

Stepakov turned his clownish face towards him with a look of sadness. 'All too soon you will have work to do, my friend. I promise you that. But here we are in four walls. You know what this means. In Russian it is like your saying, walls have ears. To be frank with you, actually, we don't like this. KGB operational training and all our instincts are against the use of safe houses. Briefings between four walls. But we have made a room here that is as safe as it can be. Tomorrow. First thing tomorrow morning, we shall start. I too need to hurry this along or things won't work out as we wish. By tomorrow night you'll both be out there in the cold of a Moscow winter. I promise you.'

★　　　★　　　★

96

Most large cities of the world have a particular smell or sound. With New York it is sound—that series of man-made caverns which distort traffic noises, and the wail of police or ambulance sirens echo as though they are in low, narrow rocky valleys. In Paris it is smell—a mixture of coffee and strong Gauloise cigarettes. The Irish city of Cork is identifiable by the aroma of fish which grows stronger the nearer you get to the docks. London, in the old days, before the Clean Air Act, had a special scent, sooty and distinctive. Berlin still has the tang of burning wood when it rains, a reminder of the terrible destruction at the end of World War II. Moscow, even in the freezing cold, smells slightly sour. This gets worse in summer and jokers have been known to say that Lenin's body, lying in state in the Red Square mausoleum, is responsible.

Nigsy Meadows caught the scent as soon as he stepped off the plane from Berlin. He knew that within a day he would have got used to it. It had all been very fast. Fanny Farmer, his replacement, had come in within three hours of receipt of M's signal. There had been quick exchanges of information, mainly of an operational nature, and an hour later, Nigsy was on a Lufthansa to Berlin, Tegel, and from there direct to Moscow, Sheremetyevo.

The Russian passport control officer flicked through his large black book, then raised his head and smiled. 'Nice to see you back, Mr Meadows,' was all he said in Russian, but to Meadows the unspoken words were there. 'Ah, Mr Meadows, British Embassy spook, what're you doing back in Moscow?'

There was an embassy car waiting, and Owen

97

Gladwyn, the number two to the SIS resident, sat in the back seat. He thrust out a large pugilist's hand to greet him. 'Bloody cold weather you've brought with you, Nigs. How's tricks?'

'Much the same. I hope there's some spare winter clothing knocking around in the shop.'

'Doubt it.' Gladwyn had a battered face, the inheritance from rugby football. It made him look like a first-rate hoodlum, though in fact he was a quiet, unassuming man who always got on with the job and never complained. 'Give the Centre a bell, they usually have plenty of hard-weather gear to spare. Number's 91, though nowadays you might even get a Porsche dealer.'

'Very amusing.' Nigsy was really unhappy. 'Is Jupiter at home?' Jupiter was this month's crypto for head of Moscow station.

'Never goes out. Got a light in the window for you, old boy. Can't wait.'

An hour later, Meadows was seated across from Jupiter, a rather smooth young man who had come up in the world like a rocket and was known back in the UK as the whizz-kid, for he was certainly uncannily talented. His true name was Gregory Findlay.

They faced each other in one of the two bubbles, as the hygienic rooms were called, deep within the embassy, safe from electronic or any other surveillance.

'So, I have an operation running on my turf with a big notice stuck to it telling me to keep out.' Findlay did not sound as peeved as his words indicated.

'Come on, you don't have to keep out, Greg. You'll know everything. I'll go through you all the

98

way. Fact is . . .'

'Fact is, old darling, you can override me at any time. That's what M says, and I presume he has a reason for it.'

'*Fact is*,' Meadows continued, speaking over him, 'I'm bloody tired, not to mention bereft of any proper clothes for this climate. Also, *you* have to brief me. Fanny only brought in the rudiments.'

'Don't really know what it's all about.' Findlay now did sound riled. 'I have a pile of "eyes only" signals for you and a long one for me which I have to pass on to you immediately on arrival, which is now.'

Meadows nodded.

'Right. *Operation Fallen Timbers*. We have two men in the field. Cryptos Block and Tackle, which sounds a bit muddied. I gather, however, that Block is of great operational importance, and word has it that he's a former 00 Section man. Could even be Bond, for all I know. They are working in close harmony with Centre, which sounds far-fetched but appears to be part of bloody *glasnost* which is emptying our ricebowls faster than a plague of locusts . . .'

'It won't last for ever, Greg. We both know it, so don't carp. Just give me all the contacts, map refs, signals, words, the usual.'

It took over an hour for head of Moscow station to hand over the long and involved list, then another hour for Meadows to unzip the 'eyes only' signals. None of it made much sense, except the part about *Chushi Pravosudia*, the *Scales of Justice*. Findlay told him they had picked up two signals on the previous evening leading them to believe a terrorist act had been threatened and then carried

99

out. They even had the name of the victim, Colonel General Victor Gregor'evitch Mechaev, 'And it couldn't happen to a more deserving guy,' Findlay had said as though he had ice in his veins.

So that was that. Meadows was aware. Meadows simply had to wait. Twenty-four hours a day until they either told him he could go home or there was a sudden panic alert from the ludicrously cryptoed Block or Tackle. Nigsy Meadows, a man of great intuition, just did not like the smell of it. But, then, Nigsy's nose had always been sensitive in Moscow.

*   *   *

James Bond dreamed he was reading a great encyclopaedia and had come across some odd reference to an ivory plaque which was handed from the monarch to a new head of the Secret Intelligence Service as a badge of office. When he woke, the dream was so vivid that he could see the entries above and below the ivory plaque paragraph. They were 'Ivy League' and 'IZL', and he knew what the latter meant. *Irgun Zevai Leumi*; the Irgun, the Jewish right-wing terrorist group active in Palestine in the late 1940s. The whole thing was so real that he wondered if he were reliving an actual experience.

Alex, Tweedledum, had shaken him gently awake and told him there would be breakfast in half-an-hour. The room was light and airy, and he recalled standing in the dark by the window on the previous evening, noting the tiny wire mesh and the telltale plastic nipples of sensors on the glass. There had been enough light from outside where the area around the dacha had remained like day. Just

100

beyond the edge of the light he had seen shadows moving regularly as though guards were walking the perimeter at timed intervals.

There was a bathroom off the bedroom, and he showered, shaved, and dressed in record time. Twenty minutes later, wearing slacks, a rollneck and soft leather moccasins, he went down the stairs and into the dining room where they had eaten so well the night before.

Natkowitz had beaten him to it and was sitting with Stepakov at a round table set in an alcove. Nicki gestured to the long table which now displayed an array of chafing-dishes containing bacon, eggs, kedgeree, ham, tomatoes and mushrooms. At the far end, there were large silver coffee pots and a dark-haired girl, who had not been on display the previous night, was making toast to order. She smiled at Bond, wished him good morning in English and was delighted to oversee the boiling of two eggs for exactly three and one third minutes.

'You slept well, James?' The large Stepakov rose to greet him. 'Pete, here, tells me he was off like a top. Yesterday must have been tiring for you.' His face remodelled itself into a comical expression. 'And if yesterday was tiring, wait till you get through today.' His laugh reverberated through the room and Bond thought that, for all Stepakov's friendliness and his vaunted brilliance in his particular field, the man could be exceptionally irritating.

He was just attacking his first egg when he saw the Russian look up towards the door. 'Ah,' he exclaimed. 'James, Pete, you haven't met our other guests yet. Let me introduce them.'

101

They rose, and Bond turned towards the door.

'Surprise. Mr Boldman's an old friend of mine,' said Stephanie Adoré as she approached the table. Behind her loomed the tall figure of Major Henri Rampart.

CHAPTER EIGHT

STEPAKOV'S BANDA

Bond had followed Stepakov's lead of the previous evening and was wearing, in plain sight, his ASP 9mm tucked into his waistband behind the right hip. Now, as he turned, his hand flashed to the weapon, but Stepakov's fingers were faster, clamping round Bond's wrist like a mantrap.

At the same moment, Pete Natkowitz bent his knees, his right hand going to an ankle holster, but Nicki, the street fighter, was on him like a dog, freezing him in a powerful hold so that he remained in an odd, half-squatting position.

'Nina!' Stepakov's voice cracked, like a sheriff in a Western, firing his old Buntline Special to gain attention.

Bond saw the dark girl who had boiled his eggs, flick at her skirt. There was a flash of exquisitely long leg and lace as the pistol appeared in her hand, jackdawed from a thigh holster. She moved with extraordinary grace and speed as though levitating across the room, the gun never wavering, held close to her left hip. She was beside Stephanie and the GIGN major, covering them.

It was impressive, Bond thought. All four of

them had been neutralised almost in the time it took to snap a finger. The exits were covered and Stepakov appeared calm while still continuing the pressure on Bond's wrist.

'I feared something like this. The British and French were not my ideal partners, but it had to be, so I'm going to ask you to relax. I also want you to make your peace.'

'The major, over there, tried to fly-swat me in London the night before last. Damned nearly did as well.' Bond's voice was level, with no hint of anger.

Stepakov grunted. 'I thought fly-swatting went out in Berlin. Late sixties. KGB used it a lot until the bills came in. It was too expensive on cars.'

'This was a very old car.' It was the first time Henri Rampart had spoken. The English was good, and though the muscles on his face remained set, nobody could miss the undertow of humour.

'Mlle Adoré also had me on a piece of string.' Bond shook himself free of Stepakov's hand, which, in effect, meant that the Russian had released him. 'She lied and had us waltzing around London looking like idiots.'

There was a strained pause in which the invisible daggers passing between the injured parties like missiles could almost be heard.

'This is the London incident about which you told me?' The Russian glared at Stephanie.

She nodded.

'Nobody said anything about attempts to kill or maim.'

Natkowitz had been allowed to straighten up. 'Bet they didn't tell you about the shooting either. We had a drama they'll be talking about over little lunches in smart Kensington for the rest of the year.'

Stepakov growled, then nodded towards Rampart. 'You wish to explain to Mr Betteridge and Mr Newman.'

Stephanie gave her tinkling laugh. 'Is that what they're calling themselves? In London your Mr Betteridge passed himself off as Mr Boldman, and he is, in fact, Captain James Bond.'

'You think I don't know this?' Stepakov raised his eyebrows. 'Just explain. Our arrangement didn't call for hostilities in London.'

Henri Rampart took a step forward, looking from Bond to Natkowitz. 'My sincere apologies to both of you. Captain Bond, I had no desire to kill you. I just wanted to rough you up a little...'

'In a brick and metal sandwich?'

'Maybe I'd have broken a few of your ribs. Things got difficult when your friend started shooting. At that moment I thought you were a junior member of the British Security Service. If I'd known ...' his voice trailed away like smoke on the wind.

'Tell us about it.' Bond stood his ground. 'You mean if you had known you had the Secret Intelligence Service or the SAS on your back you'd have been more gentle?'

'I think,' Stepakov's voice had completely lost its boom, retaining the crack of a whip or pistol shot quality. 'I think we should let all this drop for the present. It's sensitive and we'll have time to put this incident into perspective in an hour or so. Time is precious. So, let us eat breakfast, then go into details. You all know it is against my natural training to be doing this here, in a moderately secure dacha, so I am also on edge. Now, eat.'

104

'At least you should tell us why the French are here,' said Bond. 'This is something quite unexpected, something never mentioned. The Secret Intelligence Service has sent us to assist. We have the right to know why the DGSE and GIGN are involved.'

Stepakov sighed. 'Captain Bond, all in good time. You will be told everything at our special briefing. Enough.'

End of story for now. Bond realised that, while his first view of the Russian in the semi-darkness of the car at the military airport had been of a powerful man, his guard had dropped during the journey to the dacha. Now he saw clearly that Stepakov was indeed a very tough, uncompromising man, his physical attributes complementing a very high IQ—a person used to giving orders and one who was normally obeyed.

'A man of awesome knowledge,' Bill Tanner had said. Bond believed it as the Russian gave him a wide smile as though embracing him.

He went back to his eggs which were all but spoiled, and the look on his face must have betrayed him, for the dark girl Stepakov had called Nina came over and asked if she could do him two more. 'You are fussy about the way your eggs are cooked, I think.' She smiled at him, looking him in the eyes as though testing him.

He nodded and thanked her. She gave him another hard look, as though trying to see which one of them would blink first, then turned away. She wore a crisp blue dress not unlike a nurse's uniform and he realised that his eyes hardly left her as she walked back to the big table. He could sense the way in which her body moved inside the material which crackled as she walked, and his mind filled with that tiny glimpse of the long, stockinged leg and the hint of lace as she had drawn her pistol.

He picked up his coffee cup and saw Stepakov's eyes on him, smiling as though they shared a secret.

'Nina Bibikova,' he said, low and almost confidentially. 'A handful, I tell you, but one of my best. She worked in the Washington Embassy for two years and the Americans never made her. Secretarial cover, and I know for certain they didn't even keep a dossier on her. Both your Service and the Americans have the idea that our only employment for a woman is as *lastochka*, for honey traps.' He used the Russian word for 'swallow', KGB slang for the prostitutes or skilled seductresses they used for entrapment, an old speciality of their service.

'But, you see, they're wrong. Nina is very special.'

'Yes.' In the back of his head Bond saw the girl's large black eyes, the small crescent scar to the left of her mouth, the high cheekbones and now, her long slim fingers as she placed a plate with two freshly boiled eggs in front of him.

Again their eyes met, and he felt a distinct frisson of challenge. Unsummoned, his mind screened a clear picture of Nina's face above his, her lips descending on to his mouth. For a moment, he was filled with an almost tangible sense of yielding flesh.

'Thank you, Nina.' He wondered if his look betrayed the lust that had stirred at the winking centre of his manhood.

Her lips parted in an expression of acknowledgement and, though she did not speak,

106

the quick sliding of her tongue over her lips and the signal in her eye came directly from that all too human lexicon Bond already knew by heart.

There was very little conversation over the rest of breakfast. Stephanie Adoré tried to make it clear to everyone that she had enjoyed an evening at the Café Royal with Bond, hinting that this had been more than just a simple meal. Natkowitz made two remarks about the *Scales of Justice*, framing them as questions directed towards Stepakov who simply parried them and again made it clear that he would not be drawn. Henri Rampart ate three rolls, dry, with not even butter or a film of jam. When the Russian expressed surprise, he simply said that the doctor at his unit outside Paris maintained people should eat more dry bread. 'It is better for you than all the high-fibre diets the Americans hurl at you.' He lit a Gauloise, drawing hard on it, and continued to talk. 'The Americans are obsessed with diets, health, cholesterol and smoking. This is so crazy. At one time you had the simple choice, and smoked or you did not smoke. Now you cannot smoke for fear of people getting secondary inhalation. If this were so serious they should look to newsprint and books. Printers' ink is dangerously full of the same carbons they fear from cigarettes. So what do you do? Burn the books? Ban newspapers? Wear respirators in the streets to ward off all those fumes from the internal combustion engine? I guarantee that two hours reading a book will do as much harm as walking through a cloud of secondary smoke.' He spoke like a fanatic, and with some anger. Nobody commented. This was a well-worn monologue, the diatribe of one who wanted to defend the indefensible.

Alex and Nicki stood by the door and the lovely Nina walked between the round table and the coffee, filling cups and bringing extra toast. She did all this with dignity and no sense of servility. The fact that she was obviously on the team did not make her role as table-server demeaning.

*　　*　　*

The sterile room was in a basement carved out and cemented like a bombproof shelter. The walls, Bond noted, were lined with the thick anti-electronic material they used in embassy bubbles, the bubble that had been more or less stolen from the American practice, as it took up little space, and was one hundred per cent secure, though it caused much discomfort to those who had to use the igloo-like facilities in embassy bowels. Here, at the dacha, there was a whole large room and it was clear that no expense had been spared. Though the walls and ceiling were well-lined, there were also small electronic bafflers, grey boxes with winking red lights, fitted into the roof and at each corner of the room. The door had an extra sliding section which sealed it off from the crude wooden stairs and there was no telephone—an extra precaution lest security was somehow breached and the instrument made live.

They sat in comfortable leather chairs, arranged in a half-circle, and nobody was given a chance to take notes. No pens, pencils or paper were allowed in the room.

'This must be absolutely secure,' Stepakov began. 'We have taken great pains to make it so, for I suspect we know far more about *Chushi*

Pravosudia—what you call the *Scales of Justice*—than any of our visitors from France and the United Kingdom. Let me first explain my position in all this. My name, as you know, is Boris Ivanovich Stepakov and I hold the rank of General KGB. More than that, because of our fears of internal terrorism, I do not report through normal channels. I don't present myself to the Central Committee or the Praesidium. I don't have to make a physical report to dva 2 Ploshchad' Dzerzhinskogo, the postal address of KGB Moscow headquarters as I'm sure you know. I answer directly only to the Chairman, KGB, and the General Secretary, who is now also our President. You will realise why in a moment.

'You have met my immediate staff—Alex, Nicki and Nina. They are my most trusted people, and we have others, both here and at another dacha a couple of miles away in the forest. They act in a number of ways—they are bodyguards, go-betweens, analysts and keepers of my closest data bases. We are a kind of task force, and apart from these, others work unseen—in the Kremlin itself and secretly both in and outside our borders. We make up what is commonly known over here as Stepakov's Banda. In English, I suppose it might be translated as Stepakov's Mafia. Many within KGB and the army do not like us at all, and I have to be exceptionally careful both with information and my personal movements, particularly in Moscow.

'You must understand that we in the Soviet Union have not been in this business of international counterterrorism for very long. We have not yet started to share completely as you in the West share. This is, I suppose, the reason we have not altogether been forthcoming about the organisation you call the *Scales of Justice*.'

He coughed, clearing his throat before continuing. 'The *Scales of Justice*, or *Chushi Pravosudia* as we call them, first came to *your* attention in the October of last year. I fear we have had knowledge of them for much longer than that, and our knowledge will undoubtedly alarm you.'

It was as though he had begun to soften them up for something sinister—facts which possibly had escaped the West entirely. Whatever it was, James Bond felt an old familiar stirring—the desperate need to know everything about his enemy. He also sensed something else. It was as though all his experience had brought him to this one point. He had squared off against evil many times in his long career. Larger-than-life evil. Criminal, political and military wickedness. At the time, much of it had seemed unreal. Now it felt as if he were about to come up against a kind of reality he had never faced in the past.

The *Scales of Justice*, Stepakov told them, had come into being within the Soviet Union and her satellites of the old Eastern Bloc as early as 1987. Primarily, they had been Russian in concept, and at first KGB had believed they were another manifestation of unrest. Early on there had been informers. They knew, by the autumn of 1987, that *Chushi Pravosudia* was organised much as a network of agents was organised. 'Initially there were three rings, or cells, here within the Soviet Union. They have now amalgamated these into one.' Stepakov's manner was grave. His natural happy and boisterous personality seemed to have retreated as though the people of which he spoke were too

110

dangerous to laugh at or joke about.

'We know there was another ring in what used to be East Germany, one in Poland, one in Czechoslovakia. We were also aware of American, British and French connections. We detected this through informants. People we trusted. And this is significant—even those who informed did not know the full reality. From the autumn of 1987 until the autumn of 1988 we followed up on forty-two of these informants. They took us only to the people who made the first approach, the primary contacts. Let me tell you how it worked.

'It started with a whispering campaign. First, simply the name, *Chushi Pravosudia*, repeated over and over, passing from ear to ear. It spread through Moscow in a strange, confused manner. Through the more luxurious apartments along the Nevsky Prospect, among students at the university, like wildfire in the eggbox apartments of the workers, in the factories, in the illegal markets and bargaining places, in GUM and the other department stores, inside military barracks, and so into the Kremlin itself. Within days the name was known to everyone except foreign journalists from whom people instinctively kept this strange name. So *Chushi Pravosudia* became a household word. It also became something tangible. Through the repetition of the name, the organisation took on a life of its own.

'Then the informers began to pass information which was routed into my relatively new counterterrorist department. They used the MVD and special units of the police, following up on each reported case. But it led to nothing. Dead ends littered the filing cabinets and in-trays of my Banda.

111

'It was an exceptionally clever and ingenious ploy, when they ran traces back to those who had contacted the informants they came up against a frustrating wall. For the recruiters had been chosen by the *Scales of Justice* because of their own innocence. These recruiters fell into several distinct types: they were often people who lived alone, sometimes simpletons with only enough intelligence to carry out easy tasks, sometimes old women whose lives had become barren and useless, people who yearned for some task to keep themselves occupied. The call came to these innocent folk from strangers in a meat line or a bar, even in a group waiting at a bus stop. Those with telephones were contacted quietly, often early in the day, and always there was a promise. This is good work, they were told. Easy work. Work for the State. Nothing criminal. Each was given a name—usually it was someone they knew, even slightly. They had to ask this one person a number of questions: do you wish to serve your country so that life will become better? Are you willing to undertake some special job, for which we believe you are well-suited? Always there were the mystic words, *Chushi Pravosudia*. Always there was a special promise—a few roubles, a new television set, a food parcel.

'These simple, mainly good folk were lured into recruiting like men and women in Britain or the United States are offered lucrative work from home—addressing envelopes, canvassing over the telephone. We all know how *that* works,' Stepakov said. 'And the hell of it was that these people received their rewards, the few roubles, the television set, in one case a week's vacation. These were truly unwitting agents. They had no idea that

112

they were canvassing for an illegal terrorist group. When they had the answers to their set of questions, they would pass them on. They would be told to await a messenger or a telephone call. The messengers were often children they had never seen before or even someone in the very place they had first been approached. All insubstantial. Traces which led nowhere.'

The main worry, during this period—autumn '87 to autumn '88—was that the informers, reporting back to Stepakov's Banda were obviously only a fraction of those who had been approached.

'We knew,' he told them, 'that the *Chushi Pravosudia* was now a reality, and we were also aware they had started to spread out of the Soviet Union into the satellite countries of the old Eastern Bloc, even into other Western countries. Our agents caught traces of similar recruiting techniques, and from these we made calculated guesses about the locations and the number of cells. The *Scales of Justice* was exactly what Winston Churchill once said of the Soviet Union—a riddle wrapped in a mystery inside an enigma. But Churchill also predicted that there might be a key, and there *was* a key, but one which, initially, took us only a short way. It led us into the ante-room of the *Chushi Pravosudia*, and what we heard there made our blood run cold.'

It had happened almost by accident. The interrogation section of an MVD unit had hauled in a language professor who taught at Moscow University. He was suspected of what the authorities loosely termed 'Black Market Activities', which meant anything from dealing in illegal currency, to luxury items, right on up to straight and unadulterated espionage.

In the case of Vladimir Lyko, a senior professor of English, it was several illegal currency transactions amounting to some $100,000. There were no doubts, the evidence was there, the money had been traced, and one of the professor's pupils had informed.

'It was January 1989.' Stepakov placed his large rear end against the back of a chair, as if settling to tell a good tale. 'They got me out of bed at one in the morning, and I went straight to Lefortovo. The MVD had a direct instruction to contact me if they ever came across any evidence leading us to *Chushi Pravosudia*. The officer in charge of the interrogation told me that Lyko had things he would talk about. He wanted to do a deal, and, as you must know, this is strictly against our operational practice.' He gave a big smile. 'We never do deals. Except when we will gain much. From tiny acorns ... Well, Lyko was a very small acorn and he has grown into a very large tree.'

*   *   *

At the airport Bond had considered that the Russian would be a good story-teller. Now, with his mobile clown's face and a knack of graphic description, Stepakov told them about his first meeting with the professor. Bond had been right. He did all the voices.

Lefortovo is a grim, haunted place at the best of times. In winter it is truly bleak. They had Vladimir Lyko in a small interrogation room. Bare and unfriendly, with a table and two chairs bolted to a stone floor. The prisoner sat with his back to a

114

wall, and directly behind him, high in the stone, was a small circular opening. In the old days victims had been shot from that tiny aperture, usually just as the interrogating officer took their signed statement from the table and moved to one side.

Stepakov wore his heavy greatcoat for there was ice on the walls. Lyko looked, rightly, terrified. He was a typical academic from the university. A fussy little man, about forty years of age, with dusty short hair and the thin face of a zealot, in which the once fervent eyes now reflected his terror. His hands shook as Stepakov offered him a cigarette and the KGB man had to hold his wrist to steady him as he lit the smoke for him.

'Well, Vladi, you're in a fine pickle now. They tell me over one hundred thousand dollars cash. This is a great deal of money. Enough money to give you one year for every ten dollars. One year for ten in the Gulag. You think this is cold? Wait till you get to one of the camps. This'll feel like a summer vacation.' He paused, looking at the dismal, cringing figure who saw himself, at best, as one of the living dead.

'The boys here will be back. They'll take your statement, your confession, and you'll sign it. Then you'll be up in front of a tribunal, and away you'll go. Someone who's had it soft, like yourself, feels bad about that, and the shame will stretch into the very heart of your family.'

For the first time, Lyko spoke, 'I can provide information.'

'Good. Provide it. If the information is fact, then you could get fifty years knocked off your sentence.'

'I am one of the ...' he stopped, as though

115

making a huge effort. 'One of the *Chushi Pravosudia*.'

'Really?' Stepakov evinced surprise. 'Who are these *Chushi Pravosudia*? Can't say I know them.'

'You know very well what I'm talking about. I can give you a lot of help. Details.' For a second, Lyko seemed to have tapped a source of inner strength. That was good. This pitiful apology for a human being had found some self-respect.

'You can give me names?'

'Names are difficult. But I can give operational procedures; organisation; methods and, best of all, what *Chushi Pravosudia* is really doing.'

'Go on then. Talk.'

Little dusty-haired Lyko shook his head. The moment of courage seemed to have put new life into him. 'I'll talk to you, even work with you, only if charges are dropped.'

Stepakov slowly got up and began to walk towards the door. Then he turned back. 'If you have good information about *Chushi Pravosudia*, you'll give it to the interrogators here and they will pass it on to me. They're very good at that kind of thing.'

Lyko lifted his head. He actually smiled. 'I know,' he said quietly, his voice shaking, fear just below the surface. 'The problem is that the kind of information I have is useless without me. Information by itself cannot help you. For instance, do you know what *Chushi Pravosudia* really is?'

Stepakov stood, just looking at him for a moment. Then, quietly, he said, 'Tell me.'

Vladimir Lyko smiled and motioned for another cigarette. 'Now tell me,' Stepakov repeated after he had sat down again and lighted cigarettes for both

116

of them.

The professor gave a little mirthless laugh. '*Chushi Pravosudia* is an organisation up for hire. They are terrorist mercenaries, with no political aims, no morals, no set ideology. If the Islamic Jihad require assistance, then they will provide it, for money; if the German Red Army Faction ask for help with a particular target, *Chushi Pravosudia* will use its people in Germany, strictly for cash; any terrorist organisation in the entire world can look for logistic support, sometimes active field support, from *Chushi Pravosudia*. The *Scales of Justice* is their joke. There *is* no justice from them. They're in the game for the money, and what better place to use as a base than the USSR? The cradle of Communism. They have made it into a cradle of capitalist horror.'

Back in the present, in the hygienic room below the dacha, Boris Ivanovich Stepakov looked at Bond, Natkowitz, Stephanie Adoré, Henri Rampart and the three assistants. He arched his eyebrows, shrugged, and said—'The terrible thing is, he was telling the truth. That is exactly what *Chushi Pravosudia* were doing, are doing, and will go on doing if we don't stop them.'

The Russian continued to talk, filling in the gaps, putting things into perspective. Names and locations were difficult because the *Scales of Justice* were, by this time, expert in the art of concealment. Their work was always done through numerous cut-outs. The main cells merely planned. The plans were put into operation by paid couriers, or men who worked like agent handlers. One subject possibly led to another, but, as you went down the line, so the chain of command split into fragments,

117

tributaries, dead ends. Just as they had done their initial recruiting, so they ran operations, terrorist strikes, disruption, assassination and every conceivable kind of attack by covering tracks.

'Even the funds generated by their work come back to them in ways so complex that I have asked for, but not yet received, an entire department of accountants who are familiar with the global movement of money. Often the payments are made in cash, which is broken up into relatively small allotments, and passed hither and thither, until it seems to disappear. My friend Lyko's original $100,000 was payment for help in the murder of an Italian politician.' He said the name aloud. Then, '*Chushi Pravosudia* actually did the whole of *that* job.'

Bond could not be silent any longer. 'Bory, if what you're telling us is true, then these people must have access, must have a way into all kinds and conditions of organisations. Can you name any worldwide terrorist operations in which you know they have had a hand?'

Slowly, Stepakov nodded. Then he began to reel off a list of horrors and atrocities, from car bombs and fire bombs to shootings and kidnappings which crossed every continent and infiltrated every border.

'I don't believe it,' Bond said finally. 'The terrorist organisations we know about, scattered through Europe and the rest of the world, are well documented. We know names, places, operations. None of them leaves room for outside help, particularly help from some crackpot secret plotters within the borders of the Soviet Union.'

'There you're so wrong, James.' Stepakov had

118

not moved. He remained leaning against the chair back, unsmiling. His voice was steady, almost hypnotic. 'What should concern us is that *Chushi Pravosudia* has been able to provide arms, explosives and support to hundreds of incidents. Your normal counterterrorist experts take for granted that should the Hezbollah or the Red Army Faction or any one of the established terrorist groups claim a particular "event", as we so callously call them nowadays, we tend to believe them. There are clues, the well-known code words to the media, the kind of explosives, the handwriting. You think these cannot be copies, cannot be forged? Of course they can. They *are* forged by this group within the Soviet Union. It is a new kind of private enterprise, Captain Bond. You had better believe me.'

'So, what has all this really got to do with our being here?' Bond snapped back. In the depths of his mind a cloud of concern rose, black and threatening.

'Two reasons.' The room was very still, as though those listening were about to be given some terrible sentence. 'First, the long march of this our Motherland to a new, more open and free, kind of society is under threat. There are those who would see us back in the dark ages of something akin to Stalin's Great Terror. Second, the United Nations deadline to the Iraqis is getting very close. We have a hint that the *Chushi Pravosudia* have their fingers in both of those pies and, strangely, the entire business of this war criminal, Joel Penderek, is tied to each of these items.'

'How?'

'How?' the Russian echoed. 'I'll leave that for

119

you to discover first hand, Captain Bond. You and your colleague will have the opportunity of actually going out and, in all probability, meeting members of the inner circle of *Chushi Pravosudia* here in Moscow.' He nodded to Alex who stood by the door. 'Make sure he's been brought over.' Alex slid back the screen and hurried away.

'We are very much on top of present events, and the man we have been running as a ferret within the *Scales of Justice*, Professor Vladimir Lyko, should be the one to brief you. He will be here in a moment.'

'Then, if we have time,' Bond was still not completely convinced, 'are you yet prepared to tell us what our French friends are doing here?'

'The question is really what have they done?' The Russian treated them to one of his big smiles again. 'We could have asked *your* Service, but I doubt if you would have done it; the Americans would certainly have said no; the Israelis have a vested interest. In the end, we asked the French, and they performed very well indeed. Stephanie, my dear, would you tell Captain Bond exactly why you're here?'

Stephanie Adoré nodded elegantly, turning towards Bond. 'Oh, yes, James, I'll tell you. Our DGSE, in co-operation with the force to which Major Rampart belongs, ran an operation in the United States. We brought out the real Josif Vorontsov from right under the noses of the Americans and, I believe, an Israeli snatch team. It was a great success. We have Vorontsov safe, should the world require real evidence of his existence.'

'Uh-huh.' Bond nodded, glancing towards Pete

120

Natkowitz who seemed to be amused by the whole business. As Stephanie Adoré hit them with the news that the French had abducted Josif Vorontsov from Florida, Natkowitz had simply thrown back his head, mouth open in a silent laugh.

The French girl had the knack of delivering tidings which were neither comforting nor joyous, like someone cracking a walnut with a sledgehammer. Her sweet, tinkling manner was the velvet glove surrounding a steel fist. Stephanie Adoré, the name went through Bond's head. Stevedore, he thought automatically.

'Where the hell're you holding him ...?' Bond began, edgy and annoyed. But Natkowitz' amused restraint was a calming influence. Instead he smiled. 'You obviously did very well. Forgive me, but, if you have Vorontsov safe, what're you doing here? And why the visit to London?'

'Because we had a problem here. With Vorontsov.' Stepakov spread his hands as if to indicate that this answer was enough.

'What kind of a problem?'

'Okay.' Stepakov inclined his head towards Stephanie.

'You're familiar with hostage-taking techniques?' She was telling Bond, not asking him. 'In the situation we had with Vorontsov it was essential to get his confidence. To begin with we had him doped up to the eyeballs. You see, we had no clandestine way to get him out of the country. He had to walk, come of his own volition. No restraints. Just like Adolf Eichmann with the Israeli snatch team in 1960.'

Bond recalled that when the Israelis had lifted Adolf Eichmann, one of the main instigators of the

121

monstrous Nazi Holocaust, from Argentina to stand trial in Israel, they had persuaded him to walk out to an El Al scheduled flight disguised as a flight attendant.

'Yes.' He indicated that Stephanie should continue.

'I don't need to give you all the technicalities, but we drugged him initially. After that it was my job to be his friend, to reassure him and make certain he was not overanxious.' She gave a very Gallic shrug. 'This, of course, meant lying a great deal. Telling him that no harm would come to him. Making him totally pliable.'

Bond again made a little gesture to show he understood. Indeed he did. He knew the ways of hostage-takers and political kidnappers. You either scared the victim out of his wits or you made him feel at home. As a rule one person did exactly what Stephanie had been instructed to do, and should the victim have to be killed, it was usually the trusted one who did the killing. 'So you did all that, obviously. You got him to do as you wanted.'

'But of course. He even followed Eichmann's footsteps. We all walked on to an Aeroflot jet dressed as flight attendants. It was very easy.'

'So, why are you here now?'

'There was a small problem. Bory ...?' She appealed to Stepakov.

The exaggerated clown's smile. 'For obvious reasons we did not want to have Vorontsov sedated. Who knew when we might need him? Stephanie handed over her duties to Nina. Things didn't work out.'

'You see, it's like a psychiatrist and a patient,' Stephanie chimed in. 'What do they call it...?'

'Transference,' Bond supplied. 'When a patient has so much trust in a psychiatrist that he becomes completely dependent. If it's a difference of sexes, the patient often persuades himself, or herself, that he's in love with the shrink.'

'Right. Happened just like you say,' Boris Stepakov sounded excited.

'I was removed,' Stephanie looked pleased with herself. 'He pined for me, poor monster. Wouldn't accept Nina. Even tried to attack her.'

'Was very difficult,' Stepakov made gestures with his hands as though mimimg a great physical problem. 'Nina came to me. She couldn't deal with it, so she suggested we bring Stephanie back.'

'And Henri came for the ride?'

'I came as muscle, Stephanie's minder, as you'd say.' Rampart did not even look in Bond's direction.

'Mmmm.' Bond still did not sound completely happy.

'James,' Mlle Adoré's voice dipped seductively. 'It was a kind of contract operation. We were hired. Money in the bank.'

'Mice,' Bond muttered, and they all knew what he meant. Mice was the English acronym used by all intelligence communities to indicate the four principle motivations of espionage agents: Money, Ideology, Compromise or Ego. The French had been attracted to the operation by money. It was often the strongest motive these days.

'Why London? Why did you . . . ?' Bond began. But at that moment the door opened, the screen slid back and Alex returned with a short, thin-faced man who had dusty-looking hair and wore spectacles.

123

'Come in, Vladi. Welcome.' Stepakov pushed back the chair and opened his arms to embrace the newcomer.

CHAPTER NINE

LYKO'S LITTLE ADVENTURE

Stepakov's effusive greeting and his previous description left none of them in any doubt that the man brought in by Alex was Vladimir Lyko. Indeed, he was almost a caricature of an academic: for one thing, his shabby jacket had leather patches on the elbows, the Western badge of office within the groves of academia. His whole appearance was untidy, a person divorced from the real world, small, cowed, a grey man. Yes, Bond realised, this was the archetypal grey man—the ideal spy—one who had difficulty in catching a waiter's eye. That was the old definition of the perfect agent. So here he was, the immaculate dissembler, moving into the room.

As Stepakov embraced him, the professor seemed to shrink back as though embarrassed by this show of affection, and his eyes bore that restless quality associated with someone who has suddenly been released from the prison of a library, the jail of study, and is now blinking in the unaccustomed sunlight of the real world.

'My former prisoner,' Stepakov boomed, all his heartiness up and operating at full strength, the lick of hair falling across his forehead, the long, clownish face frozen in a look of surprise, eyebrows

124

arched and mouth split like a watermelon segment. 'My former prisoner, now my long-term penetration agent within *Chushi Pravosudia*.' He gave everyone the benefit of the major smile, ushering the small, nervous figure on to centre stage, talking as he did so. 'Professor Vladi Lyko has much to say. You will be given a chance to question him afterwards, but you, Captain Bond, and you, Pete Newman,' pause and a laugh, finger stabbing the air in their general direction, 'you should realise his is the only true briefing you will receive. He has the answers, if you have the questions.'

The dusty-haired little professor cleared his throat, hands moving forward as though to arrange lecture notes on an invisible lectern. When he realised there were neither notes nor lectern, he dropped his arms and, for a few seconds, did not know what to do with his hands. He cleared his throat a second time, then started in with confidence that seemed at odds with his appearance. He spoke in English, clear and precise, with the hint of a South London accent.

'General Stepakov will have told you part of my story,' he began, glancing up, his eyes almost glowering and challenging the assembled company. 'I was a fool who wanted material gain offered to me by the *Scales of Justice*. When my folly was revealed, it became clear that my country, and the Party, would be best served by my working undercover.

'Let me first explain what the general has probably hinted at. *Chushi Pravosudia* is a truly cunning group. In my time working for them, I have yet actually to meet another senior member of

125

their controlling body face to face.

'These men and women could have been trained at the greatest espionage schools in the world. During my many debriefings with General Stepakov, it's become clear that they operate by rules so strict that the innermost cell of the organisation is always at arm's length.' He turned to look at Stepakov, asking if he had explained the initial recruiting methods used by the *Scales of Justice*.

Satisfied, Lyko continued. 'My first duty with the organisation was, as you know, the collection and dispersal of funds, mainly in US dollars. It was during this phase that the good general showed me the error of my ways.' Another little bow towards Stepakov.

Bond wondered how much of Lyko's script had been written for him. In spite of his confidence, the professsor seemed intent on making an apologia, a public confession which might even require a public penance.

'I was able to carry out the duties given to me by *Chushi Pravosudia* very effectively, especially once the general took over my secret life. He made it easier for me to launder the funds which passed through my hands and I began to make a great impression. Within a few months, the leadership decided that I was ready to organise recruiting for them abroad. Because of my command of English.' He gave a small self-satisfied smile and then bowed towards Nina Bibikova. 'Not as brilliant as Nina, of course, for she has an advantage; yet I was good enough and they gave me most detailed instructions. My target would be the United Kingdom, and they were specific about the kind of people they wished to recruit. The most interesting aspect, you will probably agree, is that whenever I was required to go abroad, the necessary documents were always there for me. They were also genuine. Never first-rate forgeries. The passport and visas given to me, together with the other documents, were *always* the real thing. I have been out of Russia a number of times, but never with the freedom these people gave to me.

'General Stepakov has rightly drawn attention to this. For it is another indication that *Chushi Pravosudia* either have powerful assistance from the authorities, or that members of the leadership are themselves high-ranking officers within the military and KGB. This concerns us greatly.'

He continued to talk for some twenty minutes on the type of persons targeted for recruitment in the United Kingdom. All were fervently left-wing in political outlook, and the accent was on assisting towards a better understanding of freedom within the Communist countries. It was also noteworthy that people with special skills were marked as high-priority objectives. Men with military experience, particularly those who had been trained for the modern electronic battlefield, also journalists, certain specialist doctors and nurses and people with experience of theatre—actors, make-up artists and designers. The reason for the inclusion of such a wide variety of specialists was hard to determine and if the little professor was to be believed, he enrolled a fair-sized network, even though it was sprinkled with notional non-existent recruits—a trick as old as the trade itself.

'None of us working within the General's Banda could come up with reasons, or any logical scenario, which would call for people of such variegated abilities. However, we now stand at a most urgent point, for with the latest events there is a chance that, with your help, we can break through into the command structure and so discover the final aims of *Scales of Justice*. So far, the main objective as you know, has been money—terrorist mercenary operations taken on and carried out solely for gain. You might not agree with me, but I have the distinct impression that, with this present action, we are seeing a change, a move towards some possibly ghastly end game.

'It started,' he told them, 'with what *Chushi Pravosudia* designated *Operation Daniel*. The prime object was to shame the Soviet President and the Central Committee into mounting a full-scale war crimes trial similar in nature to the Eichmann case. When Adolf Eichmann was finally tried in Israel back in 1961/62, the world applauded, and saw the trial and subsequent execution as true justice. It was put to me in very clear terms,' Lyko continued, 'that the arrest of Josif Vorontsov, formerly a Russian citizen, and his return to the Soviet Union would force the Kremlin to conduct a fair and absolute trial against a war criminal who was guilty of committing appalling crimes against Russian Jews during World War II. The very fact of a trial would signal to the world that the Central Committee—the Government of the USSR—was serious, and that its attitude of active and passive anti-Semitism had changed. For me, it began when I was informed, in a message brought to me at night, that the criminal Vorontsov was about to be arrested and brought back to Russia. This was a week before Joel Penderek was abducted in

America.'

Carefully, Lyko went through the various stages of *Operation Daniel*. The abduction, followed by *Chushi Pravosudia*'s demand and deadline. 'Naturally, I knew nothing of the operational arrangements,' he told them. 'But, from the moment they alerted me to the impending kidnap, I was told to be ready to move at a moment's notice. Even before the facts were made known to the world, I was equipped with documents and tickets so that I could travel to London, make contact with two of my recruits and bring them into Helsinki prior to seeing them safely transported to Moscow. They gave me the code word Optimum. As soon as I received this word, I was to follow rigid procedures.' He looked closely at Bond and then turned his eyes on Natkowitz. 'I received Optimum on the day after the deadline was delivered to the Kremlin, and there are two impressions which have remained vividly in my mind. I stress that they are only impressions and I cannot back them up with any hard facts. First, I am ninety-nine per cent certain that *Chushi Pravosudia* is *not* being paid to carry out this *Operation Daniel*. In other words, this is not another piece of contract terrorism but something devised solely by the organisation. It is as though much of the money made from previous acts of terrorism is now being used solely for a long-term plan. Secondly, I believe that the inner circle of leadership fully expected their demands to be rejected by the Kremlin. That rejection, as you all know, came yesterday. It was followed at great speed by a political assassination. General Stepakov agrees with me on these points and we both await a further act of terrorism in the name of the *Scales of*

Justice—probably within the present twenty-four hours.

'Now, it is very important for you to understand that at this moment, as far as my controllers in *Chushi Pravosudia* are concerned, I am not in Russia, but sitting in the comfort of the Hotel Hesperia in Helsinki, waiting for our British contacts to join me.' For the first time he smiled in a way which indicated that inside the reserved, serious, somewhat self-important shell, there was humour in the man.

'The British recruits are, in fact, hidden not far from here. Yet, when *Chushi Pravosudia* contact me, as they do practically every day, they firmly believe that I am still in Finland.' He gave them a bold, conspiratorial wink. 'Naturally, we have to thank General Stepakov for these clever deceptions, and I should tell you what has happened in some detail, for your own lives might well depend on the things we have done and the lessons that have been learned.' He paused as though suddenly short of breath.

'So, I went into London on Friday December 28th last year two days after Joel Penderek was snatched from Hawthorne, New Jersey...'

James Bond's concentration did not waver. His mind, trained to seek out key words at briefings like this, had automatically picked up and logged the serious facts. In some ways he had leaped ahead and could already divine a few of the things that had happened. He listened with all his senses to what Vladimir Lyko now said, as though living the little professor's adventure with him.

★   ★   ★

130

Vladimir Lyko had received a thick envelope, dropped through the letterbox of his apartment sometime during the dark hours of Christmas night. He had not made any attempt to watch for the messenger, though he knew that one of Stepakov's Banda was probably keeping the block under surveillance. They had done so before, and to little effect. Those who carried messages for *Chushi Pravosudia* were usually picked off the street, or from a bar. They were people chosen at random, like winners in a sweepstake, their prize a few roubles and the assurance that they were not breaking the law. Stepakov's people had yet to hit a jackpot of hard information concerning the random communications network. No courier was ever selected twice, and should the messages arrive by telephone, the conversation always lasted for less than two minutes. With the wire-tapping facilities of KGB, coupled with Moscow's telephone service, a good five minutes plus was required to trace the source of an incoming call.

The package contained a thick wad of travellers' cheques, some cash in English and Finnish notes, a valid American Express card, plus a Visa card issued by one of the major German banks, air tickets, travel documents and a passport which said Lyko was a German computer programmer. Other papers and pocket litter suggested he was en route to London for a course due to begin at the British offices of a multinational software firm, on January 2nd. Lyko's new name was Dieter Frobe. As ever, the professor's wife, an untidy, listless, heavy drinker, remained in the dark about her husband's double life. She asked no questions as long as there

131

was a good supply of Stoly in the apartment. The activator, Optimum, came, over the telephone, at 2 a.m. Friday, December 28th. The flight left at 8.40 a.m.

Herr Frobe came into Heathrow on time, passed through immigration and customs without setting off any bells or whistles, and took a taxi to one of those richly named, utilitarian hotels which litter the warren of streets around the junction of the Edgware Road and Oxford Street. This one, which he had never used before, lay behind the large department store, Selfridges. By midday, he had walked into Oxford Street itself and eaten a meal of shrimp cocktail, rump steak and trifle at an Angus Steak House near Marble Arch. At three in the afternoon he made his first telephone call, from a public box in Orchard Street.

A woman answered, her voice immediately recognisable. The moment he heard it, Lyko became obsessed with the idea that there might be a problem.

'Can I speak to Guy?'

'Sorry, Guy's out. I'll take a message ... Hey, is that Brian?'

'Yes, it's Brian. Will he be long, Guy, I mean?'

'No idea, Brian. Where've you been hiding yourself?'

'Helen, I need to speak with him, it's ...'

'He's over at the Beeb. Something to do with a job. Seeing some producer who says he can use him. Is this urgent? Is it ...?'

'Yes. Very urgent.'

The Beeb, Lyko knew, was the way people spoke of the British Broadcasting Corporation. He cursed, silently. If Guy was at the Beeb, heaven knew when

132

he would be back. The Beeb often used freelance cameramen like Guy on overseas documentaries or with second units for drama series. They could call a freelance and within a couple of hours he would find himself at the other side of the country. Again Lyko told Helen that this was extremely urgent. 'Tell him Lazarus.' This was the activator agreed with all the British recruits. 'We have to go tomorrow. Say I called. Just tell him, Helen.'

'Lazarus? Really?' Her voice had become breathy. Oh, God, he thought, Helen should have been kept out of it. He had told Stepakov that the woman was possibly a weak link. Mouthy, he had called her, meaning she was insecure. Stepakov said that was *Chushi Pravosudia*'s problem.

'Can he phone you? I'll get him to give you a bell the minute he gets in.' She was obviously excited, knowing her lover was committed to the cause of a new Communist freedom. You could sense that she felt Lazarus also included her.

'No. I have to be out,' he said, very quickly. 'Out now, in fact. But this *is* urgent. Ask him to stay by the dog, would you?' Lyko was particularly proud of this last. As often as not, someone from South London would call the telephone the dog. Rhyming slang, dog and bone, phone.

'I walked along Oxford Street, turned left, and made my way through to Marylebone High Street,' he told the silent, slightly cynical audience in the sterile room below the Russian forest. 'Give them the tradecraft,' Stepakov had instructed him. 'Don't elaborate. They'll want to hear you did the job well. These people believe in the rituals. They're old Cold War veterans and won't be impressed by your usual flamboyant lecture style.

133

And no shoddiness, Vladi. Understand?'

So he said nothing of what was going on in his head. Nothing about the pain of coming to England and only spending time in London. Lyko had learned, studied and taught English for the best part of his life. He loved, lived, and breathed Chaucer, Shakespeare, Dickens, Scott, the poets Wordsworth and Shelley. He had even instilled a love for Shelley in the clown-faced Stepakov. In England he wanted to visit the libraries, the old sites. He wanted to take a train to Stratford-upon-Avon and see the views that Shakespeare had seen. His mind was always on the great writers and poets when he was in England, but he told them none of this.

Lyko walked on into Marylebone High Street where he used another public telephone to call George. George was in and said, 'Yes, yes, of course. God, I thought this would never come. When do we leave?'

'As soon as I can get hold of Guy.'

'I'll stay in. Let me know as soon as you've got it organised.'

'I'll call you sometime tonight.'

Lyko walked back into Oxford Street, hailed a cab and asked to be dropped at the Hilton. He had not spotted the surveillance, but knew it would be there. Stepakov's people were good, and they were everywhere. He relied on them to pick up any watchers *Chushi Pravosudia* might have on his back. There had never been any sign of people following him, and Stepakov's men and women had come almost to second guess the little professor. They certainly knew his haunts and his morals. He had given no signal of success, so they would probably be in the Curzon Street/Shepherd Market area before him. 'All the time,' he told them in the sterile room, 'I doubled back. I lingered at shop windows. I detected no surveillance. I even spent half-an-hour in the Selfridges department store. People were returning gifts that were sub-standard, or broken. I saw a lot of women returning underwear.' A schoolboy snigger. 'Then I checked the street again.'

In telling the story, the professor was as honest as possible, though he clouded the next hour and a half by simply stating baldly, 'I went with a whore to pass the time.'

There was a splutter from Stepakov who was well aware of the way in which Vladimir Lyko passed the time with whores. He did it regularly on *Chushi Pravosudia* money whenever he got out of the country. His favourite was a tall black girl with immense breasts who worked the Shepherd Market area blatantly, unconcerned by the laws that banned prostitutes from the streets. Stepakov knew all about her. How they called her Shiner, and how she specialised in helping men like Lyko live out their fantasies. Stepakov's people had even bugged her little work apartment near Curzon Street and heard her tell of the client who liked to crawl around on all fours while she pelted him with oranges. He even brought the oranges with him while she provided the strange leather underwear on which he insisted. Stepakov considered this a great waste of oranges and was pleased that Lyko's sexual fantasies were more comprehensible. Why, he could supply Vladi with *lastochka* who owned whips and chains, right there in Moscow.

By six on that bitter cold evening, the professor

135

was back in Oxford Street and called Guy again, from another telephone kiosk. This time the cameraman was in, and elated by the news. They set up the meet for Gatwick airport the following afternoon.

'Where're we going?' Guy asked.

'You'll see soon enough. Tomorrow. Three o'clock.'

The professor glossed over the following hours, leaping ahead to the next afternoon. 'Here it began to get difficult. Helen turned up with the two men. They all insisted on her being with them. I had no papers for her. No visa. Nothing.'

This was real trouble. His instructions were clear. You will bring in the cameraman and sound assistant, they had told him. Now the two major players would not move without Helen who had often worked with them in the past. They argued that she was one of the team, so Lyko aborted that day's departure, returned to London and made a crash call to Sweden.

At ten o'clock the following morning a special delivery reached him at the hotel, direct from Stockholm. These people were very efficient. He thought they must have prepared documents for all the recruits, for the package contained a visa stamp and extra papers for Helen.

'You must understand that *Chushi Pravosudia* recruits from Britain, or anywhere else, were to use their own valid passports. They provided visas and other control documents. I was very concerned about being watched, because they seemed to have everything so tightly sewn up. Knew everything. So I made the next move quickly.'

He telephoned Sweden again, saying he was

136

heading into place. Helsinki. The group would follow as he instructed them. They met at Gatwick, and he gave them the tickets, all rescheduled by telephone, once more from a public kiosk.

He flew out to Helsinki that night, direct by Finnair from Heathrow. Stepakov's people picked him up at Vantaa. 'The most delicate part was about to begin. If we pulled it off, we would be very close to penetrating the *Scales of Justice*'s inner circle.'

The man who checked into the Hesperia Hotel under the name Dieter Frobe was not Lyko, but a trusted Stepakov agent, a former First Chief Directorate field agent who physically resembled the professor. They had briefed him thoroughly, and it was this man—in the sterile room they simply called him Dove—who had next made a crash call to the Swedish number, telling them there was a hold-up. The pigeons, he said, had been delayed. He would let them know as soon as they started to fly.

'Sweden appeared to accept this calmly at first.' Lyko was standing straighter, occasionally walking up and down as he went through the story of his little adventure. 'By two days ago they had started to get frantic.'

'We need the pigeons. We need them now.' The voice from Sweden was sharp, commanding.

'It's no fault of mine,' Dove told them, whining and laying it on with a trowel. 'I've ordered them. It is a domestic matter. Be patient.'

'The window is not large,' by which they meant there was a serious time-scale problem, a window of opportunity.

The people whom Dove talked of as the pigeons

137

were, in fact, long gone. All three, two men and a woman.

Lyko waited for them as they came off the Finnair flight from London. There was a car outside, he told them. He even helped them with the luggage. 'We must make a short helicopter trip,' he said.

'Never been in a helicopter.' Helen was more excited than the others, and was almost like a child once they were in the car which took them to the private flying area at the far corner of Vantaa airport.

The chopper was a big Mil Mi-26 with Aeroflot markings. The Finns were quite used to Aeroflot making unscheduled flights in and out. As always, they had co-operated with the request for his flight plan.

'They suspected nothing.' Lyko meant the 'pigeons' and gave a self-satisfied smirk. 'Within three hours we were here, or within a few miles from here.' He turned deferentially to Stepakov who motioned him to one side as though swatting an insect out of the way.

'Captain Bond, Mr Newman, you will now become Guy and George. Nina would pass as an English girl anywhere, being half-Scottish. That is correct, yes?' Bond nodded, and Stepakov laughed. 'I read bad English sometimes. Some people say Scotch.'

'Which is a drink,' Bond supplied grittily. Concern, the possibility of duplicity and a regiment of problems had already marched through his mind.

'Right, Scotch is a drink. You won't see much Scotch where you're going, I fear, Captain Bond. *Chushi Pravosudia* have instructed that you should

138

be at the Dom Knigi bookshop on Kalinina Prospect at seven thirty tonight. All three of you will enter and purchase a copy of *Crime and Punishment*—apt, huh? You will linger for a short time, and then leave. If contact is not made, there is a fallback at Arbat restaurant, nine o'clock. We shall be following you all the way. I have enough forces at my disposal to make absolutely certain that you are tracked wherever they take you. Now,' he put his head back and glanced from one to the other, 'you have many questions. You have also to spend time getting to know Nina, and we have to talk about signals, codewords and the usual trappings of an operation like this. There is much to do before seven thirty when you enter the most secret circle of the *Scales of Justice*. Questions?'

As James Bond opened his mouth to frame his initial concern, he knew they were in over their heads.

'What if you lose us?' He wanted to let Stepakov know he was not happy with the small amount of information. He wanted the Russian to feel he was anxious, if only to make the man more fearful, to pause and reflect. He repeated, 'What if you lose us?'

'Then you will be—what is the English slang? You will be in dead lumber? Is this correct?'

Bond nodded. 'I'm not ecstatic about the dead part. And what of our two French friends?'

'What indeed?' Stepakov made his clownish features go blank.

Then Natkowitz spoke, leaning back, looking lazy and unperturbed. 'Before we take this on, can you tell us your own assessment of the situation? The general objective of the *Scales of Justice*? What

139

they expect to accomplish?'

There was a long pause during which Bond counted to ten.

'Yes,' Stepakov's voice dropped almost to a whisper. '*Operation Daniel* might hold a clue. I think *Chushi Pravosudia* are planning what terrorists nowadays call a world-shattering spectacular, and I think you, and Captain Bond, and Nina here are going to be at the vortex of that spectacular. It might be that they know exactly what we're doing. In fact, it wouldn't surprise me if they're pulling our strings. Does that help you, Mr Peter Natkowitz? Please let's dispense with the Newman rubbish.'

CHAPTER TEN

DAUGHTER OF THE REGIMENT

It started to snow as they reached Kalinina Prospect, taking the slip road off Suvorovsky Boulevard. Flakes the size of silver dollars drifted sluggishly through the night air. Some hung motionless, for there was hardly any wind. Within a few minutes it began to thicken. The traffic moved slowly and bundled-up people trudged along the pavements, badly wrapped parcels silhouetted against the lighted shop windows. The scene had all the makings of a Christmas card.

Lyko drove. He said the snow would not last long. 'The blizzards are over for now. This means it's a little warmer, so it probably won't freeze again until the early hours. The city soon gets back to normal once the blizzards are gone.'

Hard dirty snow packed the gutters and was piled against buildings, leaving only two-thirds of the pavements clear.

Sitting in the back of the old, souped-up Zil, James Bond tried to make sense of the day. Since they left the dacha, he had immersed himself in everything he had seen and heard, his mind circling, buzzard-like, trying to pounce on one fact that made sense. The windshield wipers lazily pushed away the build-up of snow while the inside of the windows started to steam. Lyko swept his open hand across the glass, clearing a view for a few seconds. The road ahead looked bleak, rather than romantic. To Bond, everything looked bleak. He could make no sense of any part of the operation in which he and Natkowitz were engulfed. There was no shape, no form, no logic whichever way he looked at it.

When Stepakov had revealed the Natkowitz was an Israeli and an officer of the Mossad, Pete simply sat back and laughed at him, his face looking even more like that of a gentleman farmer in an English pub. You could almost see the phoney horse-brasses hanging around imitation Tudor beams.

Nicki had moved, blocking the door, his dark face threatening. Alex pushed his Tweedledum figure from the wall against which he had been leaning. Henri Rampart looked at his shoes as if displeased with their shine. The lovely Stephanie Adoré seemed to be posed for a glamorous photograph, her head cocked and one jewelled hand poised under her chin, while Nina Bibikova sat very still, her dark eyes fixed on Boris Stepakov.

'Look, Bory, I've always had great respect for

141

KGB. What makes you think, because my true name is Natkowitz, I'm the Mossad?'

Stepakov guffawed. 'Because, Pete Natkowitz, your handwriting has been on a hundred operations carried out by the Mossad, some of them against KGB. I know you. I have your dossier. In the Mossad you're as famous as Bond in his Service. Come on now. We know who you are, and I'm not going to become difficult about it. If the Israelis want to be in bed with the Brits, that's none of my business. My business is splitting open the *Chushi Pravosudia*, finding out what makes it tick. I needed two agents from British SIS. I now find I really need three, two men and a woman, but we can provide the woman. I'm not concerned if SIS send us one officer and a member of the Mossad. It'll be a neat trio—SIS, Mossad, KGB.'

'If you could provide a woman officer, why not the two men, Bory?' Bond asked, a whole chain of questions forming in his head.

Stepakov sighed, put one large hand on the chair against which he had earlier leaned, turned it around and sat down, straddling it, his thick arms resting along the back.

'James,' his face looked pained, 'do I have to explain the concerns we have about *Chushi Pravosudia*? It should be obvious to you that they are very well-organised. It doesn't take a huge intellect to see them for what they are—hardline, old-guard extremists with a lot of pull. We look over our shoulders all the time. These people have admission through doors we can barely open these days. Have you not yet worked out what Russia is really like now, poised over the abyss of ruin, economically scuppered and with the Neo-Stalinists

142

fighting to regain control? A year ago they said the Revolution had failed, now they tell us *perestroika* has failed. It's chaos. The hardliners have agents within KGB, within the Central Committee, they have friends at court. I truly believe they're everywhere.'

'So you're saying they probably hack into the computers at Dzerzhinsky Square and out in the Yasenevo complex...'

'Exactly. I...'

'So they will have all relevant details of your department, the Stepakov Banda. This means they probably know about this dacha, they have names, dates, photographs, personalities...'

'No!' Stepakov whip-cracked. 'No, not quite all.'

'Why not?'

'Because the important aspects of what insiders call the Stepakov Banda are just not in the computer systems. We made it that way. We organised it in that manner because we consider ourself an élitist force. At the end of 1989 all our records were removed from the data bases. We regrouped, we reorganised...'

'Then why no men? Why nobody who can successfully pose as a British camera crew?'

'Because we have very few new agents available, James. People like Alex and Nicki, here, were *never* listed. They were *never* field agents. We're long on executive personnel, but very, very short on field people. Those I have are men and women trained since November '89, and they're at full stretch. It took eight people to babysit Lyko in London and that was only one fragment of an operation. It hasn't been easy. I have *no* spare male bodies, James. I *do* happen to have one, and only one,

143

female who can do the job off the top of her head. I have Nina because she doesn't appear on any lists. Nowhere. I told you about that. Even Washington doesn't list her and as far as current KGB data's concerned, she doesn't show because ...' he paused, looking towards Nina Bibikova as though awaiting her permission to reveal something about which there was great secrecy. Bond just caught the small nod, the almost imperceptible jerk of her head, allowing Stepakov to continue.

'She doesn't show,' he paused again, swallowing. 'She doesn't show ... because she is dead.' He was not smiling as he said it.

'Shall I explain, Bory?' Nina had the kind of voice that made Bond think of velvet and honey. A voice smooth and deep as a cello. The brief words they had exchanged above ground in the dining room had not prepared him for the instrument that was released now as Boris Stepakov nodded.

'My father,' she began, standing unselfconsciously and looking at each person in turn, 'my father was Mikhail Bibikov, and that probably means nothing to any of you, for you all knew him under another name. Michael Brooks.'

'Jesus!' Contradictions, fears, all kinds of devils shrieked in Bond's head. '*The* Michael Brooks?' The name stuck in his throat.

'Yes,' she smiled, looking directly into his eyes. '*The* Michael Brooks. KGB never released his true name. Not even when he died. He returned to Moscow, followed shortly afterwards by my mother, in 1965. I was born later that year. I don't know if you knew my mother, Captain Bond?'

'Barely—as a young recruit.' His throat was dry, and as he looked at Nina, he suddenly realised

144

where her dark, wondrous looks came from. 'I certainly remember all the pictures. Emerald Lacy was quite a lady.'

Nina gave him a tiny nod. 'She was certainly a lady.'

In his mind, he saw the famous photograph of Emerald Lacy hanging in the Rogues Gallery at headquarters, the one used by the press and T.V at the time—Emerald leaning over one of the copying machines, chatting to the other girls in the cryptography pool—dark hair, lustrous complexion and the smile old hands said would make you think you were the one person who interested her. Senior officers used to call her the jewel in the crown, she was so good. The whole story returned, complete and unadulterated in all its disturbing detail, an epic film played out on the wide screen of his mind.

*   *   *

Michael Brooks began his career with the Secret Intelligence Service working for the old Special Operations Executive during World War II. He had been a contemporary of Philby, Burgess, Maclean, Blunt and Cairncross—those Cambridge graduates who had so successfully penetrated the British secret world at the behest of their KGB masters—so effective that they were known in the corridors of Dzerzhinsky Square as the Magnificent Five. Michael Brooks' name had never been associated with them, not even after his story came out—or that part of it which was allowed to be released and put under the public microscope.

Brooks had an incredibly successful war. He had run agents out of Lisbon, was parachuted into

France and, much later, Jugoslavia. When the peace came he was a natural for the Secret Intelligence Service and spent some time on the Middle- and Far-East Desks before moving, in the early years of the Cold War, to the Russian Desk, flitting between London and Berlin—debriefing agents, running three networks which Philby's final unmasking in 1964 caused to be closed down.

In the Secret Intelligence Service they said that should you write a history of operations from 1945 to 1965, Michael Brooks' handwriting would turn up in every chapter. He was omnipresent, you could sense him everywhere, from Malaya and Hong Kong to Berlin and the Soviet satellite countries. More, he seemed unstoppable, this tall, lean man with the patrician nose and iron-grey hair matched by the colour of his eyes. Impeccably turned out, always a military man in mufti, in some ways an anachronism next to the sweaters and slacks brigade who looked like mad scientists or refugees.

In the end, Brooks was just pipped at the post for Deputy Chief. Then, for a reason never revealed to either the public or his colleagues, he was suddenly cut adrift. Early retirement on pension and with no hint of dishonour.

A few weeks later, Michael Brooks disappeared. A fortnight after that the alarms went off. Emerald Lacy flew out to Bonn on a routine assignment, went missing, and reappeared, complete with photographs, at Moscow's main Soviet wedding place. The groom was Michael Brooks and it was only then that people began to wake up in horror, claiming the happy couple had been Moscow Centre penetrators, at it for years.

146

The story was played down. Brooks even issued a statement from Moscow. He had simply decided to live out his retirement in the Soviet Union. His political views had altered over the years.

The press kept it going as long as they could. Brooks' name appeared in the so-called true espionage books. Accusations flew around, but only those with immense, stratospheric security clearance were allowed to peep into the hall of distorting mirrors which constitutes the real world behind the myth of modern espionage.

Within the deep paranoia which surrounds intelligence communities the world over, the name Michael Brooks became taboo. At the very mention of the man, cabinet ministers became tight-lipped; D-notices showered on to editorial desks and journalists who were heavy-handed and stupid enough to mention him found themselves out of the door before they knew what had hit them. Stories persisted. Rumours remained rife, even with the passing of time.

James Bond was one of those who had been Sensation Cleared, as the wags dubbed the Michael Brooks/Emerald Lacy case, cryptoed Brutus, for reasons best known to those who make the decisions on coding. Now Bond looked at the lovely Nina with a renewed interest.

*   *   *

'I was educated in Russia and, later, England; my maternal grandmother took care of that side of things. I was passed off as her orphan grandchild.' Nina had a disconcerting way of standing perfectly still. She did not emphasise anything by using her

147

hands. It was as though her voice and a slight change in expression were enough.

'When I was seventeen, it was a *very* good year.' She gave a smile which lit up her face, her eyes alive, her mouth changing shape, showing the two small creases of laugh lines bracketing her lips.

'I spent a year in Switzerland,' Nina said, 'then came back to Moscow and, given my father's history, did the training and became an illegal. The Chairman wanted to keep my name off the official lists, and that was done. I spent two years in Washington with straight secretarial cover. I've never been blown because I've never been on an official KGB file.' She bit her lip, just a tiny movement, quick as a finger snap. Again, Bond saw the photograph of her mother. The girl was a mirror-image, looking up from under her eyelids, a hair's-breadth from flirting.

'As you probably know,' she was swallowing Bond with her eyes, 'my father and mother were both killed in a car wreck in January 1989. I was just getting over the shock when Bory came to me. He came, as he always does, at night and very well guarded. Bory can get around the city and the country like a ghost. He wanted me for his department, but he wanted me in absolute secrecy. So, I died.'

Bond did not blink. 'In a riding accident, I believe. I recall one of our more sensational tabloids carried an exclusive. The tragedy of Michael Brooks' family. A curse on your house. Something like that. You've ceased to exist, then? Though I suppose, as far as KGB's concerned, you're really the daughter of the regiment.'

She gave him another smile, and he saw a gold

148

light reflected off the taut, silky skin running from jaw to ear. 'Something like that,' she said, and sat down, flicking her blue skirt with the back of her left hand, as though to brush away stray crumbs. Bond recalled, from somewhere, that Brooks had been left-handed. Strange how trivia lodged itself persistently in the mind.

Stepakov still did not smile. 'She was riding. Horseback. In the woods west of Moscow. The weather had been bitter. Earth like bricks. Treacherous. The horse bolted. Threw her. The body was missing for three days. Two foresters found her. She was frozen stiff as a board. It was in the papers, this terrible tragedy. Could have happened to anyone. Just bad luck it was her. As you say, James, the tragedy of the Bibikovs.'

'Okay, Bory, so you've made your point.' Bond was polite, but firm, casting the Michael Brooks legend to one side. 'But there're other things I'd like to know. Things about our comrades in arms. Our French friends. They claim to have snatched Josif Vorontsov. What did they do with him, and why are they still among us?'

Stepakov gave a small burp of laughter. 'Don't the British say the French are always with us, like the poor?'

'Hadn't heard it that way.'

'Well, they *are* here, and they're going to stay here until it's over. In a way they're a little bit of collateral, James. They've given us the real Vorontsov. Believe me, we have him, safe and secure. Mlle Adoré and Major Rampart are our guests, just as they are part of this operation, in case we need them again.'

As he spoke, Bond was conscious of a tiny

149

electronic noise like a whining in the ears.

Stepakov nodded to Nicki who slid back the inner door and let himself out.

'The little noise. The singing in the ears.' Stepakov started to laugh as though to himself. 'It is our alarm signal down here. We have no telephone, so there is this small sound to alert us in case there's news or a message.' The laugh welled up. 'There's an old joke we make about it. We say it is dogs blowing people whistles.'

Bond moved the questions in close again, fast before Stepakov could sidetrack them. He wanted to know many things from Vladimir Lyko. Did the professor have any idea if any other recruiters were working for *Chushi Pravosudia* in England? The professor was obviously impressed with their techniques—the concealment, communications network, the tradecraft. Could he point to any weak link in his dealings with them? Why did he have the impression that *Operation Daniel* was not a contract piece of terrorism? Why did he think they required the types of people he had told them about—trained electronic battlefield technicians, doctors, nurses? Why actors? Could he give any hint? Why, at this moment, did they need a couple of freelance British cameramen?

Lyko answered as best he could, but threw no new light on things. When Bond came to the last question the door opened again and Nicki returned carrying sheets of paper. 'I think this might give you a hint, Captain Bond.'

Nicki did not even look in Bond's direction but walked fast, full of self-importance with his street fighter's swagger to where Stepakov sat and handed his chief the papers with a flourish.

150

Everyone waited, for Stepakov's whole body seemed to shut down as he read. There was a silence so dense and concentrated you could hear the breathing of various people. You could almost identify individuals by the different rhythms.

Stepakov looked up, then stood, his right hand flicking the papers so that they made a distinct crack. 'I must go and make some calls.' He began to move. *'Chushi Pravosudia* have done it again. They've killed and issued another statement.'

He was out of the room before anyone could ask further questions.

There was an uncomfortable shuffling, broken at last by Natkowitz who asked, 'Stephanie, am I reading Bory correctly? You're staying here by choice? He made it sound like the Iraqis holding foreigners as human shields. Which is it? You never *did* tell us why you came back into this country via London.'

Henri Rampart gave a mirthless bark. 'Let me.' He touched Stephanie's shoulder, but she shrank away from him.

'No, I'll tell him.' She leaned forward as though trying to make some intimate contact with Bond. 'James, *chéri*, you don't think we're *that* foolish do you? My darling man, we knew what we were doing. Bory asked the Piscine direct.' (They always called the DGSE headquarters La Piscine because of its proximity to the municipal swimming-pool on Boulevard Mortier. It was a vaguely pejorative term.)

Mlle Adoré talked on, her accent full of sparkle. Each word semed jolly, even touched with sarcasm. When a Frenchwoman speaks good English, Bond thought, it takes on a new tune. It is either a merry jig or a dirge. Stephanie made it all sound terribly amusing, in the old Noël Coward sense. 'La Piscine okayed it,' she shrugged, 'though you'd probably have some difficulty finding it in legible writing. It was not the easiest operation, but we did it or, to be correct, Henri's people did it. Snatched the man from his doorstep. Waved magic wands and brought him out on a flying carpet. Turned him over to Bory's people. But I've told you this already.'

'Stephanie,' Bond stayed cool and very correct. 'I've only met you once, in London a couple of days ago. I've read your file. I know we're in the same business, but we're not bosom friends.' He realised that, for some reason, he was distancing himself from her for Nina's benefit. 'Come on, Stephanie, what were you doing in London?'

She scowled, slightly taken aback, for she never imagined that James Bond, whose reputation was that of a gentleman, would speak to her like this. 'What can you mean?'

'We met *once*,' he repeated, 'in London. And on the same night after we had dined innocently at the Café Royal, you had a clandestine tryst with Oleg Ivanovich Krysim, known also as Oleg the Fixer, third Moscow Centre bandit in London. If it was all straightforward, why bother London?'

Her eyes cut towards Rampart, who twisted his mouth and said, 'Tell him. Bory would tell him.'

Stephanie Adoré gave a nod, curt as a death sentence. 'Simple. The Soviet Embassy in Paris ...' she trailed off as though still trying to make up her mind about revealing anything.

'The embassy in Paris is leaky,' Rampart supplied. 'Bory would not go through them. Not at

152

any point. Initially he came over himself to set things up in Paris. After that, our only contact was through Krysim, in London. He's Bory's man. We had a crash call from him, because of the Nina/Vorontsov business. So we came into London ... You know the rest.'

'I suppose we do,' Bond said grudgingly, and at that moment Stepakov returned.

He went straight back to his chair again, mounting it like a horseman. A sad clown now, with the blond hair hanging over his forehead. 'It's true, I'm afraid.' His voice was quiet and Bond could have sworn that the dark patches around his eyes took on the shape of the elongated stars used by so many clowns in their individual make-up. But it was only the way the light hit his face.

'At seven o'clock this morning, Anatoli Lazin, an Air Force colonel currently on the advisory staff to the President, came out of his office within the Kremlin. He always took a walk when the weather was clear. This morning he went into the Cathedrals Square. He was standing by the Queen of Bells, when someone shot him. Just once. Through the back of the head with a small calibre pistol. They have not captured the assassin. Colonel Lazin was a fine officer.'

'Loyal to the ideology of *perestroika*?' Bond asked, and Stepakov nodded. 'Of course. Very loyal. Believed absolutely that an open market, free trade, the new aims were the only way to go.'

'What of the KGB man who got himself killed yesterday?'

'Colonel General Mechaev?'

'Him, yes. What about his loyalty?'

'In line with the President. Why?'

153

'It makes sense if *Chushi Pravosudia* is really carrying out the assassinations, they're not likely to take out hardliners. It's about the only thing that does add up.'

Stepakov gave a little sideways nod. 'It's *Chushi Pravosudia*. No doubt of it. They've issued another communiqué, claiming responsibility. I should read it.' It was not a question. Everyone waited for Stepakov to compose himself. Finally he read, in a flat, unemotional voice:

'Communiqué Number 3: The governing body of the USSR remains adamantly stubborn. There has been no hint or sign that they intend to carry out our wishes and relieve us of the burden by taking the criminal Josif Vorontsov into custody and giving him a fair and open trial to show the world exactly how Russian people treat racial murderers. In our last communiqué we said we would place video recordings into the hands of the authorities proving our point beyond doubt. After much thought we have decided to take more drastic measures. We are now poised to carry out a trial under the current criminal laws of the USSR. This trial of the prisoner Vorontsov will be recorded on videotape and copied to every existing world television network. The trial will begin first thing tomorrow morning: January 5, 1990. We still urge the authorities to accept our demands. Meanwhile, we will ensure our outrage is felt at the highest level. This morning, a member of this organisation executed Colonel Anatoli Lazin of the Red Air Force, a senior adviser to the President. This execution was carried out within the Kremlin walls to show that

154

our reach is long and deadly. A member of the governing body or of the armed forces or the Secret Organs will die each day until the authorities remove the responsibility of Vorontsov from our shoulders. Long Live Truth: Long Live the Revolution of 1991.'

There was really no reason for Stepakov to add the signature *Chushi Pravosudia*.

'And the Kremlin?' Natkowitz asked.

'Have replied.' Stepakov hung his head, once more the sad clown. 'They have refused. On the same grounds as before. That the man held by *Chushi Pravosudia* is not the real Vorontsov. It seems as though we will soon be required to produce the man you brought from Florida, Stephanie. It is also clear why they require a British camera crew.'

'That's rubbish,' Bond said angrily. 'If they have Penderek holed up somewhere, and are going to proceed with some farcical trial, they could use anyone. If all you've told us is true, it doesn't matter a damn what nationality the camera crew is.'

'Obviously it matters to them.' Stepakov focused his baleful eyes on Bond. 'Just as it's clear they are determined to use you. Just as we are going to use you. I think we should now get our operational logistics together. We will all have to be very precise about what we do.'

They spent the rest of the day going through the nuts and bolts of the operation—telephone codes, hand signals, names and times to make contact should they get the opportunity. There were numerous telephone codes, seemingly innocent sentences and responses—all the safeguards and, sometimes ludicrous, tradecraft which, if used automatically and without thought, could turn individual intelligence agencies into microcosms of villages, where gossips tweak at lace curtains and watch with glee while lovers and petty villains go through sly charades, obvious for all to see. Tradecraft for the sake of tradecraft, an experienced instructor had told Bond years before, eventually becomes a nervous tic.

All the time, Stepakov maintained his people would have them covered. 'However fast *Chushi Pravosudia* move with you, we will be there,' he said. 'I have all my people back in Moscow and within a hundred miles of the city now, at this very moment. There is nobody left abroad. Even the surveillance crew used to watch Vladi in London is back here. We will not lose you, and you will take us right into the heart of *Chushi Pravosudia*.'

During the late afternoon, while they were getting their various items of gear together, Bond, dressed in his outdoor cold-weather clothes, excused himself and made for the nearest bathroom.

He checked the place as well as possible, screening himself from any mirrors, examining walls and ceiling for any hint of the pinhole lens of a fibre optic camera. When he was satisfied, he unzipped the inner lining of his parka, found the hidden studs and opened the lining which contained a miniature short-wave transmitter, complete with a tiny tape recorder, all held in place by strong velcro straps. From the lining of the parka's hood he removed a notebook-size computer, no larger than a deck of cards, and half the thickness of a packet of cigarettes. There was no form of disk drive in the

156

notebook computer. All the programs were stored on tiny chips. There was, however, a space at the back which accommodated a minute tape recorder.

Sliding the minicassette into place, he switched on the battery-powered notebook, then carefully typed in a message, using his fingernails to hit the keys accurately. The tape slowly moved, copying his input. When he completed the message, he rewound the tape, returned the notebook computer to its hiding place and put the tape back into the transmitter, which he set to the required frequency before that was also slipped back into the parka's lining.

He made a last check, to be sure his finger could reach the concealed transmitter. Then he went back to join the others.

They left at around four thirty, and it was only when they reached the suburbs of Moscow that Bond slid his hand into the parka. He pressed the transmit button as they passed through Vosstanya Square with the barbarous twenty-four storey building, the Gastronome grocery store, lit but empty, with little on its shelves, the cinema with a dejected line of people waiting for the next performance. The Vosstanya, he remembered, had been one of the great sites for barricades during the Revolution. He wondered how the old comrades of 1905 and 1917 viewed this tawdry, ugly place now.

He was certain the range would be right as the sudden two-second squirt-transmission leaped silently and invisibly into the air, guided straight to the heart of the British Embassy. He wondered what good it would do, and whether anyone really cared.

'We're half-an-hour early, what shall I do?' Lyko

asked, sudden panic in his voice as they came up to the Dom Knigi, Moscow's famous bookshop.

'Keep on driving, Vladi,' Nina snapped. She could have been talking to an unresponsive horse.

'Someone'll pick us up, if we just drive around aimlessly. I'll let you out.'

'Drive!' she all but shouted. 'But don't drive aimlessly. Do what you've been taught. Do a couple of blocks to the left, then go west again another two blocks. God, Vladi, hasn't Bory taught you anything?'

The professor hunched over the wheel and did not speak again until, at just before seven thirty, they drew up in front of the shop.

So, now here they were, Guy, George and Helen, a British camera crew, climbing from Lyko's car. Thanking him in Russian, laughing among themselves, they waved goodbye as they lugged their backpacks towards the Dom Knigi bookshop where they would purchase a copy of Fyodor Dostoyevsky's classic novel, *Crime and Punishment*. Bond wondered what irony lay at the heart of that choice by *Chushi Pravosudia*: the tale of Raskolnikov's demonic self-will, the murder he commits out of contempt for his fellow men and his redemption through the prostitute, Sonya.

Inside, the shop was warm, though the assistants looked bored, and only half-a-dozen people browsed among the books—two men and four women, dressed well enough in furs. He saw the flash of diamonds on the hand of one woman as she reached forward to take a foreign language espionage novel from the shelves.

The men, he thought, would be the ones to make contact. But the two quiet, studious-looking men

158

took no notice of the trio. One was in his early twenties, the other old with straggling hair and bottle-thick glasses.

They spent almost ten minutes deciding on the copy of *Crime and Punishment* they would buy, and it took a further fifteen minutes for the listless saleswoman to stir herself, take their money, check the copy and wrap it for them.

So it would be the fallback, Bond thought. The Arbat restaurant at nine o'clock. They had a lot of time to kill in the cold outside. But, as they left the shop, close together, turning right, looking as though they had a purpose in their walk, three young women closed in upon them from the street. One wore a magnificent fur with the collar turned high, the others had long, waisted coats, also with high collars. They looked like film extras from *Anna Karenina*. All of them wore fur hats and they giggled as they jostled close. Their black leather boots seemed to send sparks showering from the snow. Three girls out for a good time.

Natkowitz first thought they were high-class whores. Bond saw light-coloured curls peeping from under one of the fur hats. Then, between the giggles, the girl closest to them muttered, 'Turn right and keep walking until a car reaches us.' She spoke in English with no trace of an accent. The girls dropped back a little, still laughing and bumping shoulders. For a second, Bond and Nina were separated from Natkowitz, and Nina slid her hand through Bond's arm, nudging close and whispering, 'Trust nobody. Please trust none of them, not even Bory. We must talk ... later.' Then she just hung on as the long black car pulled up in front of them, doors opening and two men on the

159

pavement barring their way, stopping them gently, urging them to get in. The trio of girls was close behind, crowding in, pushing them into the car, laughing and giggling as though it were a great lark. The car resembled a stretch limo.

'Come. Fast,' one of the men, who looked like a tough bouncer for an illegal nightclub, hissed at them in bad English. 'Fast. You must be fast.'

'Quickly,' one of the girls cried, between giggles. 'Wake up! Quickly! You haven't got all night!'

'Listen to the sergeant major,' another of the girls said, and they all thought this was real wit.

The interior of the car smelled of garlic and cheap wine. Bond had hardly seated himself when they pulled away and he felt all reality spinning into a whirl of darkness. The last thing he remembered was Nina Bibikova's head falling towards his lap.

★   ★   ★

Professor Vladimir Lyko drove straight on after dropping the three at the bookshop. The snow was not too bad and he peered towards the pavement, looking for the familiar figure he knew would be there. Never had he let him down. When he said he would be at a certain spot, he would inevitably appear, like a genie.

There he was. Lyko would have recognised the walk anywhere. He pulled the car over towards the pavement, leaned across and opened the door for him to get in.

'There,' his passenger said brightly. 'There was no need to worry. Like clockwork, Vladi. I'm like clockwork.'

'Where do I go?'

160

'Keep driving. I'll show you. I'm your guardian angel, Vladi. You know that, don't you?'

The little professor nodded energetically as he concentrated on driving, following his friend's directions. As they neared the Moscow State University buildings, the streets became deserted.

'Pull over here,' the guardian angel told him, and Lyko had scarcely put on the handbrake when the bullet took off his face. The car filled with the smell from the pistol and from Lyko's bodily reaction. There had been no sound, only the light plop from the noise-reduction device on the gun.

Lyko's guardian angel had performed his last service. He stepped from the car and vanished quickly into the snowy Moscow night.

CHAPTER ELEVEN

HÔTEL DE LA JUSTICE

Greg Findlay, the SIS resident head of Moscow Station had limited resources at his disposal. While there was a natural tincture of resentment over a former resident, Nigsy Meadows, being attached to the embassy to run *Fallen Timbers* at his own discretion, Greg was duty bound to give Meadows all possible 'assistance, succour and help', as they described it in the textbook jargon. His two juniors, with second secretary cover, did not have need-to-know, so could not be used. Nigsy, however, had pleaded for two of the resident's four minders. The minders did any dirty work, from the occasional pick-up, to emptying dead-drops, to

161

babysitting, guarding, or even flushing out the competition. Certainly the Cold War was officially over, but you did not abandon regular operations overnight.

Findlay wondered what the Americans were about when he heard reports that certain senators and congressmen actually wanted to disband the CIA. That lunatic measure, he confided in anyone who would listen, was like removing a burglar alarm from your house in Mayfair because the police had caught one thief in Kensington. There were also strange claims being made in much-praised novels about a close co-operation between SIS and KGB. He prayed it was not so. By the shades of Richard Hannay and Bulldog Drummond, this would have been catastrophic folly on a grand scale.

Findlay also had at his disposal four cipher clerks who dealt with routine embassy work as well as performing extramural activities for the SIS resident. This quartet had to be closely involved with *Fallen Timbers*, and one of them, Wilson Sharp, was there to field the first catch.

Sharp had the swing shift—four to midnight—so had been on duty for less than three hours when the squirt-transmission came in, a few seconds after six thirty-five. There was no surprise when the needles flicked and the warning went off in his headset. He punched the rewind button, started a new tape on the secondary channel on the main receiver and picked up the telephone, all in three fast moves. Nigsy Meadows was in the communications room within seconds, snatching the tape from Sharp's hand and going down to the electronics bubble to work the decrypt machines. Ten minutes later he had Bond's signal *en clair*:

SoJ to lift self, Tackle plus Brutus's daughter from Dom Knigi, Kalinina Prospect, seven thirty this night. Fallback nine pip emma Arbat restaurant. Switched on. Please track. Block.

Nigsy was shouting for the car and one of the minders for protection should he need it before the decrypt had finished shredding into the burn bag.

Nigsy's own car was an old Volga he had bought on the black market during his last stint at the Moscow Embassy. He could have used one of the many British cars in the pool—in fact as SIS resident he was allotted a splendid Rover—but Nigsy felt less visible in the Volga. He had spent much of his spare time working on the vehicle, replacing engine parts and making it generally more roadworthy. When they had moved him on to Tel Aviv, Nigsy had put the Volga in mothballs as he knew some day soon he would return.

His priority, after arriving in Moscow, had been to check out the Volga, draw the dodgy equipment that had been shipped in under diplomatic seal, and install it in the vehicle. The Volga came out of the embassy gates just after seven. It was logged by the KGB surveillance team, who still carried out the routine, in spite of the official cancellation of Cold War activities. They immediately fingered the driver as Bolkonsky Two, their identifier for the former resident, together with a member of the British *boyevaya gruppa*—their own outdated jargon for a combat team used as a hit squad—riding shotgun.

Even in the snow, which came and went like a

163

tide, Nigsy drove just within the speed limit, turning left, then right, doubling back to get on to the Kamenny Bridge. He could see the floodlit gold onion domes of the Kremlin rising up to his right, for the Kamenny Bridge provides one of the best views of the Kremlin. In the far corner of his mind, Meadows thought that this had once been an ancient stone bridge, the very one Dostoyevsky's character, Raskolnikov, crossed on that sultry July afternoon in the opening chapter of *Crime and Punishment*. Everyone did a course of Russian literature, among other things, before being posted to the USSR, but Nigsy's thought could have been put down to some kind of ESP, for he knew nothing of Bond's task that night, to buy *Crime and Punishment* at Dom Knigi.

Years previously he had worked with Bond in Switzerland. Together they had set up a snare for a Soviet agent engaged in laundering money for pay-offs to support networks being organised in the United Kingdom. They had become close, and Meadows often thought he had learned more about fieldwork from the six months in Berne than from any other experience. He had an affinity for Bond which had lasted through the years and prided himself that he could read 007 like an ophthalmologist's chart at two paces.

They reached Kalinina Prospect via Marksa Prospect, skirting the hill topped by the old Pashkov Palace, now the Lenin Library, its circular belvedere just visible through the snow. As they made the first sweep, Meadows saw a grey MVD security van parking about a hundred metres from the bookshop and another one further down the street. They had all the telltale signs of watchers' vans—the tall, thick aerials and mirror windows at the rear.

He spoke rapidly to the minder, Dave Fletcher, as they drove, telling him what to look for, describing Bond, giving him the possible location in which the agent might be spotted. He circled the area in imprecise patterns, first left, then right, then doubling back and making an approach from a different direction, knowing he could not keep this up for long, as the MVD vans almost certainly had the licence number of the Volga from the embassy watchers. He did not want the vehicle stopped and scrutinised. It bore no CD plates, in direct contravention of standing orders, and he was also carrying highly illegal electronics—a modified Model 300 receiver, originally made by Winkelmann Security Systems of Surrey—adapted for field use by Service electronics wizards in London.

One of the buttons on Bond's parka contained a micro-transmitter, a strong homing device designed to talk only with this particular receiver, or one of its clones. The bleep came up just as Meadows thought it was time for them to be safe rather than sure. It showed that Bond was somewhere off to the right of them, behind Kalinina Prospect, moving at around thirty kilometres an hour.

'You read it,' he told Fletcher. 'Just tell me which way to go.'

They lost the signal five times over the next half-hour, but on each occasion it came up again, moving faster now and heading out of the city, going east. By nine o'clock they were out in the countryside, Meadows worrying that they might have problems getting back to the embassy. The snow was thickening, though the signal remained strong. Then, unexpectedly, the track changed, moving very fast indeed, coming towards them as though on a collision course.

Somewhere above the engine noise in the car they both heard the heavy thrum of helicopter motors.

Meadows cursed as he watched helplessly. Within three minutes the signal went out of range, travelling north-west. A couple of hours later, back at the embassy, he checked with Findlay to make certain the embassy would not wish to know about the operation, and sat down to cipher an 'eyes only' to M. All his experience told him that the *Scales of Justice* almost certainly had Bond out of Russia by now. M's detailed briefing, delivered in the main by Fanny Farmer in Tel Aviv, had suggested as much. 'The Old Man doesn't believe for one moment that these jokers have their main base anywhere near Moscow,' Farmer had said. 'His bet is on one of the Scandinavian countries, though it might be even further away.'

If M was on the ball—and when was he not?—Nigsy Meadows thought there would be a flash priority for him to get himself elsewhere first thing in the morning.

★　　　★　　　★

James Bond returned to consciousness like a man waking from a perfectly normal doze. There were none of the usual side-effects. No floating to the surface. No dry throat, fuzzed vision or disorientation. He was deeply unconscious one minute and wide awake the next. He smelled wood, and for a second, thought he was back in the

166

relative safety of the dacha. Then his brain leaped again. This was not the same polished scent. This was more like lying in a pine forest. The pleasant odour of the wood enveloped him and he wondered if *this* was some strange after-effect of chemicals. He knew they had used some form of drug. He saw the pavement and the car, like a limo, pulling up, heard the giggling of the girls and, clear in his head, a picture of the two young men. He even recalled the glimpse of a female leg, encased in a tight-fitting black leather boot, then Nina's head slumping onto his lap.

There was no sense of urgency. Bond simply lay there, smelling the wood and sifting through his last memories. Then he recalled the dreams—the incredible colours and the mists swirling around him as he levitated, the great waves of sound as though he were on a beach shrouded in this multicoloured fog with the roar of the sea he tried to see by peering through the murk. It was all real, immediate and vivid in his mind. He could almost believe it had happened. He seldom remembered dreams, so was surprised at the clarity of these images.

He heard the voices, urgent, shouting, over the noise of rolling breakers which came ever closer. He had felt himself being lifted up as though floating on an agitated sea. There was no fear of drowning, even when his body was picked up and slammed down again in the boiling ocean. This had gone on in his dream for some time, then suddenly the bumping stopped and quiet came. After that there were moments of erotic awareness, as though his body were wrapped around that of a woman he could neither see nor hear. He had dreamed of the

167

sexual act, knowing that he was performing it with someone for whom he felt great warmth and affection.

The ceiling above him was made of wood, untreated, not finished or varnished, simply plain pine worked into smooth planks which waited to be sealed and painted. Distantly he was aware that the scent emanated from the ceiling and, probably, from other parts of this unfinished room.

Automatically he tried to sit up, and this was the moment when Bond realised all his faculties had not been released from whatever they had inserted into his body. His brain and vision had been returned to him, but his limbs remained captive. It was a strange, not unpleasant, feeling, one which he accepted without really questioning the final outcome.

There was no sense of time passing, so he could not tell how quickly the memories of his dreams altered and became more substantial, but it seemed as though, quite suddenly, he knew some of the memory was not a dream.

The coloured swirling mist had been snow, with blue, green and red lights refracted through the whirl of flakes. He had not levitated. Strong arms had lifted him. The increasing sound of the sea was the steady engine noise of a large helicopter, and the voices were those of the crew, and others, who were strapping him down inside the body of the craft. The roller-coaster ride on the sea was the helicopter flight. Into his mind now came clear pictures, flashes of Pete Natkowitz and Nina Bibikova within the metal hull of a large Medevac chopper.

Lastly, he realised the erotic dream had been no dream. There had, indeed, been drug-induced sex, though he had no clear picture of his partner.

It was as he was pondering this last truth that Bond felt the chemical begin to leave his body, slipping from muscles and flesh, moving downwards. He thought this must be like death in reverse. Does death sometimes take you slowly, so that you feel each part of your physical make-up sliding away until the final enemy, the brain death, overcomes everything, plunging you into the seamless darkness? The unknowing?

He moved a hand, then started to reflex, lifting his head, and finally sitting up, propping himself on one elbow.

The room was large, high with a single, wide, arched window reaching up and almost covering one entire wall. Everything was in the same smooth, unfinished pine, even the long dressing table with mirrors set deeply into the wall behind it. There was a circular table and chairs, two stand chairs at the table and three cushioned chairs with long curving backs. The design of the room and everything in it, from the chairs to the bed on which he was now lying, was modern, functional and very Scandinavian. Not that this meant anything. The Russians had used the Scandinavian countries to supply furniture and design for many of their new hôtels.

He took in the size of the room, the doors—one leading to a bathroom—and the big window, before his mind began to monitor the bed itself, a great king-sized creation, a boxed framework holding a firm comfortable mattress. It somehow did not come as a shock to realise that someone else lay next to him on the bed, or that they were both naked.

Nina Bibikova was stretched out beside him, her

large dark eyes dancing with pleasure and her mouth trembling as it puckered into a smile. Neither of them felt embarrassment, and he saw that she lowered her eyes to search his own body just as he also raked her nakedness. She was on her back, the long legs slightly apart, one bent at the knee as though by way of invitation. For a second he took in the dark pelt at the apex of her thighs, then the smooth curve of her belly, with a neat, almost finicky dimple of a navel, and then to her breasts which thrust upwards to the deep dark aureoles and erect pink nipples like wild raspberries. They did not flatten and spread as the breasts of many women do when they lie flat on their backs. Nina's were firm, poised and hardly moved as she shifted her position.

It was Nina to whom he had made love at some point before his body—could it have been both their bodies—became trapped into immobility?

'Good morning, darling.' She spoke in the same, almost upper-crust, English she had used at the dacha. 'Sleep well?' As she said it, Nina turned on her side, still holding him with her eyes, one hand close to her face, a finger raised, making an almost imperceptible circle, the warning they all used to signify *son et lumière*, sound and light, audio and video bugs.

'Like a log. We'll have to sweep the bark out of the bed.' He was immediately aware that he was supposed to be Guy, the cameraman, and she was Helen. He raised a questioning eyebrow. 'Where are we?'

The Russian girl devoured him with her eyes. 'No idea, Guy. But wherever it is, we're very comfortable. They said there would be a job to do,

170

so I reckon this is where we do it.' Her hand went to his loins, practised, her fingers knowing and experienced.

At the rap on the door, they flung themselves apart as if they were guilty lovers. Bond called out as the double rap was repeated, then lunged from the bed, looking around for something to cover his body. Their backpacks were placed side by side against one of the more comfortable chairs. They were still fastened as though nobody had touched them or examined the contents. Then he spotted two towelling robes laid out on a long stool at the foot of the bed.

'Just a moment,' he called out, as he threw one to cover Nina's nakedness and wrapped his body in the other, pausing again by the door to ask, 'Who is it?'

'Breakfast.' A male voice, accented, though he could have been from anywhere—Spain, Italy, France.

Bond wondered which one of them had slipped the safety chain in place the previous night. The wood on the door was as smooth as Nina's skin. He felt it with his palms and then the back of his hand as he took off the chain and opened the door.

The man could have stepped straight from any major European hotel—black pants and a white jacket, swarthy, tanned, smiling and pushing a large room-service trolley.

''Ope you sleep well, sir, madam. Where you wan' the breakfast? Over by the win'ow?'

'That'll be fine. Thank you.' Bond expected him to produce a chit to be signed, but the waiter simply opened up the trolley, corrected the place settings on it, and then removed covered dishes from hot

171

boxes stored under one end before reciting the menu. 'You have bacon, eggs, hash-browns, tomatoes, juice, rolls, toast, confiture, coffee. This okay for you?' Then, as an afterthought, 'On the house. Is all on the house.'

Bond blanched slightly. Breakfast was the best meal of the day, though he normally did not eat eggs and bacon. 'Fine,' he lied. 'Splendid. Where are we?'

'Ah,' the waiter gave him a bland smile, 'you are in the complex we call the Hôtel de la Justice, sir. I am to tell you it will be explained.' He paused to look at his watch. 'You have plenty of time. Is only eight thirty. Your guide will come for you at ten thirty. Is enough time, yes?'

'Ample, yes. Thank you.' What else could he say? Intuition told him to behave normally, as though this were an everyday occurrence. As the waiter was bowing himself out, Bond asked, 'The building? It's not quite finished?'

The waiter smiled and shook his head. 'Not quite, sir. No. Soon it will be completed. It was built well, but in a short time. Eventually, they tell me, it will be splendid.'

'Hôtel de la Splendide Justice,' Bond muttered, half under his breath, as he looked under one of the plate covers at the pile of beautifully arranged food. 'Come on, love.' He grinned at Nina. In the far corner of his head, he realised that he was automatically slipping into the role of Guy, the cameraman. He even thought of the girl as Helen, his London lover, and wondered if, during the strange night journey, they had meddled with his mind.

As he began to tackle the food, he did some

172

mental stocktaking, questioning himself at each turn. He knew exactly who he was, what his orders had been; there was total awareness of Stepakov's plan and the swap that had been made for the three Londoners.

'You're very quiet, Guy?' She was looking at him in the same disarming manner across the table.

Bond shook his head, as though to rid himself of daydreams.

'It's been a remarkable couple of days, Helen. Or are you used to being put under and carted to Lord knows where?'

'Living with you, darling, has prepared me for anything. I mean messages like "Get your knickers on, we're off to Saudi in an hour..."'

'Only once. Only once did we do a trip like that.'

'Okay.' She sipped coffee, then took a mouthful of bacon and eggs, a little yolk escaping from her lower lip, running down her chin so that she had to mop it off quickly with the crisp, starched white napkin. 'Okay, so only once to Saudi...' another mouthful swallowed. 'But you've dashed all over the country at the drop of some producer's whim. That's why I was such a bitch about this trip.' She tossed out the last sentence lightly as though laughing at herself.

Bond shrugged. He was taking his cues directly from her. It was quite possible that she had watched the tapes of the real Guy and Helen, locked away in the other dacha they heard so much about.

'Remember when you forgot to tell me you'd left for the Hebrides?'

'It was the Isle of Skye as I recall.'

'Hebrides, you dolt. "Back in the morning, love," and I'm sitting there like a lemon for three

173

days.'

'You knew what the job was like before you moved in. Love me, love my job. Never held out on you. Couldn't afford to pass up work. Still can't.'

They kept up a pretence of bickering while demolishing the bacon and eggs; then through the toast and coffee, Nina leading him like a dance partner, making sharp comments about their supposed London lifestyle, even accusing him of being in league with George, the sound tech.

'I know George was covering for you when you were tripping the light fantastic with that dusky bit in Liverpool. George lied his head off for you. Lied to me—"He's still working, setting up shots for the morning. Out with the director, Helen." I *know*, Guy...'

'There was no dusky maiden in Liverpool.'

'No? Right. She was no maiden, Guy. But I forgave you, so you're bloody lucky.'

Finally, she rose, leaned over and ruffled his hair, saying she was going to take a shower.

'Well clean out your ears. That might help you to hear the truth for a change,' Bond called out, and a few minutes later she shouted from the bathroom, asking if he'd like to scrub her back.

Naked, in the shower, they soaped each other's bodies, standing very close. This was, possibly, the only place they could have some clandestine conversation as long as they both kept their heads turned towards the steaming tiles so that watchers could not lip read. Certainly sophisticated equipment could filter out running water which, in the old days, was a perfect foil for audio bugs, but if they whispered, there was a good chance that tiny amounts of information could be passed between

174

them.

'Any ideas?' His lips brushed her ear and she shook her head, camouflaging the action as she washed away soap.

'I don't know where we are, but it can't be good. The whole thing stinks.' She had her chin resting on his shoulder, standing on tiptoe to accomplish it.

'Really stinks?'

'The entire operation. Bory never levelled with you. He certainly didn't tell me everything, and my intuition says we've been measured for our coffins. I thought that from the moment they brought you in.'

They were able to talk like this by shielding their mouths, moving themselves so that it simply looked like lovers sharing a shower, allowing lips and ears to connect, then shift away. A couple of sentences and they would change position, soaping, turning their bodies to get the spray of the shower on one part or another. It was like a carefully choreographed, complex and strange surreal ballet.

'You ever sit in on the interrogations?' he asked.

'Which ones?'

'The real Guy and Helen—George.'

'I didn't even see them.'

'Then we don't know if they exist.'

'I only know some of the things Lyko and Bory told me. I've been trying to feed you some of the audio. They let me listen to one tape.'

'Like going to Saudi at a moment's notice?'

'That was on it. Bory said they argued about his work all the time. She was almost hysterically jealous. Didn't trust him out of her sight. With good reason probably. That's why she insisted on coming on this trip. That's what he said. What

175

Bory said.'

'You offered to do the job—this job?'

'More or less.'

'How much more and how little less?'

'It was a direct order, but there *is* another reason.'

'What?'

She ran her face under the spray, then shook her head, allowing it to touch his cheek. 'I want to be with my parents.'

So, he thought. Everything began to fit into place. It was as though fragments of a jigsaw, hidden away secretly in his head for five years, had suddenly come together and formed at least part of a cohesive picture.

He stepped from the shower, towelled himself down, then went through to get his shaving gear from the backpack. Before leaving the dacha he had taken the usual precautions. Just before closing up the top of the pack he had lined up the rear pocket of a pair of thick jeans with a crease he had made, tacking the material lightly with cotton. There were also two thin threads, laid across one another, over the clothing.

The searchers had been careful. The threads were back almost exactly as he had laid them, but the pocket and the crease were a long way apart, and it could not have happened by accident as they were hefting the packs around.

He went to the louvred doors of a built-in closet and found his parka neatly put away on a plastic hanger. It looked as though the transmitter and notebook computer had not been detected. They were skilfully hidden. Unless you knew exactly where to get into the parka's hood and lining, they were protected by the heavy windproofing of the garment. Nobody appeared to have played with the micro-transmitting button either. But he must assume someone had done so. At least he was not carrying a weapon. Stepakov was adamant that no weapons should be taken. Reluctantly he had left the ASP back at the dacha.

He heard the hairdryer come on in the bathroom. Certainly the Hôtel de la Justice complex was equipped with every convenience. Why, he wondered, as he pulled his toilet gear from the backpack, had they left the wood unfinished? Not enough time? Had the place been purpose-built, and the schedule had proved either too tight or was changed suddenly because of events? The questions would remain until they saw more of the building.

He paused by the window on his way back to the bathroom. Outside it was murky and dawnlike which meant they were far north, for it was almost nine fifteen. The room looked down into a kind of courtyard which had four trees set symmetrically, as though landscaped. All was covered in snow, and icicles dangled from the trees. They were some five storeys up, and the other three walls surrounding the courtyard, or garden, appeared identical. There were rows of tall arched windows like this one, sets of rooms and suites rising up to seven levels. The entire structure appeared to be wooden, carefully built on a great framework of thick beams. He could see, even in this light, that some of the beams were intricately carved. The entire exterior reminded him of something, though he could not reach over the horizon of his mind to grasp what it was. There was a familiarity about the building which he found disturbing.

177

Only at ground level did things change. Down there the windows were high and close, as if a wooden cloister had been preserved by glazing. There were tall arches joined along their vertexes by long carved struts. He could see lights behind these windows and caught sight of a group of people walking along a corridor—about ten men and women, carrying clipboards and talking to one another. Very normal, relaxed and civilised.

Nina was coming out of the bathroom, her hair in a towelling turban, as he went in. She stopped for a moment and put her face up to be kissed, then her arms went around him and she whispered, 'We're a very loving couple, I'm told.'

Twenty minutes later Bond emerged from the bathroom still wearing the robe, his face stinging from aftershave.

Nina sat at the dressing table, wearing only a clean change of underwear. She fiddled with her hair, oblivious that he watched her from the door. She was not a true beauty, he thought, but her face had incredible mobility. A lover would have to spend much time with her before he could accurately detect the sea-changes of her moods.

Now, she took a long strand of hair and pulled it down, holding it under her nose. 'Jawohl, Herr Oberst,' she muttered, and Bond began to laugh.

She stood and opened her arms to him. 'Come here,' she said, and her voice sounded as loving as any newlywed.

They held each other close. Then she guided him to the bed where he stripped her of the flimsy garments. It was a time of great passion, with Nina's legs wrapped around him, crying out for him to be harder as they rode towards their climax.

178

Bond felt she needed him for some purpose of her own. A release, perhaps, from dark fears, or a way to bolster her confidence. She had, after all, told him what she really wanted—'...to be with my parents.'

She cried out as she reached fulfilment, the cry of someone who might be looking towards the last uncharted land beyond the grave.

When it was over, they were silent for some time. Bond got up at last, glancing at his watch, to see that it was almost time for their guide, as the waiter had called him, to arrive. He washed again, and dressed, still worrying at the view from the window and, at the same time, trying to arrange his thoughts.

The priorities, as he saw them, were to find out the exact location of this so-called Hôtel de la Justice, to be certain members of the inner circle, the leaders of *Chushi Pravosudia*, were there, then to extract, by direct observation or clandestine methods, the reasons for their presence. Lastly, armed with all this information, to get away, warn, bring down the wrath of Stepakov's Banda upon this strange and divergent terrorist group. Maybe that would also entail calling in the secret power of his own Service.

He still stood gazing down at the high wooden structures which formed four sides of the frozen garden when Nina came up behind him, dressed now, like himself, in heavy jeans, rubber-soled boots and a thick, enveloping cable-knit pullover which threatened to swamp her. He wore one of his favourite heavy-duty sea-island cotton rollnecks under a thick denim jacket, reinforced with leather at shoulders and elbows. It was a jacket he had

179

chosen especially before leaving London, for it carried a few surprises he was certain would not have been detected in even the most rigorous search.

'Thank you, Guy,' she said, one hand on his arm. He wondered for a second if the lovely Nina had any devious reason for seducing him as she had done—last night, under the influence of drugs, or this morning when all defences were down. It was too late to worry about the possible consequences now, and as he looked into her eyes, he thought he could see some great sadness lurking like a tiny, dangerous, quiescent dragon behind her irises.

Then there was a firm knock at the door, a sound as commanding as that of a drill sergeant.

Bond opened up to find Pete Natkowitz, looking very fit and bright, standing next to a tall young woman with exceptionally long legs encased in tight jeans. She had short blonde hair which had been teased into a row of curls above her forehead and he knew that this was one of the giggling trio who had pressed them into the car near the Dom Knigi on the previous night.

'Hi, Guy.' Natkowitz's face was filled with a kind of devilish glee, and his short stature, topped by the unruly red hair, made him look like an errant teenager out for roguery. He nodded at Nina. 'Morning Helen, this is Natasha. She's in charge of us. Going to show us where all the goodies are.'

'We've already met,' Natasha also looked as though she shared some secret with the Israeli, 'though neither of you probably remember. George certainly didn't.' She looked down at Natkowitz's perky face and her hand drifted, like a feather, tracing fingers down his jawline. 'I think we should

180

go.' The hand made a small gesture towards the corridor. 'They'll probably be waiting for us. Clive said ten forty-five and, as a director, Clive is a martinet where time's concerned.'

As they walked down the passageway, Bond wondered at the normality of the place. It appeared to be like any other hotel. Doors were open while maids worked inside, and you could peep into suites and rooms like the one they had just vacated—all in the same condition, the woodwork smooth and unfinished.

At the end of the corridor they came to a bank of three elevators. Three other people waited—two elderly women and a man, talking in voluble Russian.

'I have no doubt, as I said to Rebecca,' one of the women said. 'He *was* the man. I saw him every day for almost two years. You think I could forget that one? He killed my sister. Little Zarah he killed. Shot her there in the mud because she laughed.' Tears welled in the old eyes which seemed to look back with loathing to another place and another hated time.

'I wish to hear him speak,' the man replied. He was stooped, a short person who seemed bowed now with a terrible weight. 'I am not certain, not until I hear his voice. They will let us hear his voice, surely?'

'Most certainly,' the other woman said, more calmly than her companions. 'You're both well in character. You've worked hard and that is good. Stay in character. Remain there the whole time, for the camera will be on your faces. It will use your expressions, eyes, mouths, to gauge the truth.'

'I could never forget Zarah,' the first woman

181

said.

They did not speak again as they rode down in the elevator cage, to find themselves emerging into a large room filled with people. Most of them elderly, some of them very old. The conversation rose and fell, a babble of languages swarming around the ears.

Natasha motioned them to follow her, and Bond soon realised they were walking along the inside of the wooden well, the part which looked like a cloister. He tried to make a ground plan in his head, so he could work out exactly which way they were heading. With concentration, he divined they had traversed one wall of the four when they reached another large room, like the foyer of a hôtel. This time, though, the wall furthest from them was not a wall, but two vast metal doors. There was a small entrance, set into the doors to the right of where the doors met, and next to it, a pair of lights, red and green. The green was on and Natasha went straight for the smallest door, ushering them through.

'Ah, here, I sincerely hope, come our blessed camera crew, and about time too, 'Tasha darling. What've you been doing with them? Doesn't anybody realise we're on the tightest of schedules here. Tighter than your little backside, 'Tasha.' He was a tall and willowy man in dark pants and a shirt. Long hair flowed to his shoulders, his hands danced, playing invisible arpeggios on the air, and he was accompanied by three smaller men who seemed to hang on every word. They looked, Bond thought, like trained whippets ready to streak away the moment their master commanded them.

'Come along, then, let's all get moving. You're

Guy, I suppose.' His small eyes looked up over a pair of granny glasses straight at Bond. 'See, I'm right. I'm always right. I can spot a cameraman at fifty paces in me high heels. So you,' to Natkowitz, 'must be the sound tech.' His head whipped round to settle his eyes on Nina. 'Oh, but Lord knows what we're going to do with the pretty lady, and she won't tell, will she?'

'Clive,' Natasha muttered by way of introduction.

But Bond was hardly listening to this stream of words which seemed unstoppable. Instead, he was taking in the sight which had greeted them on passing through the door. The area was vast and hot from the huge lighting gantries which ran above them. Cables snaked across the floors and at the far end there was a massive set which was immediately recognisable as an immaculate replica of a real courtroom.

'Now, Guy,' the tone was high, peevish and irritable. 'I hope to goodness you've worked with Ikegami equipment before, because if you haven't you're going to be no use to me.'

They stood on a very real sound stage which was almost certainly an exact copy of one of the major Hollywood studio sound stages. The only thing missing was the mass of technicians and assistants usually associated with sound stages during the shooting of movies. Only Clive, his three stooges and a handful of assorted men and women—Bond counted six—who fiddled with cables and were doing things to the lighting gantries.

Clive saw the look and plunged straight in. 'Yes, I know, Guy dear. I *do* know what you're thinking. There aren't nearly enough people here to shoot a major movie, but it's make do and mend time as they used to say in the navy, and I had plenty of experience both making do *and* mending. We just have to go with what we've got, and I only hope, in the name of Ossie Morris, that you're at least competent with a camera.'

'Oh, yes.' Bond looked round, still taken aback by the scale of the sound stage. 'Oh, I'm competent. Just tell me what you want and I'll do it.'

'Ah,' Clive gave a little dance, two steps forward and two back. 'Ah, so we have a pro. Thank heaven for small mercies as my old mother used to say. Now, perhaps we can get on with the bloody picture.'

'What's it called and have you got a shooting script?' Bond asked.

'No, dear. No script. We have to make it up as we go along. As for the title, weeeellll, I suppose we could call it *Death of a Salesman* but I suppose Arthur Miller'd be a bit miffed. Let's make up a name—after all we *are* making up a movie. Let's call it *Death With Everything*, because that just about sums up the plot. Grisly, dears, just too grisly.' He gave an almost sly pout in Nina's direction. 'Hope you've got a strong tummy, dear. The people in this epic aren't exactly your normal cosy down-memory-lane folks.' He paused, sadly only for a quick breath. 'These good people *do* go down memory lane, only all the mementos are mori, as it were. It's as amusing as an evening with grim-visaged death, as the Bard would have said.' He sighed, raising his eyes to heaven. 'Lord how I miss Stratford,' then in an aside to Bond, 'I was there with Peter, you know. And how that boy's got

184

on, bless him. Get him now? Oh, well, we can't all be visited by a good fairy in our cradles, can we? I think they let Karabos into my nursery.'

At the far end of the sound stage, people had begun to drift in, and even at a distance, a cold chill descended blotting out the heat from the lights.

CHAPTER TWELVE

DEATH WITH EVERYTHING

Nigsy Meadows was right—and wrong. As he had expected, M sent him a flash which came in at three in the morning. They woke him and he tottered down to the bubble to deal with it. After that, he found it difficult to sleep. The signal did not contain the instructions he had expected, ordering him back to London. Instead, he was told to meet M personally at the Grand Hotel, Stockholm. The wording indicated that the Old Man wanted Nigsy there yesterday. For breakfast and, preferably, on toast.

He arrived in the middle of the afternoon. The people at Aeroflot were their usual uncommunicative selves. Even under the twin turbos of *glasnost* and *perestroika*, very little has changed in the manner in which the Russians run their hotels, restaurants or state airline. In his short time back at the embassy, Nigsy heard stories of couples trying to get meals in Moscow hotels. They were usually turned away from half-empty restaurants because they were not 'a party'. When it came to booking a flight on Aeroflot, they wanted to

185

know, as Nigsy's old father would have crudely put it, 'the far end of a fart'.

Finally he had got out with the help of the third secretary (Trade) who was the embassy's travel agent. He was left with the distinct impression that Aeroflot would have been happier if he had travelled British Airways, even though BA did not run flights direct from Moscow to Stockholm.

The Grand Hotel, Stockholm, is more large than grand, though none can deny that the views from the rooms at the front, looking across the canal towards the royal palace, are spectacular. People were known not to book wake-up calls, relying on the military band playing during the Changing of the Guard. The music floated loudly across the short spit of water and on a good day you had to raise your voice to be heard above the military marches.

Meadows thought he spotted the first signs of M's presence at the hotel some two hundred metres from the elaborate entrance. One of the British Embassy's pool cars, aptly a Saab 9000 CD, was tucked into a parking slot with its nose protruding so that the driver and observer had good sightlines along the approach. In Stockholm, the SIS preferred to be in plain sight unless a particular situation demanded otherwise. Hence the CD plates and British registration, shouting that the embassy had interests nearby.

In the foyer, replete with high-priced glass-cased baubles and a grand curving staircase, two Special Branch men tried to look like tourists, an exercise which made them only appear more like policemen. Nigsy even knew one of them by name, but they all behaved with perfect decorum. Nobody nodded,

186

smiled, or even passed a raised eyebrow. He wondered what these kind of people did when they went off to the Canaries or Madeira, or wherever policemen went on vacation nowadays.

As a pillbox-hatted pageboy led him to the elevators, Nigsy saw someone slightly more perturbing who also hid in plain sight—a short, muscular young man, dark and self-confident with the restless eyes and air of a street fighter. He stood close to the elevator doors, scrutinising anyone who approached. This man was definitely neither Branch, SIS nor the local Swedish versions. He had KGB written right through him, like the wording inlaid in a stick of English seaside rock. No psychiatrist wheeled on by the Service could have told how Meadows knew, but he did. Part intuition, part long-term Moscow experience. His nostrils twitched, the mental antennae beeped, and the answer came up, KGB thug. To Nigsy it was unnerving because he knew that, had Bond been there, his answer would have been the same. On the flight he had started to realise he was feeling guilty about 007's disappearance.

The message light was winking on the telephone when they got to his room, but the pageboy insisted on showing him the luxurious amenities of the accommodation, even though the word luxury is practically an insult in the Swedish lifestyle.

Nigsy tried to intimidate the lad by advancing on him, edging him from the room, thrusting money into his hand, tipping to excess multiplied by three. The pageboy would have none of it. He went through the long spiel, praising room service, the minibar and the wonders of the television system, which, besides the usual programmes, would give

187

him excellent adult films as well as three normal choices plus Sky and CNN. All for a fair price.

He was still talking, showing off his English and obeying hotel policy as Meadows closed the door on him, turned, threw himself across the bed and grabbed the phone to ask for the message.

Would he please call the Bernadotte suite? Should they put him through? Please.

'Franklin Mint's suite.' Bill Tanner's voice was balm to his ears.

'It's Bert. Home is the hunter.' There was none of the 'grey goose is flying tonight' rubbish. Just plain Bert would do it, followed, of course, by the key phrase.

'Come on up. Quick as you can, old boy.' Some three-decimal-nine minutes later, Nigsy Meadows stood in the famous rooms which had been home to people like Gigli, Henry Ford II, Richard Burton and Elizabeth Taylor.

M sat in a comfortable chair nursing a cup of tea. 'Have some, Nigs?' His smile was that of a wily old alligator. Meadows declined, asking if the place was secure.

'Safe as a tomb,' Bill Tanner supplied. So Nigsy told them they had KGB in the lobby.

'Yes,' M looked unruffled, 'we're hosting a small, and very private, meeting.'

'Ah,' Meadows said. Then, 'They all laughed when I sat down to play.'

'Always the wag, Meadows,' M gave a tired sigh. 'You lost one of our favourite sons, I gather.'

He nodded, inwardly furious. 'Snow. Ice. Moscow nights. The whole show. Thought we were right on top of him. Then they flew him out, straight over my head in a damned great chopper.'

188

'Yes.' M took another sip of his tea. 'This is really rather good. Sure you won't have any?'

'No, sir.' Meadows spent a lot of his life telling his wife, Sybil, that when he refused food or a cup of tea, he meant it. She always pressed him when he said no.

'We've put people straight into the field.' M seemed to be talking at the teapot. 'You *did* get a good signal from him?'

'You could hear it chime from ten miles, sir. Then there was only the usual intermittent loss. It wasn't the equipment.'

'So, you came a pearler, Meadows.'

That triggered another memory. His father laughing over a line in one of Graham Greene's books—he could not remember which—where the head of a private detective agency greeted one of his errant sleuths with almost the same words. 'Another of your pearlers...'

'If you mean they got away so fast that I couldn't follow, yes, sir. You can't very well take to the skies in a Volga, especially when it's snowing and you've only got limited liability.'

'*They* did.' M smiled to show he was playing with his agent. 'Not your fault, Nigs.'

'No, not my fault, sir. But that doesn't make it any easier.'

'Course not. Sit down and go through it with us. I want the minutiae.'

So he talked, giving them the whole story from the moment Wilson Sharp fielded Bond's squirt-transmission until it was over. They put a spiral-bound map of Moscow and environs on the table for him to trace every move, and M constantly interrupted. He had said he wanted the trivia and he pressed for it—other cars in the vicinity, the exact holding patterns Meadows had driven while trying to lock on.

'The MVD surveillance vans,' M growled. 'You get their numbers?'

Meadows surprised himself by rattling off the licence plates without even thinking. That kind of thing was second nature to a good field man. In training, at the SIS prep school, they spent hours playing a complicated version of Kim's Game—the one where a tray of objects was uncovered for a minute, then the subject was asked to write a list of everything on the tray. In their field games they learned mnemonics to aid memory and stored away licence and telephone numbers like jackdaws.

M circled his finger around the streets Nigsy had driven with the minder, Dave Fletcher. 'You went quite close to the Moscow State University. That annexe they have downtown, not the main buildings out in Leninsky Gory.'

'Within a block, yes.'

'Nothing untoward? No oddities? Cars driving in a strange manner?'

'Everyone was moving slowly. At times it snowed quite hard.'

'You didn't see an ancient Zil?' M repeated a plate number, and Meadows shook his head.

'You were very near to a violent death. Did they report a murder before you left Moscow?'

'Not that I know. There are always murders in Moscow. Every night. It's getting like Washington.'

M grunted.

'Something special?' Nigsy asked.

'A professor in English from the university had half his face blown off. Sitting in a parked car. Man

190

called Lyko. Vladimir Ilich, if I've got it right. It's possible he was the driver who brought them into town for the contact. The *Scales of Justice* have done another one as well.'

'They seem to keep their promises.'

'This was a double event, as they say. One of the foreign policy advisers. They garotted him and his wife right in their dacha. It was his day off.'

'What a way to spend a vacation.' Meadows had always been prone to making sick remarks which slipped out before he could stop them.

M scowled at him, his face twisted like a man who has tasted spoiled fish. 'They scrawled *Chushi Pravosudia* over the mirror with the woman's lipstick. I blame these serial-killer films for all the sensationalism.' Then he turned to Bill Tanner. 'I think we should ask Bory to come up. Make sure he knows we had no ulterior motive in keeping him waiting. I'd hate him to think we were pulling a psyop on him.' By psyop, M meant psychological operation.

While Tanner was away, M told Meadows whom they were about to meet. 'Boris Ivanovich Stepakov,' he filled in the details, 'head of their counterterrorist department. Lives outside the law, as it were. Reports only to the top. Has no dealings with the rest of the KGB. None of his files are on Centre's mainframe computers. This is the man who asked for our help, and I trust him eighty per cent of the way.'

'What about the other twenty per cent?' Meadows asked.

'We must always leave room for doubts. If there were no X factors, we would be obsolete. Accountants could do your work.'

'I sometimes think accountants are taking over the world.'

'Perhaps they are,' M replied, and at that moment Bill Tanner returned, bringing with him the tall man with the long clownish face and a lick of blond hair which he constantly kept brushing back from his forehead.

'You mind if I smoke?' Boris Stepakov pulled a packet of Marlboro from the pocket of his shabby crumpled suit and lit a cigarette with a Zippo lighter. The lighter had the sword and shield KGB crest affixed to one side in gold and red. Stepakov threw it in the air and caught it. 'A friend brought it in from LA,' he laughed. 'We couldn't get such a thing, not even in the new Russia. Anyway, the crest is incorrect. We've removed the sword.'

'Yes, but for how long?' M asked.

Stepakov shrugged. 'Who knows? History teaches us that man is basically a psychopath. He never learns. This is why history is circular. One day the sword will return.'

He did not want to talk in the hotel suite, and they understood that, for it was against all his training, so they went outside and walked along the quay in front of the hotel. M's people surrounded them at a distance and Stepakov's two men—the street fighter and the one who looked like Tweedledum—stayed very close, though just out of earshot.

'We also tried to follow them,' Stepakov said. 'We had vans and two surveillance teams followed *you*,' he nodded towards Nigsy Meadows. 'The helicopter was large and powerful, a new version of the Mil Mi-12. What NATO calls a Homer. Its range is nearly seven hundred kilometres. They were very efficient. They even took out the man who drove your agents into Moscow.'

'Mine, and *yours*, Bory.' M had his head down as a chill wind blew along the quay. 'You also infiltrated the operation.'

Stepakov nodded, then continued. 'Lyko was murdered within half-an-hour of the drop, which means *Chushi Pravosudia* have close inside knowledge. It is also clear their links go right into the military and, almost certainly, as I have feared, KGB itself. Probably the Politburo and Central Committee also. But I still hold strong cards. There is a man, one of my men, who works deep within the military air traffic control. I think we have the flight plan of the Homer. Therefore, I think I know where they are.'

'Out of Russia? Somewhere not far from here? One of the Scandinavian countries?'

Stepakov shook his head. 'No, they are in Russia. But only just. In the forests close to the Finnish frontier. In the Arctic Circle.'

He told them the exact location. Two years ago, he continued, the Red Army had started to build a luxury hotel protected by forest high in the Arctic Circle. It was to have been used for officers of the special forces who do much training there under harsh winter conditions. 'It was never completed—one of those things phased out even though a fortune had been spent, and many people had been relocated to work in the place. The army calls it the "Lost Horizon". Intourist didn't really want it, but it was passed to them. They did nothing. The staff lived there, but it was not a functional, going concern. Then Mosfilm asked to use it for a movie. They had many technicians flown

193

up. A few stayed. I suspect these people are still there. *Some*, I believe, are controlled by *Chushi Pravosudia*. It makes a wonderful safe house. I should imagine they're holding the poor Mr Penderek up there.'

'Can we mount any kind of rescue from here?' M asked, as though he already knew the answer.

'I doubt if we can mount a rescue from anywhere. The only way in is by helicopter until the spring. The place is isolated. It looks like a monastery from the Middle Ages, but built of wood, not stone.'

'Have you no way?'

Stepakov shrugged, tossing his head, holding it against the breeze as though to let the wind run through it to tame the unruly lock which fell across his forehead. 'Only if I can convince some Spetsnaz senior officer to go—how do you say it? Out on a limb?' The Spetsnaz are the Soviet *Troops of Special Designation*. The real élite, equal to SAS or Delta. Once more, Stepakov tossed his head in the wind. 'But they are controlled by GRU, Military Intelligence.'

'You have no levers?' M's voice was suddenly urgent. Stepakov shook his head.

'I might be able to help you there.' This time M sounded almost self-satisfied.

*   *   *

Several years before, James Bond had travelled to Los Angeles with orders to kill a man. This was both unusual and highly illegal in the great game played by superpowers. Contrary to popular belief, intelligence services are not in the assassination business, for it is counter-productive. If you know

194

about an agent, or the leader of some network, there are more sophisticated things you can do to neutralise the threat. The first rule, however, is, better to live with the enemy you know than remove him with violence and risk a more cunning, undiscovered person succeeding him.

Certainly there have been revenge killings, but they are squalid affairs. Yes, there was foolish talk by officers of the CIA, putting up many ridiculous ways in which Fidel Castro could have been assassinated. But, in the main, killing is not an option.

The man Bond was sent to kill had been run as a double in London for nearly ten years. His demands had become more grandiose as each year went by. He gave less and wanted more. He had started to display all the symptoms of *folie de grandeur*.

When, at last, the storm was about to break and threaten him, he had been pushed over the edge by a woman. The beautiful girl with whom he had been living in London, left him and ran to America, to LA. The man followed her and was doing foolish things, like creeping up to the house in which she sheltered, leaving flowers in the dark on the doorstep, telephoning her in the middle of the night. He was also telephoning the British Embassy in Washington, demanding to talk with the chief spook, making threats which would have caused much embarrassment to the British intelligence community. So Bond was dispatched to operate, without American sanction, in the United States.

He tracked the man down and killed him by running his car off the road in the Hollywood hills. He could still recall that night—the car turning over

195

and over, its headlights strobing the darkness before it landed against rocks and blew up in a fireball.

On the following evening he engineered a casual meeting with the man this spy's girl had run to. His name was Tony Adamus and he was a professional TV News cameraman. They dined together, and Bond made certain that neither he nor the girl suspected foul play in the spy's death. He already knew the LAPD regarded it as an accident. They talked for a long time about Adamus' work.

During the conversation, Adamus told him, 'There's nothing difficult about a studio cameraman's job. He has to have a good memory and excellent reflexes, he must have a good eye so that he can focus the camera quickly and correctly, good hearing to obey the orders that come from the director and he must be strong enough to move the ped or pedestal on which the camera is mounted.

'The real skill in being a news cameraman is when you work in the field,' Adamus had said. He was, naturally, a field man.

Bond was obsessed with the detail of other professional people's lives. He also knew that it was best to know everything about journalism, for journalistic cover is often the most secure. On returning to the UK, he had gone out of his way to learn more about TV crews, cameramen and those who worked alongside them.

Now, on the large sound stage, the knowledge bore fruit. On the first day, Clive instructed them that they would be taping many people giving evidence, though the accused would not be present. The court was soon revealed to be a kind of military tribunal. Three senior officers sat in judgement while a prosecuting officer took turns with a defending officer in questioning clouds of witnesses.

Bond was amazed to see that Pete Natkowitz appeared at home with the sound equipment, swinging the big overhead sound boom on its silent mechanism and fine-tuning the words which came from the witnesses. Most of these were Russian, though there were some who were questioned and cross-questioned through interpreters. Clive said the final cut would be in Russian, though subtitles would be added so that the non-Russian people's replies would be clear to an audience.

The first half-dozen witnesses were German. Each identified the absent accused as Josif Vorontsov. They all said that, in 1941, he was an SS-Unterscharführer in the Waffen-SS Special Duties Brigade, just as they evidenced the fact that on September 29th, 1941, he had been at the Babi Yar massacre. They had been there also, as soldiers. The prosecuting officer told the court these men had all been purged of their sins. No action would be taken against them. They had been given immunity.

These old soldiers of the Third Reich gave ghastly details of the massacre. Two of them wept as they told the story and one fainted and had to be revived by medical orderlies. They were shooting the video in black and white. Clive said it would give more credence to the final result. People remembered the Nuremberg trials when the Nazi leaders were accused, filmed in grainy black and white. Also the Israeli trial of Adolf Eichmann had been relayed to the world mainly in black and white. It was fitting. Psychologically the impact would be strong.

It was also horrific. Bond watched Natkowitz and Nina Bibikova and saw that, in spite of the fact they realised this was all a performance, they were deeply moved and disgusted by what they saw and heard. It was all convincing. You could hear the screams, the pleading and the bullets.

They completed the 'testimony' of the Germans by late afternoon. Then came the other witnesses—Jewish people, either very old or middle-aged, who had, supposedly, come up against Vorontsov in the death camp at Sobibór. If the Germans' evidence had been harrowing on a scale of one to ten, the new evidence rated sixty.

By nine o'clock that night they had heard memories which could strip sanity to the bone. These old people described, in excruciating detail, the beatings, clubbings, stranglings—the casual violence meted out as daily normality in the death camp. After the first three witnesses, the mind became numb with revulsion. This was certainly death with everything as the director had warned.

Clive decreed they had time for one more. An old woman, supported by her equally aged husband, took the stand. They looked drained, haunted, as though living lives which had been taken away from them long ago. They gave their evidence in Russian, answering questions slowly. They had met in Sobibór and married later.

'We did not expect to survive,' the old woman said. 'Even though we were still strong enough to be made into trusted prisoners, we did not dare hope for a life after the camp. Nobody remained trusted for long. Vorontsov, that man over there,' she pointed with a trembling, aged finger, in the direction of the empty box, out of shot. By this

198

time, as they all agreed, it was as though the shade of Josif Vorontsov stood there in reality.

'That man. Vorontsov,' the old woman stumbled over the words, 'he made certain you did not remain trusted. One morning, we had two young girls assigned to our group. Our job was loathsome, for we had to help pick over the corpses for any jewellery or personal items that could be salvaged. These two girls were strong. In their twenties. They had worked on a farm, but they could not stand this. One of them began to retch, and this set off the other. Vorontsov was standing near the pile of bodies that morning. It was a gloomy day—every day was grim but today it was drizzling and worse. He ... he gave an order to one of the guards.

'The girls were dragged away. He considered them unfit for the job, so they were put in a special hut and used continuously for two days by the soldiers. On the third day they were dragged out. He had dressed them in some kind of finery, clothes taken from the dead, but considered sexually arousing. He paraded them in front of the whole camp. Then ...' she paused, unable to continue with the revolting way they had died. When she did manage to get the words out, everyone was shocked and stunned. It was one of the most horrific stories of atrocity Bond had ever heard. He could not even bear to picture it in his head and he blotted out the words, concentrating through the viewfinder of the camera, obeying Clive's trembling voice which came in through the headphones clamped over his ears. Clive told him to move in very close. 'Get her head. That's it. Right in. Now close on the lips. Just the eyes, nose and lips.'

Bond watched, seeing the lips moving but

199

blocking out the words of her terrible description. And as he looked at this face, close in, he realised that, under the make-up, he saw something else which suddenly tangled his mind. His brow furrowed, his back straightened in involuntary reflex. His chest felt tight. He glanced towards Nina and saw that she was weeping, but her eyes were fixed on the old woman.

Behind the mask of this aged, haunted person, Bond saw laughing eyes and a young mouth, perfect lipstick and arched eyebrows. He knew who this broken old woman really was. Beyond the work of clever make-up artists with their latex, putty and paint, he could see the face of Emerald Lacy in the photograph that hung in the headquarters building in London—Emerald Lacy back in the sixties, telling some secret tale, leaning over the Xerox machine. Only then did he dimly recall that she was supposed to have been a wonderful amateur actress, and that theatre was a passion she had shared with Michael Brooks. His eyes shifted to the old Jew, the woman's husband.

CHAPTER THIRTEEN

THE MAN FROM BARBAROSSA

'The problems are incredibly complex. Byzantine really.' Stepakov appeared hardly to have heard M's offer of assistance. He spoke the word 'Byzantine' as though proud of his choice of English. They still walked along the quay near the Grand Hotel. The canal was a black sheet of glass, and what light

200

there was made the buildings across the water look like grey cardboard cut-outs. 'The military are split. After all, the President promised a new country, and it seems to have slipped into chaos. He has promised a way forward through the Communist Party—so much for the Western belief that Communism has failed—but the disorganisation and hardship are worse than before. The army is unhappy. Some returned from Afghanistan to receive nothing, not even homes in which to live. The Americans have collective guilt over their returning troops from Vietnam. There is no collective guilt in Russia.'

'But Misha will give you authority,' M spoke soothingly, as though to give the KGB man confidence.

Stepakov flapped his arms. 'Of course. Yes, the comrade President would give the order through me, but I have no idea whether the military would take any notice. Local commanders seem to be making their own rules.'

'As I said,' M put his face close to Stepakov's ear, 'I can help you. This would have to be done by Spetsnaz, wouldn't it?'

'They're the only troops who could ensure a containment at the Lost Horizon, yes.'

'Colonel Berzin,' M screwed his eyes against the breeze. 'Gleb Yakovlevich Berzin.' Even his tone was cryptic. 'You know him, Bory?'

'Spetsnaz Training School commandant at Kirovograd? That son-of-a-bitch?'

'Personally I know nothing of his ancestry.' For a second M held the Russian with eyes bleak as an ice floe. 'I *do* know that Colonel Berzin owes me a favour.'

201

'He's a general now. What the Americans would call hard-nosed. The course at Kirovograd has been made even more difficult since he's been in charge. It was hell before him, now it is purgatory, hell, and a nightmare all at the same time.'

'A general, eh? Come up in the world.'

'Owes you a favour.' Stepakov sounded as though he found that hard to believe, but he was not questioning.

'I do assure you, Bory, that whatever his allegiances are now, there's more than a ninety per cent chance that he'll obey the President's orders if you give him a message from me.'

'You mean it? You're not just hoping...?'

'Oh, I mean it. Whoever's in control, Berzin will want to keep his job.'

'You're not telling me he's an asset of your people?'

'Hardly. Someone like Berzin would've been very difficult to control. No, he's not an asset. But, as I say, give him a message, together with the President's orders, and you should have no problem.'

'And the message?'

'Just tell him, "All I ask is a tall ship." He should reply, "And a star to steer her by."'

'This is your poet, Masefield. I prefer Wordsworth.' Stepakov's mouth was fixed in the permanent clownlike smile that was also a look of despair.

If there had been light enough, the Russian might have detected a flush on M's face. 'Don't know much about poetry,' he growled. 'Know what I like. Songs of the sea, that sort of thing. Just give Berzin the orders, then tell him what I said. Don't

202

even mention I said it.'

'And he will obey the comrade President's orders, no matter how he feels? Even if he's allied to a possible military revolt?'

'I've told you, Bory. The chances are high.'

'You have a secret with him. Obvious. Tell me.'

'People who live in secret houses should not throw answers. Now, let's go.'

They watched Stepakov leave with his two bodyguards in a car he had conjured from a trusted secret source which M said could even be a PLO cell in Stockholm. 'Bory is accepted by the strangest people,' M told them as they walked back to the elevators. 'That's why he plays it so close to the chest. He's made counterterrorist work into an art form, and he doesn't just play both sides of the street, he plays the entire neighbourhood.'

Back in the Bernadotte suite he told Tanner to order dinner from room service. 'Just a light supper for the three of us. Then I'm going back to London.' He fixed Meadows with bleak eyes, the colour of the North Sea in winter. 'Nigsy, you'll go further north. Join a couple of people up there. Chief of Staff will give you the mumbo-jumbo after he's telephoned London. We'll pinpoint this Lost Horizon hotel. You can try to run interference for Bond if he makes a break for it. Intuition tells me this isn't just an internal power struggle or a genuine attempt to shame the government into putting Vorontsov on trial. There's something more at stake here. Something which could affect all of us. Global, as the strategists say. I'm very unhappy. It feels as dangerous as trying to ride out a hurricane in a ketch.'

They had *Ølebrød*—that devious beer soup which

203

is a favourite in Stockholm—followed by *Janssons frestelse*, a wonderfully simple casserole of potato, onion and anchovy, something which suited M's jaded palate, and while they ate, Nigsy asked about General Berzin. 'How, sir?' not expecting an answer.

M filled his mouth with a forkful of the casserole, closing his eyes. It was the nearest Meadows had ever seen him to admitting that the taste of food could be a beautiful experience. 'You know,' he said, 'a literal translation of this dish is Jansson's temptation. I have a recipe at home, but nobody can make it in London.'

He ate more, washing it down with an aquavit flavoured with rowanberry and a long draught of beer as a chaser.

'Berzin,' he said the name and gave a grim smile. 'You recall Berzin, Chief of Staff?'

'Like yesterday.'

So uncharacteristically, M told the story. 'You remember Savall?'

'The cipher clerk?' Meadows knew people who had worked with Stanley Savall at the Moscow Embassy. The rumours were that he was a spy who had committed suicide.

Savall, while in Moscow, had been honey-trapped into a homosexual relationship with one of the KGB's male prostitutes. The ones they called *voron*—ravens, the counterpart of their *lastochka*. In the space of a year they collected massive amounts of audio and photographs. This was in the late sixties. When Savall was posted back to London, the Russian service laid the news on him. They could destroy his life. So Savall agreed to do what was asked of him. Over two years he systematically stole classified information and fed it to his control in London. Then he was caught, in a routine security check. There was no fuss. The Security Service kept it quiet and spirited him off to a safe house where they dried him out. The safe house was a fifteenth-century manor house in Wiltshire, near the ancient city of Bath.

While the British and American Services did not go in for assassination, the Russians had never been shy of it, so the interrogators ringed the old manor house with experienced members of the SAS. They knew that Savall could give them a lot of information regarding KGB operational practices in the UK.

On the third night after they had moved Savall into the house, two members of the SAS stalked and caught a man dug into a skilfully concealed position, giving him a view of the garden area where Savall was allowed to exercise. The man wore a camouflage suit and carried a Dragunov SVD sniper rifle. He would answer no questions, so they passed him on to M who carried out the interrogation himself in the secure rooms underground, below the headquarters overlooking Regent's Park.

Before he began the inquisition, M had the prisoner's photograph run through their vast filing system which they called 'the magic machines'. The machines put a name to the face, so, when he began the first session, M seated himself opposite this hardened, tough young soldier, offered him a cigarette and began to talk. 'Colonel Berzin,' he began. 'I wonder how your wife, Natalie, and your two children, Anatol and Sophie are getting on in your quarters in Kirovograd. I would speculate they won't be allowed to stay there for long.' He then gave the colonel a rundown of his entire life history, his training and the present mission. He even guessed, correctly, at how Berzin had come into England, via France and Guernsey. There was no doubt what his mission had been. Then M threw a packet of cigarettes on the table and left Berzin alone for two days.

When he returned, M told the soldier what they intended to do. 'We're simply going to send you home. When you arrive back, you can carry on your normal life. But I have to tell you that a full report of your capture, together with a copy of the secret information you have given us in this interrogation, and a tape, will be sent to the GRU.'

'I have told you nothing,' Berzin laughed.

'They'll only have your word for that.' M gave him a warm smile which said he loved all mankind. 'You won't be leaving for a week or so. In that time we shall put you under drugs and question you.'

'I know nothing that would interest you. I am a soldier with no access to the greater secrets of the Organs.'

M nodded. 'Probably, but we'll have your voice on tape, and from it my technicians can produce amazing confessions. By the time we send the transcript and tape to GRU and KGB, you'll have told us things you did not even suspect you knew.'

'I am a soldier,' Berzin protested again.

'Then that will be the end of it. You will probably die like a soldier, while your wife and children will be packed off to the Gulag. Good riddance.'

Berzin broke about an hour later. He claimed that he was merely on a training exercise. He had no orders to kill Savall. Then he spilled all he knew

206

about the training and use of Spetsnaz forces—how they would be used in any war and how they were used now as an élite force undertaking difficult military espionage and clandestine operations in the NATO countries.

'He talked himself dry,' M told them in the Bernadotte suite. 'Gave me everything, then said he needed asylum for himself and facilities to get his wife and children out of Russia. We refused.'

M had asked him if he enjoyed his life as a soldier. It was all Berzin had ever wanted. He was also a high achiever who *knew*, as high achievers always *know*, that he had a marshal's baton in his knapsack.

'We simply told him that we wanted his happiness. He could return to Russia. We would even provide him with photographs showing that he had eliminated Savall. Already we had done a deal with *him*.' Savall was to be given a new identity and shipped off to Australia once he answered all the questions. 'He was pretty spineless,' M said with disgust.

Before they allowed Berzin to leave, M had spent an evening with him. 'We will never ask you to spy for us,' he told the Spetsnaz officer. 'But there may come a time in the future when you can be of some small service to us. I swear to you that it will never be in time of war, nor will it be against your country's interests. If that moment ever comes, someone will be in touch with you.' He then gave Berzin the code phrases, together with a lurid description of how he, personally, would see that a tape of all their conversations went to the right hands in Moscow if the officer did not do the favour asked.

'There is a lesson in this,' the wily old spy said. 'Keep everything. Never throw anything away. Use every scrap that's given to you. I imagine the general will come up trumps.' He smiled gleefully now, and turned immediately to the orders he had for Meadows, letting Bill Tanner do the detailed briefing.

★   ★   ★

That night James Bond and Nina Bibikova showered together once more, to escape the fibre optic lenses and the invisible ears. 'I know,' Bond said, close to her ear. 'I saw both of them. You knew they'd be here, I presume?'

She nodded fiercely.

'It's okay. I am one of the few people who has the whole story. This is why you wanted to be with us? Because they were here?'

'Yes,' she whispered. 'But something truly terrible will happen. We must try to find a way to get out. All of us. Pete and my parents as well. Look for any way of escape, James. Please look hard. The *Chushi Pravosudia* are obviously using actors from various companies throughout the Soviet Union for this charade. My parents were in a theatre company based in Leningrad. That's where they went after they staged the accident.'

They went on washing each other, going through the ballet they were quickly perfecting. Bond asked if she knew why it had been necessary to use two technicians from England to do the camera work when any Russian team would have done it just as well. She had no idea. 'I think, however, that we shall all be disposed of as soon as the video is

208

completed. Nobody will be left, but there is more to it than this.'

They slept in each other's arms that night, rising at dawn, when summoned, to begin another day with the horrors of the past.

More and more witnesses were taped, each with his or her terrible description of life at Sobibór which was run like a sickening mass production factory, the final product being dead Jewish people.

They described how the Germans and their Ukrainian turncoat assistants had meticulously organised the place. It was similar to all the nauseating stories anyone had heard of the Nazi death camps. It was the efficiency that was as distressing as the amoral mass executions. All those who gave evidence were people who had been saved from the gas chambers either by their skills or strength. Some had been tailors or cobblers, working in special areas for the camp staff. Others had escaped by doing the revolting work—the picking over of possessions left by an intake of prisoners, the 'dentists' whose job it was to remove gold teeth from the victims and the sanitation squads who cleaned out the cattle trucks in which the doomed were transported to the camp. One old woman told how her entire time at Sobibór had been spent in a shop which specialised in picking the yellow Star of David patches from the discarded clothing of victims.

The witnesses had been trained by experts, so when he was behind the camera, Bond knew, with part of his mind, that they were actors performing as former victims. Yet the achievement of these men and women was so real, so brilliantly good, that as the day wore on, he became deeply depressed and mentally torn by the endless abominable repetitions.

It was late on the second afternoon that he realised some of the actors were appearing more than once—giving evidence, then being freshly made-up to return and perform as a new character with a slightly different story.

Michael Brooks himself came on to the witness stand for a second time towards the end of the day. Ordinarily, Bond would never have recognised him, now an old, bent and quavering man. It was the face behind the mask that Bond saw clearly and this performance was bravura. The old man told of one day at the camp, a day when the camp was visited by the architect of the so-called 'Final Solution', the Holocaust—Heinrich Himmler himself. On that day a special train arrived with several hundred Jewish girls from a labour camp in the Lublin district. Himmler watched the whole extermination process from arrival to the end.

'He gave no sign of remorse,' the aged Jew, who was Michael Brooks told the 'court'. 'He simply watched each phase with a growing interest. The victims might have been cattle for all the humanity Himmler showed. I was near the party when they left. I spoke some German in those days. Before he got into his car, Himmler said to the commandant, "You're doing well, but if things go as they should, you'll get some bottlenecks. That could prove difficult. I will order more chambers to be built. You need to be able to process more. I'll see to it." Those were the words he used, "to process more".'

They wrapped up for the day and Clive came down on to the sound stage floor. 'They're expecting some big cheese from Moscow tonight.'

He looked tired, as though he also felt the strain. 'I'll be up late in the editing suite. I've got permission for you to take a walk outside so that you can get fresh air.' The effect of the day seemed to have removed his cheery, camp manner. 'It's quite cold, and you can't go far, but I think it might do you good.'

Bond, Nina, Pete Natkowitz and three of the wardrobe people went outside through a door which led directly from the sound stage. They could not speak freely because of the wardrobe trio, and the darkness hit them like a wall, so that it took several minutes for their eyes to adjust. Then the lights around the Hôtel de la Justice came on and Bond realised why he had thought it familiar. From the outside it looked like some large medieval monastery fashioned in wood. He had once seen a drawing of a building just like this one. There was even a hexagonal gate tower, projecting from one side of the building, while the arched windows in perfect rows along the exterior could easily have been the windows to monastic cells.

The place had been built in a great circular clearing cut out of the forest. It must have measured a good half-mile across, and the perimeter where the clearing turned into thick woodland was lined with a high fence of barbed wire. It was lit at intervals by small floodlights, giving all of them the impression that they were at this moment in the awful camp of which they had heard so much during the day.

In the trees behind the perimeter, Bond thought he could sense movement. He saw nothing but experience told him there were armed men hidden in the forest. Nina was probably right. Nobody who

211

worked on this video would be allowed to leave. The Hôtel de la Justice would become their own personal death camp.

As they returned to the door, through which they had been allowed to leave, floodlights came to life on the far side of the building, revealing a circular hard standing marked with a white H. As the dazzling illuminations cleaned the darkness around this area the sound of helicopter engines roared in from above, getting louder until one of the machines dropped neatly from the sky and settled on the pad.

About a dozen men emerged from its body and were met by men in uniform who rose up out of the ground and ran forward to help them. As soon as this group had disembarked, the helicopter took off, to be replaced by a smaller machine from which three men climbed and walked briskly towards another knot of figures who seemed to be a special reception committee. Just before the lights flicked off, Bond saw men exchanging salutes. The leader of the arriving group was tall, silhouetted for a moment. There was something forbiddingly familiar about him, even at this distance. Throughout the night his shape returned again and again to Bond's mind, but he could not think who the man might be. He was certain of one thing, that should they escape it would not be through the trees, for they were a killing ground.

In the early hours, Nina cried out, coming to the surface from some dreadful nightmare. She clung to Bond as though the spectres from Sobibór were at her heels. 'James,' she whispered in terror, her body soaked with sweat, 'I dreamed we were all there. You understand? All?'

He shushed her, making the noises with which one calms a child.

'Bory was sending us all to the showers,' she sobbed. The showers were the gas chambers. The victims were told they had to shower before being given camp uniforms. Inside the showers they were gassed. In the first year or so of Sobibór's macabre history, they had used primitive methods and the gas had been carbon monoxide produced by a 200-horsepower engine in a shed near the showers. Later they progressed to the lethal Zyklon B, hydrogen cyanide, manufactured in Frankfurt and Hamburg.

* * *

There was a different atmosphere about the sound stage when they were taken down on the following morning. For one thing there were more uniforms, extra armed men at the doors and a smarter military ambience which had been missing for the past two days.

Behind the camera, Bond heard Clive speaking into his earphones. Even *his* usually languid voice had a clipped tone to it. 'We're going to do the Judge Advocate General's opening speech, first,' he said. 'I want you to focus on the doors to the right of the tribunal's stand. They'll bring the prisoner into the dock. Then the JAG will enter and address the tribunal. I'll be cutting you between him, the tribunal and the prisoner.' Then he began speaking to Pete about sound levels.

The prisoner was instantly recognisable, even in the grey, drab, shapeless jacket and pants, even with the shaved head of a convict. Bond had studied his photographs in London and again outside Moscow. He had no doubt that the man they were calling Vorontsov was, in fact, the hapless Joel Penderek from New Jersey. But Penderek behaved like a guilty man. He did not act like someone wrongly accused. His eyes constantly moved around the set which was the courtroom, and his demeanour was that of a man guilty of terrible crimes. The shifting eyes did not hold fear, but a kind of arrogance, as though he were saying, you have caught me, now do your worst.

Then the doors again opened and a tall figure in the uniform of a Red Army general strode into shot. The general looked more like a scientist than a soldier, slim and tall, with an almost ascetic, scholarly face. Clear blue eyes traversed the courtroom from behind heavy rimmed spectacles.

It was the man whose silhouette Bond had seen on the previous night, but now he recognised him. The supposed Judge Advocate General was Yevgeny Andreavich Yuskovich, Commander-in-Chief of Rocket Forces, Red Army.

As he kept the general in shot, closing on him, Bond wondered if, at last, they were getting close to the real leadership of *Chushi Pravosudia*, the *Scales of Justice*.

Yuskovich, the man known to be a cousin of the real Vorontsov, turned, looked at the prisoner and then at the tribunal. When he spoke, it was not the voice of a parade-ground slave-driver, nor of a man who commanded thousands of troops by example, coupled with an authoritative manner. His voice was soft, almost gentle, and mild in quality.

'Comrades, we are here to listen to stories of dread, for we are here to sit in judgement over a
214

man who assisted in, and carried out, heinous and deplorable crimes. These are crimes against humanity itself, crimes carried out to the relentless drum beaten by an enemy some fifty years ago. But this man, Josif Vorontsov, this old man we see before us today, was born of Russian parentage. The soil of this country, the very roots and seeds, were part of him. Yet when the enemy came, when the Nazi tanks rolled on to the beloved Motherland, for what Hitler called Operation Barbarossa, this Russian, born of Russian parents who were the children of Russian parents, decided to throw away his glorious birthright and join the ranks of the infamous Adolf Hitler's war machine. Not only that, but Josif Vorontsov also turned coat and allied himself to the most barbarous of Hitler's troops, the SS. This pitiful object we see before us, this apology for a man, should terrify us. He comes to us, comrades, like an apparition from the past. He is, verily, a man from Barbarossa.'

The speech was so quiet and gentle that its impact became all the more menacing. Bond felt the short hairs stand up on the back of his neck, and as he looked into the wide frame of the viewfinder, he saw that General Yuskovich's eyes seemed to be staring directly at him, as though boring into his very soul. The calm stillness of those eyes was more frightening to Bond for deep within them he saw a burning coldness and recognised it as mighty ambition. Though there was no way for him to know what plan had already been set into action, Bond could be sure that this man alone was the central organ, the pumping heart of *Chushi Pravosudia*, the *Scales of Justice*. It is difficult to fight an enemy you do not know, Bond considered,

215

realising with the thought that he knew nothing of Yevgeny Andreavich Yuskovich except the bare facts in a dossier read far away in London.

CHAPTER FOURTEEN

THE HUSCARL

Boris Stepakov's aircraft was a spacious variant of the Antonov An-72 with two huge turbofans, seating for fifty-two people and a STOL ability. It was the same kind of plane used by the President and the Chairman of KGB. Now he flew from Stockholm to a secret airfield west of Moscow where a car waited to carry him and the two bodyguards, Nicki and Alex, back to the dacha. There was news of yet another killing by *Chushi Pravosudia* while he had been in Sweden. A young woman, Nicola Chernysh, aged twenty-six, who held the coveted post of Supervisor to the President's Secretariat, had left her work in the Kremlin at five that afternoon. She had driven straight back to the apartment building in which she lived with her elderly mother, a block from the Central Concert Hall. Two men had shot her as she left her car. They had pumped eight bullets into her from handguns, then escaped in an unidentified foreign car thought to be of British origin.

Nobody came forward as witness to the actual shooting. The car was seen by six people: 'Driving away furiously,' one said. 'There were two men. They went very fast, nearly knocking down an old *babushka* who was crossing the road,' another reported. 'These men were hoodlums. One had a scar across his right cheek, the other wore a hat like in American gangster films,' a third reported, but he was very drunk and five blocks away when it happened.

At six thirty, an unidentified male voice spoke to the duty editor at *Pravda*. He said, 'Romany. *Chushi Pravosudia* have executed Nicola Chernysh, an enemy of the true revolution. We ask the authorities to take Josif Vorontsov off our hands and bring him to public trial. One member of the present regime will be executed each day, as promised, until some action has been taken.' Romany was the code word the *Scales of Justice* had now established with the Soviet media.

Stepakov spoke for half-an-hour with Stephanie Adoré and Henri Rampart who were still held at the dacha. He then summoned his car and drove into Moscow. The President had arranged to see him at nine.

The interview began on a sour note. If General Stepakov had wanted to see the President urgently, he obviously did not know how urgently the President wanted to see *him*. For almost an hour, the man with the weight of Russia's problems on his shoulders, upbraided Stepakov or fired questions at him like a heavy machine gun.

Why had these *Chushi Pravosudia* not been rounded up? Why had there been no progress? The comrade General had promised, nay, assured, the President that he had the real Josif Vorontsov in Russia and under lock and key. Why then had this situation not been exploited? When would these senseless killings stop? Heaven knew, he had treated poor little Nicola Chernysh—he fondly called her Nicolashenka—like a daughter. It was terrible and it must end. When, comrade General, *would* it end?

The President was exasperated, at the far stretch of his rope. The country faced grave new economic disasters every day, he did not know how long the army would remain true to the establishment, there were threats and he was being criticised every minute of every hour of every day. He was not a supernatural being. There were fresh problems showing their ugly heads in the Baltic States and in Georgia, not to mention other areas. If this were not enough, he was forced to play mediator between Baghdad and Washington. Thousands of American, British, French, Italian and Saudi troops stood at the borders of Kuwait, and the deadline of January 15 crept ever nearer. Did Stepakov not see that a truly bloody war might yet erupt in the Middle East? The conflict could be the long-promised spark that would set the Middle East ablaze. In the end it might be Arab against Christian and Jew. It could even be Arab against Arab. It was something for which the armed forces of the USSR had trained. Did General Stepakov not realise that the war planners had already spent months building plans and orders of battle for such an event? But the balance of power had changed. The whole sphere of Soviet influence had slid into a new order. Russia was now doing business with the United States. War between all the Western alliances, NATO, and Iraq had long been considered a strategic lever to be used by Russia against the other superpower.

'Now, we don't want this,' the President stormed. 'If we do the slightest thing which can be interpreted as an anti-American move, we lose the aid I have sweated blood to extract from Washington.'

Stepakov was an old hand in the Kremlin. He had seen powerful men come and go. There had been days, when, as a young man, he had even taken part in one palace revolution—that sorry time when poor old Brezhnev, still titular head of the Soviet Empire, embarrassed all around him as he sank to geriatric senility and had to be rescued by those who worked him like puppet masters.

He had been ranted and raved at before. It was like water off a goose. Stepakov closed his mind to the comrade President's wrath, isolating only those pieces of information which might just require a coherent answer. Men in power hold forth, but there is always a limit, an end to the one-way street of their sound and fury.

So Boris Stepakov waited out the storm and when it finally abated he spoke, giving the President a clear and concise picture of how he saw *Chushi Pravosudia* and how the matter should finally be dealt with.

'Bory, you should have told me straightaway. We could have saved time. Let me put in a call to Kirovograd now...'

'No, sir. No, please. You of all people realise how this must remain a closed book. Better I should have your express orders in writing. I will then present them to General Berzin personally. It is really the most secure way.'

So in the absolute privacy of the President's office where no electronic devices could ever penetrate, Boris Ivanovich Stepakov dictated the order which the President signed.

It was now late. Stepakov needed sleep. He drove

back to the dacha. If they left early enough in the morning, he could hand the orders to the Spetsnaz General Berzin by lunchtime and would expect the operation to move with speed during the following night. Things, he considered, were going very well.

★   ★   ★

In their handful of days together, Nina Bibikova had become almost a wife to James Bond. They worked side by side on the studio floor during the day, ate in a canteen, which looked like an old monastic refectory, each noon and when work was finished in the evening. More often than not they shared a section of one of the long scrubbed tables with Pete Natkowitz and their guide from the first morning, Natasha, the blonde with legs so long they seemed to reach to her navel.

Natasha did not share her surname with them, but Bond did not have to be blessed with superintelligence to realise she and Pete Natkowitz were becoming 'an item'. He hoped Natkowitz knew what he was up to, and then immediately dismissed the thought. Any officer of the Mossad, especially with Natkowitz's kind of experience, knew what he was doing.

The food served to them in the canteen was above average, considering they were locked away in impenetrable forests ringed by snow and ice. The speciality was a particularly good stew made from vegetables and reindeer meat which remained appetising for the first two eatings and from then went rapidly downhill. But the diet was augmented by smoked fish, plenty of black bread and large quantities of *Kvas*, the popular home-brewed beer of farmers and peasants.

Each night, Nina and Bond had returned to their room, showered and secretly discussed observations made during the day. On this, the third night, they collapsed into bed around nine o'clock and went straight to sleep, though Nina woke Bond later and proceeded to do things at which many wives would draw the line. They drifted off again, happy and sated, into a sleep not peopled by the ghosts of Sobibór.

Bond woke with a start, his hand snaking out to grip the wrist of whoever had their palm firmly over his mouth. He did not struggle, but twisted the wrist, and would have applied more fast and crippling pain had he not realised it was Natasha trying to rouse him noiselessly.

Still holding the girl's wrist, he propped himself on to one elbow and peered through the gloom, trying to make sense of her signals. She was nimble and expert, her free hand moving in silent and precise gestures, as though making contact with some alien being.

Wake Nina, then follow me, she was signalling. It is safe, but please hurry.

Nina came out of sleep effortlessly and with that enviable immediate alertness achieved only by doctors, nurses, soldiers, and disciplined field officers of exceptional intelligence services. Bond's feet had hardly touched the floor when she was already moving silently, fastening the tie around her towelling robe.

Natasha beckoned them, still using sign language, warning that it was important for them to make no noise. The corridor was empty and there was an atmosphere of almost holy silence as though the wooden building had been muffled by some vast blanket. The sensation was so acute that for a second Bond thought they must have been victims of an avalanche. In his mind, he saw the building shrouded in snow, then realised that this was impossible. The strange sensation remained, reminding him of being in some ancient sacred place where prayers and beliefs have seeped into the ground, trees, stones or structures, captured and locked for eternity.

Natasha motioned them to stay close to the wall, and she paused for a moment by each door they passed, checking to make sure nothing could be heard from inside the rooms. They knew these rooms were occupied by 'witnesses', though, apart from the three people who had stood near the elevators on the first morning, they had not set eyes on any of the other guests except on the sound stage and in the canteen.

Before they reached the elevators, the guide pushed open a door with an international emergency exit sign, a little stick man running down a staircase. Bond always thought it looked as though the primitive character was attempting to dash down an 'up' escalator.

On the other side of the door, a staircase led up and down, fashioned as ever in wood. He imagined it would burn quite well. For the first time, it struck him that the entire building would be a deathtrap in the summer when the wood became baked by the sun into dry tinder.

They climbed up one flight, went through the door at the top into a corridor identical to the one they had traversed from their room. Now Natasha signalled for them to move faster. She crossed the space by the elevator bank and softly opened another door which had 'Private. No Entry' stencilled on it in Russian, English, French, German and Arabic.

They were in a small bare office. The blinds were drawn and the only furniture consisted of crates and packing cases strewn haphazardly over the soft pile carpet. A single brass student lamp with a green glass shade stood lit on a packing case in one corner, and Pete Natkowitz sat on a nearby crate, his legs swinging and his face flushed. Once the door was closed, he let out a long sigh and grinned at Bond.

'They haven't come yet?' Natasha asked.

'Well, my dear, if they have, you'll find them hiding in one of these boxes. No, Tashinka, they have yet to arrive.' He turned his attention back to Nina and Bond. 'Sorry to get you up in the middle of the night, James. Natasha's been trying to find a safe haven ever since we arrived.' He told them the bedrooms were wired for sound, but the people who built the place had not got around to putting in video. 'It appears we have to be heard but not seen, which I suppose means we've become adults of some kind.' He slapped his right thigh in a gesture meant to convey amusement. 'We're not really certain if they have enough staff here to monitor the sound-stealing equipment, but the golden rule is . . .'

'Assume they're lifting the words out of your mouth,' Bond supplied.

'Naturally,' Natkowitz nodded. 'This room is free of any bugs. For the first time since we arrived we can talk freely.'

'You're absolutely sure about this?' Bond eyed

223

the room with deep suspicion. He was leery of talking in a place which, to his knowledge, had not been examined and swept. As he often told other people in the business, he preferred the Russian tradecraft of talking only in the open, and where they could not bring directional microphones to bear.

'I'm certain. Three hundred per cent certain. But for you one-fifty.' Natkowitz's eyes danced with pleasure.

'And Natasha?' Bond was asking about her security clearance.

Natkowitz's face went dead, the eyes suddenly becoming hard. 'If *I* tell you she's okay, you should believe me, James. To be honest with you, when she turned up in Moscow the other night—before they put us to sleep for a hundred years—I couldn't believe my eyes. She's *with* me, if you see what I mean.'

'The Mossad has penetrations in Russia?' Bond looked surprised, even a little awed.

'You betcha.' Natkowitz cocked his head to the left, as though to underline the statement. 'The media in the West says the intelligence agencies of Britain and America are dinosaurs now that the Cold War's over, that their minds are for ever frozen into the NATO-Soviet locking of horns in Europe. But they're wrong, as we both know, James. Even the Mossad have kept a watch on the Volga, as it were. Too dangerous not to do so. Natasha and a couple of others have been here for some years. We implanted them in the early seventies when they were children. Them and their parents; and look where it's got us. Really I . . .' He stopped short at the noise which came from the far

224

side of the door.

Bond moved like a cat, springing silently against the wall on the hinge side of the door, his right hand closed into a fist, thumb tucked into the palm and the knuckles of his first and little fingers protruding slightly, his arm bent at a right angle, making an L-shape, square with his body.

Natasha was flattened against the wall on the other side, ready, tense. Natkowitz and Nina did not move as the door handle slowly turned and a voice from outside whispered, 'All families resemble one another.'

Nina drew in her breath, and the sound seemed to fill the whole room as the door closed behind the pair of tall figures who entered.

'But each unhappy family is unhappy in its own way.' Nina's voice broke as she completed the quotation from the opening words of Tolstoy's *Anna Karenina*. Then she flung herself forward into the arms of the elderly man and woman who stood silent and erect three paces inside the room.

The three of them embraced. Together. Their arms wrapped around one another so that they became a small tight circle of loving human beings—a little knot of love and comfort.

Bond took a pace forward, but Natkowitz slipped from the crate and restrained him. The trio remained, clinging to one another for several minutes. When they separated, each of them had cheeks damp with tears.

The man still had about him the stance of an old military officer, his back straight as a plank, the hair neat but iron grey. The moustache had gone, and his skin was like old, uncared-for leather, but the eyes still carried the missionary zeal he had

225

practised all that time ago in the service of his country.

The woman had not stood the test of time as well as her husband. Gone was the beautiful jet black hair, replaced now by a short, pure white cap, still silky but thin. Her hands were those of an old woman, stained with liver spots and loose skin. There were cracks around her mouth, and her eyes spoke of a hard life since she had left the relative comfort of London. She looked, in effect, far older than her years, but, when she spoke, her voice was strangely young. 'You think we're traitors, I suppose, James? I know who you are. Known of you for a long time,' Emerald Lacy said.

'Dead traitors at that.' Michael Brooks still had his charming smile. In the old days they said Brooks could charm scorpions with his smile.

Bond shook his head. 'No.' He moved closer to them. 'No, I know that you're the *Huscarl*. I've known for some time.' He turned to Nina, 'That's why I wasn't surprised at your parents being alive. When I told you last night, you didn't question me, but you looked a little frightened.'

'Because she doesn't know quite everything.' Brooks put out a hand and fondled his daughter's shoulder.

The name *Huscarl* went back to the eleventh century, during the time England was ruled by the Danes, paying the iniquitous tax, Danegeld, which some students claim still smarts within the Anglo-Saxon collective consciousness, thus provoking the British to find more and more ways around current tax laws.

For years the English suffered Viking raids which decimated entire communities, but they fought on,

226

led by a succession of kings, such as Aethelred and Edmund Ironside. Then, in 1016, the country was finally overcome by the Danish king, Cnut.

Cnut made some changes in the kingdom's military structure, including the introduction of a kind of 'Home Guard'—the *Huscarl*, the professional household warrior, armed with the great two-handed Danish axe, ready to do battle with any possible commando raid launched by other Scandinavian countries.

It was this weapon which prompted those who chose pseudonyms—cryptos for agents, or operations—to name Michael Brooks and Emerald Lacy the *Huscarl*, for they were a new, two-handed assault upon the reigning regime at Moscow Centre.

With the scandals of the first British traitors undermining both effectiveness and morale in the mid-1960s, Bond's Service had planned a fast counterstrike. Michael Brooks had long been involved with the brilliant cipher wizard, Emerald Lacy. Now, the Service let him go, dropping veiled hints that he was under a cloud, hints which paid off handsomely.

Brooks severed all his Service connections with the exception of Emerald. He also made oblique comments to people who were suspected of being close to KGB sources in the Russian Embassy. Then he sat back and waited. Eventually, KGB took the bait and he disappeared. In fact they had only taken him to Denmark where experienced KGB inquisitors gave him what they termed 'deep analysis'. In plain language, they were drying him out, but Brooks had been very carefully briefed before leaving the Service. He had been seeded with what appeared to be first-rate intelligence concerning the NATO forces and the various connections they had with the main intelligence communities. The Moscow Centre inquisition was impressed by the ease with which Brooks passed on the information and finally they asked him to defect to Moscow.

Once the offer had been made, the trump card was played. Brooks said he would come to them only if his fiancée were included in the deal. When Moscow realised his fiancée was Emerald Lacy, they leaped at the prospect.

Emerald had also been prepared. Skilled psychiatrists had blanked out whole sections of her mind which held vital information. They did this over a lengthy period using the latest hypnotic techniques. After this, they gave her other information, what they called 'costume jewellery', because it looked real and glittered in the kind of gaudy manner beloved of KGB intelligence gatherers.

So Emerald Lacy had 'defected' to Moscow, where she had married Brooks, remaining to do much good work for the British until 1989, when their deaths were faked in a car crash. But that was another part of the story and their secret presence in Russia since their 'deaths' had been of major importance to the NATO countries.

In the small room at the top of the strange wooden building they had been told was the Hôtel de la Justice, they sat down to speak of this seemingly insoluble, inexplicable operation in which they had now become joined.

Michael Brooks began with a raw statement, arctic in its bleakness. 'This business: the trial, the taping, the whole thing about this war criminal

Vorontsov,' he said, 'is a blind, a sleight, a way to throw the Kremlin and the President off-balance. It's only part of something greater, an evil which will have appalling consequences. We know some of it but not all. The gist is that hardline military people are about to launch a plot which will destroy America and probably Britain also. And I mean *destroy*. When the influence of those great nations has gone, the Old Guard will once more seize control of the USSR. They will have the ability to plunder the West and rebuild Russia as the only major power in Europe and the Middle East—a power more repressive than it was even in Stalin's day. If this works, they will eventually overcome the entire world.'

CHAPTER FIFTEEN

STONES AND BONES

Michael Brooks told them that he felt this phase of the operation was almost over, 'If we're right in our assessment.' He spoke in a correct, near military form, as if making a verbal report to the Ministry of Defence. While he talked, he leaned across, touching his wife's arm to include her in his deliberations. 'If we really have got it right, they have to make a significant move into their next phase before January 15th when the United Nations's deadline for Iraq to withdraw from Kuwait runs out.' Personally he could see nothing for it but war.

'The Americans will be forced to lead the

coalition forces and probably demolish Iraq. It's the only way they'll get them out of Kuwait.'

They sat close on the floor, in a circle. Bond thought of it as a ring of conspiracy.

'James?' Brooks said, 'you're behind the camera and must have some idea of how the taping's gone. How much more do you think they have to do?'

'A day. Maybe two. Possibly the whole thing, with editing, can be wrapped up in three. Certainly not more. I'd guess less than three. Why?'

'We should be ready for the end to come very quickly. If Emerald and I are right, they won't want any witnesses left. I mean they won't leave anyone who has taken part in, or assisted with, the making of this so-called trial video.'

'Yes, I think you're right.'

Emerald joined in. 'Have you tried to count the number of armed troops they have on the spot?'

'They come and go,' Bond shrugged. 'I don't mean physically leave and return. They get changed around a lot. Today there seemed to be more around than yesterday.' He went on to tell them what he had felt when they were outside.

Natkowitz agreed. 'You get to sense things in this business,' he began, then, 'Sorry, you two know more about that than any of us. But out in the dark the other night, I was *sure* there were troops in the forest.'

Nina nodded her accord.

'So how many?' Brooks pressed.

'Maybe fifty or sixty in the building.' Bond's voice was confident, though he was far from certain. Natkowitz and Nina agreed.

'Heaven knows how many are out in the forest. Father, there's no way we can take on this lot.' His daughter was almost pleading with him.

'It wouldn't be a question of taking them on.' Emerald spoke with authority so that they all turned to her, waiting, as though listening to a guru.

She wore a long, caftanlike, shapeless black garment. When she smiled it was as though the young woman of her past returned in spirit. 'Michael and I have been doing little night forays. Reconnaissance. We put Natasha on to this room and there are other secret hidey-holes. Well, there would be in this kind of monastery, wouldn't there?'

'Why d'you call it that?' Bond came back sharp and quick, as though Emerald had read his mind.

She gave her beautiful smile again. 'You're thinking, what's this stupid old biddy know about this building? Right?'

'No. It's only the place has a feel to it. That and the architecture, if you can call it architecture.'

'But that's exactly what it is. A bloody monastery for soldiers. Or didn't you know? We're less than ten miles from the Finnish border and this clearing in the forest has been here for centuries. It's the site of a very ancient monastery. We know all this because we worked for the buggers at Moscow Centre when they started to build this place—the Lost Horizon they call it now, because nobody really wants it. Originally it was going to be the nearest thing to religion ever seen in the Red Army.'

'Religion?'

'Well, sort of. It was to be kind of grand hôtel-cum-monastery for the general staff of the Red Army.' She pronounced 'hôtel' like the old

231

school, 'ôtel. She paused. 'You see, they found this place. This old site. Used to be revered by the Lapps. A holy place. When the building began they even found some remains. Stones and bones. Michael and I came up here, remember, darling?'

'In summer,' Brooks sounded far away. 'Yes, they'd just cleared the site when we first visited.' He took up the narrative, telling them it had been a sound military idea. Senior officers would spend time out in what would seem to be a wilderness. 'Not far from civilisation really, but it's stuck in the middle of a bloody great forest so they'd be corralled here; they'd feel apart from the world. For a week or so each year, the general staff of the Soviet armed forces would spend some time in silent contemplation of military affairs. The idea was to make them meditate, in strict silence, on the great writings of military tactics and strategy, much as monks and nuns reflect on the works of Saints Augustine and Ignatius. When they'd done their stint, they'd have some kind of a conference, share their thoughts with one another. Then, if I know the Russians, they'd all get pixillated and falling-down drunk. In the end, they built the place, poured a fortune into it, then decided against the "retreats" or whatever they were going to call them.'

Bond nudged his way in. 'With respect, what's this got to do with our present situation?'

Emerald's eyes twinkled. 'We were just trying to explain why you might have vibes here. It *is* a little odd. The Lapps always said it was haunted, but that's probably because the land used to belong to Finland, and, by inference, them. The Lapps, I mean. The point is there *are* tunnels, hidden rooms,

232

sliding panels—the kind of thing you find back home in old country houses. Priest's holes, escape routes. And we're both pretty sure none of the present inhabitants knows about them.'

'Ah.' Natkowitz nodded. 'You mean we should lie up when it's over?'

'Something like that. Though unless we had food...'

'And weapons,' Bond added.

'It's an idea,' Michael Brooks said the three words as though he really meant it was the only way any of them would get out alive. He bit his lip as though trying to make up his mind whether to tell them more. Then he said, 'I'll be honest. We've organised things. Not much, but enough for a few days if we're forced to hide. This tunnel...'

'You'll show us the way?' Bond again.

'The truth, and the light, dear, yes.' Emerald Lacy gave the impression she was enjoying this immensely. 'I think we should all know exactly where to hide. Just in case the world caves in unexpectedly.' She stopped for a moment, then looked at Bond again. 'James, do you have any way of communicating with the outside world?'

'Why?' Bond's suspicion would not allow him to share everything with these people.

Michael Brooks nodded. 'It's all right, James. We understand you.'

Emerald went on speaking, almost over her husband. 'If you do have communication facilities, however primitive, try to keep them hidden and near at hand. Michael and I have the map co-ordinates for this place. You might wish to send them out.' She gave him a quizzical, near comic look. 'That is, if you have the means.'

Bond nodded, but remained silent, and Emerald rattled off a string of numbers—standard map reference co-ordinates. 'Got it?' She sounded like a severe teacher making certain her star pupil knew all the answers. Bond gave her a little flick of the eyes.

'So what's the time?' Michael asked nobody in particular as he looked at his watch, a cheap Russian military affair, functional and probably accurate. 'Almost two thirty in the morning. Right.' Brooks looked at his wife, asking, 'Shall we take them down?'

'There's time. Why not?' She had remained remarkably composed. Bond wondered at the dangers this woman had faced in her life—almost three decades of being under cover, existing in secret with a hidden present, a sequestered future, yet at all times with the true knowledge of another person within her, someone who had lived a different kind of history, one to which she would like to return, but in all probability never would. She rose from the floor and began to instruct them in what was about to happen.

'There are usually guards in the main foyer, but they don't seem to be running patrols or even security checks anywhere else. The area close to the sound stage has never been guarded since we've been here.' Her grin brought back the girl she once used to be. 'Michael and I have spent whole nights roaming the place without interruption.'

'Except when we've engineered it.' For a second, Michael Brooks looked like a cold, hard and calculating operator.

'Meaning?' Natkowitz asked.

'You'll see.' He gave a tight little smile. 'We're

234

going to take you down to the tunnel which was here several hundreds of years ago. When the balloon goes up, I would suggest all of us try to make it to this place. It's easy enough and near the sound stage. We'll walk down.'

He cautioned them to remain silent and stay absolutely still if they encountered any of their Russian jailers.

They went in single file. You could feel their alertness, tangible in the dark, as they retraced their steps to the emergency stairwell, then down, right to the ground floor.

They exited near the elevators and crept along the passage leading to the sound stage. The huge sliding doors were open, and away to their right, the sound of voices floated from the main foyer, but they saw nobody.

Along the wall facing the sound stage doors were the entrances to rest rooms, marked by the usual simple men and women symbols. A third door seemed barred by an 'absolutely no admission' sign.

Michael Brooks winked, removed a key from his pocket and inserted it into a lock next to a solid-looking brass knob. The key turned silently and they crowded into what seemed to be a large closet, the kind of place that would normally store vacuum cleaners and other domestic requirements. It was empty and felt unused.

There was just enough room for the six of them to stand inside as Brooks relocked the door. Shelves ran around the entire space, and it was Emerald who, in sign language, told them to watch what she did.

The secret lay in the third shelf from the ceiling. She ran her hand under the shelf, then stopped, telling them in mime to look. At the far right, hidden under the shelf close to the wall was a brass ring about an inch in diameter. She pulled on the ring and there was an audible click as the entire wall detached itself and swung slightly inwards. Only when they had all passed through did Emerald signal for them to watch her next move. She closed the wall behind her and reached down. There was another solid click as the wall locked back into place and the lights came on.

She spoke in a normal voice. 'We've tested all this. It's absolutely soundproof once you're in. The light switch is right down here on the inner wall. You can find it easily in the dark and the other brass ring is here, on the inside.' She showed them. 'Familiarise yourselves with the mechanism and the lighting switch. One of the reasons we're sure nobody's used this tunnel since we've been here is that the actual light bulbs are old and some of them are dead. There are other things which indicate nobody's been here for years.'

They were standing in a passage some ten feet wide and seven feet high, the walls covered with white antiseptic looking tiles which curved in an arch above them. The floor was made of simple concrete.

'Come,' Brooks led the way. The floor sloped sharply downwards, then after ten or eleven paces, the white tiles gave way to rough walls of large dry-stone blocks. There was no curve in the roof now. Instead the ceiling was of wood which looked very old, solid black beams laid sideways and covered in hard pitch.

There was no echo when Brooks spoke again. 'Unfortunately there's been a cave-in about half a

236

mile down, but we presume this is an original vault. At one time it probably ran right off into the forest.'

The passage suddenly widened, forming a large chamber. It was cold, but not unduly so. 'Look around,' Emerald beamed. 'This is where the monks buried their dead, or at least their important dead.'

There were long ledges cut into the stone walls and Bond felt Nina shiver involuntarily as she saw the bones stretched out in their last resting places, bones so old that some were starting to fossilise. There were other artifacts—metal crosses on chains, rusted and lying over ribcages—symbols of office.

'We've managed to store a little food here.' Michael Brooks spoke as though they had been doing this over a lengthy period. 'Also, my dear wife carefully stole a small heater and a supply of paraffin. There are a few in the storerooms on each floor, presumably in case their generators go on the blink. Next, weapons. Are any of you armed?'

All except Natasha shook their heads.

'I know about you, Tashinka,' Brooks nodded, and explained that, as Natasha had been a long-trusted member of the Russian team, she carried a weapon. 'We've managed to get three automatic pistols and a little ammunition. I suspect James, Mr Natkowitz, and you, dear,' looking at his daughter, 'should have these.' He groped among the bones in one of the burial slots and retrieved three P6 automatics, each with the noise reduction system in place. The ammunition was non-standard 9mm which Bond recognised immediately as an offshoot of the British Research and Developments' 'Spartan' rounds, designed for close-in fighting: bullets which break up on impact, do not

237

overpenetrate or travel too far. Brooks showed them that all three weapons contained a full clip and he handed out another three clips apiece.

'Where in . . . ?' Bond began, and Brooks gave him a chilling look, lowering his voice. 'I wouldn't go too far into the tunnel from this point,' he all but whispered. 'The holy monks have company, but I don't think we'll be troubled by any nasty smells just yet. It's much colder along there, near the point where a fall's blocked us in.'

'You mean?' Bond raised an eyebrow.

Brooks nodded. 'Yes. Can't work out how they haven't been missed. Emerald lured them into following her. I did the business. We did two the night before last and one last night. Should be a hue and cry, but they possibly get the odd idiot going over the wall here. Either that or their organisation's porous.'

Bond did not recall the old expression, 'porous', for a moment, then smiled as it came back to him. Porous stood for 'Porous piss'.

There were spare keys for the outer door, remodelled and fashioned from other keys which Brooks and his wife had filched. Enough for all of them. They went over the situation one more time. When the balloon went up, each person would be responsible for himself. 'No hanging back, or heroics,' Brooks said. 'It's better to get yourself down here than to lose out on a foolish rescue. We can do no more until something happens.'

They agreed to meet back at the room used earlier at three on the following morning if nothing occurred before then. Brooks obviously had a very clear picture of the building in which they were being held, so Bond did not try to intervene. As far

238

as he was concerned, it was Michael Brooks' operation now. All he had to do was try to get a signal out, if he could, and if anyone was listening.

They left in pairs, and once back in their room, Bond took his parka from the clothes closet and went into the bathroom. There he committed a message to tape from the notebook computer, then rewound the tape and put it into the transmitter. Half-an-hour later, he slipped from the room and went up the wooden staircase, working his way right to the top and out on to the roof.

The air was bitter and there seemed to be light snow drifting across the forest which spread out all around him. He calculated the direction, held the little transmitter away from his body and pressed the 'send' key. For the second time in four days a tiny fragment of signal leaped, invisibly, on to the airwaves. All he could do was pray that someone was listening.

*　　　*　　　*

Boris Stepakov left the dacha just after three in the morning with his bodyguards. He also took Stephanie Adoré and Major Rampart with him. They drove to the secret airfield where the crew of his Antonov An-72 had already filed a flight plan to the Spetsnaz training base just outside Kirovograd on the River Ingul in the Ukraine.

Because Spetsnaz are trained there, the base is one of the most securely guarded in the whole of Russia. The secrecy is so great that even those living in nearby towns and villages are unaware of its importance, for Spetsnaz are the very best troops in the world, easily ranking above the British SAS

239

or the US Delta Force and Navy Seals.

Here, and at other secret bases, these special forces undergo what is possibly the most rigorous military training known anywhere. The men chosen to serve as Spetsnaz are often hand-picked even before they enter the Red Army. The recruiting officers go out and search for suitable material while young men are still in school or at universities, for these troops are brought to perfection not only in the most secret military arts, but also in the darker arcane callings which make them ideal for covert operations.

The GRU—the Red Army's equivalent of KGB—have been known to make use of these men by infiltrating them into foreign countries to work under cover for long periods. They certainly take on a much more sinister role than their counterparts in SAS or Delta.

At Kirovograd—they call the base after the great industrial city even though it is situated some fifty miles from city limits—the Spetsnaz soldier risks his life every day. The training exercises are carried out with live ammunition, and sometimes with the added danger of deadly chemicals and real explosives. Because of this there is an allowed percentage of training deaths—just as there was among the British Commando training units during World War II.

They first learn the normal skills of soldiering, but with an accent on leadership and tactics, so that any member of the force can take over battlefield command from the highest staff officer should the occasion arise.

Following this stringent induction, the Spetsnaz soldier goes on to more specialised work. They study the customs and languages of possible target countries; survival techniques; the tradecraft of deep cover and disguise, so that they can pass themselves off as tourists, businessmen, members of trade or diplomatic missions, even as cultural groups or sports teams. For instance, a Spetsnaz officer was the winner of two Olympic silver medals in pistol shooting: in Melbourne and Rome. Because of his sporting activities, this man travelled freely throughout the world. He did not move alone, but always had two more officers in attendance, and is thought to have picked up valuable information from the West—just by being a crack shot.

Intermingled with these diverse crafts, future Spetsnaz men are taught sabotage of every feasible kind, and with every possible device: they also become proficient with all known weapons, in hand-to-hand combat and silent killing. Even while doing this distinctive training, they are constantly practising the normal skills of parachuting, skiing, mountain climbing and the basics of flying. Many active Spetsnaz troops could handle large civilian aircraft in an emergency, and most could fly a helicopter.

They are truly the cream, the best-paid and the most feared of Soviet forces. They have no special uniform, except that they are normally seen wearing the dress of the airborne and special assault forces, though, unlike the airborne, Spetsnaz do not wear the coveted 'Guards Unit' badges. There are times when they will wear only civilian clothes for months at a time.

Stepakov felt he had entered a distinctive environment as soon as he left his aircraft, dogged as ever by Nicki. Alex was left on the aircraft with the crew and the French couple. The men on this base were clear-eyed, moved with more confidence, carried themselves in a more doughty manner than even the Red Army's other crack regiments. Trying to define this odd, uneasy sensation, Stepakov had long since realised that, when he was among Spetsnaz, he lived in the shadow of exceptional soldiers who could, if they chose, be ruthless killers.

General Gleb Yakovlevich Berzin—whom he had called a son-of-a-bitch—stood by the window of his austere office. He was tall with the figure of someone in peak physical condition. When he moved, the splendid muscle tone could be detected through his well-cut uniform. Like all Spetsnaz officers, Berzin took great pride in his appearance. As he turned to greet his visitor, the hard leathery face showed no sign of camaraderie. The eyes, like broken crystal, bore down upon Stepakov as though asking why a member of the KGB dared show his face, let alone his entire body, in this elect corner of the country.

'Stepakov.' He barked in acknowledgement that his brother officer was in the room.

'Berzin,' the KGB man nodded, turning the full power of his own unreadable clown's face on the Spetsnaz man.

'Moscow said this was important. It had better be. I haven't time to waltz around with people from Centre.'

'This is *very* important, comrade General.' Stepakov did not raise his voice. 'I bring you special orders, under seal, most secret, from the President himself. The President wishes these orders to be

242

carried out with urgency.' He thrust the heavy envelope into the general's outstretched hand.

Berzin ripped open the orders and began to read. Halfway through he glanced up, looking at the KGB officer with what might have been construed as a new interest. Finally he folded the paper and gave a little laugh, like the yap of a dog.

'The President really *wants* me to do this?'

'If you read the orders carefully, you'll see that he not only wants you to do it, he commands you. He also orders you to carry out this action with me as your joint commander.'

Berzin laughed. 'You must be joking, *General* Stepakov. Why should I even take you along for the ride?'

'Oh, I think you will.' When Stepakov smiled, the already upturned corners of his mouth seemed to rise higher on his cheeks. This sometimes gave the bizarre impression that someone had taken an old cutthroat razor and slashed it across his mouth. 'I bring another, even more secret, message.'

'Oh?'

'A verbal communication, comrade General. I was told you would answer me, and it comes with greetings. "And all I ask is a tall ship..."'

For a fraction of a second, light appeared to flare behind the cracked crystal of Berzin's eyes. It could have meant anything from fear to elation, for the man was virtually unreadable. He stood, statue still, studying Stepakov. Then, in a low voice muttered, 'And a star to steer her by.' He turned away to look out of the window again. Even though Berzin's back was towards Stepakov, the KGB man sensed that he was looking far away, past the rows of hutments and wooded training areas, back to another life.

'It's been a very long time coming.' He still spoke softly. 'You must have dubious connections, my friend.'

'I don't know what that message means, comrade General. I only know that the man who told me to pass it on is also most anxious for you to do this thing. We are also to take two French officers with us. They wait in my personal aircraft.'

Berzin began to laugh. First a chuckle, then a full-blown cascade of mirth. He turned, and though he laughed, his face showed no humour or merriment. It was as though an animal was baying for no particular purpose, except to make a sound meant to convey drollness. 'Who said that life is a comedy, Stepakov?'

'I think . . .'

'I don't need an answer, you fool,' Berzin snapped. 'Of course I'll do what is asked. In fact, I'm delighted to do it. Nothing would please me more. Come. Come and lunch with my officers. We will set things in motion immediately after we've eaten. We have a long way to go before this day is out.'

*   *   *

Nigsy Meadows had done as M instructed. Now he camped with another agent and a Lapp guide, high in the Arctic Circle where they monitored radio signals from Russian military units on the far side of the border. They were one of five groups spread out as secret listening posts from the Baltic to the far North.

In the Lapp's tent they set up the sophisticated

portable electronics which grabbed signals and telephone calls from the air. The other agent's name was Wright, always known as 'Pansy', for his affectation of wearing that particular flower in his buttonhole when it was in season, which for Pansy Wright seemed to be the year round. He even had a bedraggled specimen inside his cold-weather clothing now.

Nigsy also had a portable Model 300, set, as the one in Moscow had been, to pick up Bond's homing device. On top of this, he had lugged along another piece of portable electronics. A reduced unit which would duplicate squirt signals, such as the one they had grabbed from the air at the Moscow Embassy. Like the Model 300, this would only talk to Bond's transmitter.

They took it in turns to monitor the equipment, and Nigsy was on duty, listening to radio telephone communications which seemed to be coming in to a location some twelve miles distant in the dense forest within the Russian border.

He heard the tiny crackle of static and his eyes just caught the flick of the needle as the telescoped transmission flashed in.

A minute later he was shaking Pansy Wright, bringing him out of a dream which featured a carpet of wild flowers and a young woman by the name of Marge.

'This had better be good,' Wright swore at him. 'I've been after this wench for a long time and I nearly had her tonight.'

Nigsy did not know what he was talking about, but he did have the co-ordinates which would pinpoint Bond.

CHAPTER SIXTEEN

THE BLUES IN THE NIGHT

When Bond got back to their room, he found Nina in her towelling robe, still sound asleep on the bed where he had left her. She looked peaceful, lovely and detached. The robe had fallen open to reveal part of her left thigh and Bond automatically covered it. He had known since yesterday that this casual operational necessity which had thrown them together, had, for him, gone over the borderline, making them what the Americans might, in understatement, call kissing cousins.

Quietly he stretched out next to her, staring into the darkness, his mind a cauldron of confusion. Once every couple of years the Service invited him to speak to the new entrants at the kindergarten, as they called the training establishment some ten miles east of Watford. He always began with the old saw. 'Field agents and airline pilots suffer from the same occupational hazard—nine-tenths boredom followed by one-tenth sheer terror.'

So far, this job had certainly fallen into the larger portion of that hazard, but he had followed every rule, obeyed the command given to him by M, namely, done nothing but keep his eyes and ears open. 'If the worst comes to the worst, just wait,' the old spy had told him. 'Wait for the catalyst.'

He had allowed himself to be inserted with Pete Natkowitz into what Stepakov insisted was the heart of *Chushi Pravosudia*. He had played at being Guy, the recruited cameraman, and accepted Nina

246

from Stepakov at face value. But he was no nearer to the absolute truth regarding the *Scales of Justice*. Had he been magically spirited this moment into his Chief's presence, all he could have said was that the terrorist organisation appeared to be run by General Yevgeny Yuskovich, Commander-in-Chief Red Army Rocket Forces, and that Yuskovich was passing himself off for the sake of this charade of a trial as the army's Judge Advocate General.

He supposed he could add that the innocent Joel Penderek had behaved like a docile, guilty man, but after that he was left with nothing, only the sound and fury of paradox and conflicting absurdity. Now Bond tried to put his feelings for Nina to one side, letting his mind zero in on logic and facts.

The facts were that a phoney trial was being acted for cameras in some godforsaken edifice, ten miles or so from the Finnish border, if Emerald Lacy was to be believed. Nina had been foisted on them and he had formed a sexual relationship with her. At the same time, Pete Natkowitz had fallen into similar intimacy with the girl Natasha, whom he said was a member of his own Service.

During the discussions—the ring of conspiracy—which had taken place that night, he had been struck by two things. First, Natasha had taken no part in the conversation and second, Michael and Emerald Brooks' contribution had been worthless. Indeed, the pair of them had become dubious assets in Bond's suspicious mind.

The kernel of information offered by Brooks could be summed up in the man's own words—'. . . The whole thing about this war criminal Vorontsov is a blind, a sleight, a way to throw the Kremlin and the President off-balance. It's only part of

247

something greater, an evil which will have appalling consequences. We know some of it but not all. The gist is that hardline military people are about to launch a plot which will destroy America and probably Britain also. And I mean *destroy*.' That was what he had said, and the pivot of the information was contained in eight words—'*We know some of it but not all.*'

Neither Brooks nor his wife had offered to share what little knowledge they were supposed to have. Instead, Bond and Natkowitz had been shown the inside of a box of mirrors, a story about the hotel having been built on the site of a monastery, a smoothly conducted tour around a secret hiding place. He had not really bought their tale of night-stalking through the building, of 'finding' the *Boys' Own* hidden tunnel, a tale of luring three soldiers to their deaths in order to provide them with three P6 automatics. He had not even seen the bodies of these dead soldiers.

A thought snapped into his head. It was almost audible, like the tumblers on a security lock dropping into place. Silently, Bond slid from the bed. He had put his pistol, together with the spare magazines, on the floor wrapped in a towel and had advised Nina to do the same on her side of the bed. Quietly he picked up the bundle and crept into the bathroom.

First he examined the ammunition. The weight and feel were right. The magazines slid neatly into the pistol's butt, so if anything was wrong it had to be in the gun itself. Quickly he disassembled the weapon and his fear was confirmed in a matter of seconds. The firing pin had been carefully filed away, so this particular P6 was of no value unless you wanted to use it as a bludgeon.

He reassembled the automatic, wrapped it in the towel and returned to the bedroom, crossed the floor silently and exchanged his little towelled bundle for the one on Nina's side of the bed.

In the bathroom once more, he checked the ammunition, then began to strip down the pistol. Nina's weapon was lethal, the firing pin in place and the mechanism lightly oiled. So there you have it, he thought. Nina was armed, he was not, and he could but presume Natkowitz had been left in the same position. He went back to stretch out beside Nina, knowing, as he had discerned during the night, that all was far from well with Michael and Emerald.

How in heaven's name could that be? he questioned. He had seen the files; he was one of the chosen few who were, as they said, 'Sensation Cleared'. These two were legends in the secret community—the *Huscarl*, the Service's two-handed axe sent to avenge those famous KGB penetration agents the Press called moles.

He frowned in the darkness, searching for any hint from the files he had examined, which might explain that the *Huscarl* had been tainted— tripled—because that was where logic took him. Once more, the picture of the elderly spies skulking round the building, operating like a pair of agents in some comic book, filled his mind. It was foolish, not just unlikely but damned near impossible to believe.

Never discount the impossible. He heard M's chilly voice in his ear. Dry old spies, he thought. Dry, slack with their years. Obsessed by methods now obsolete. Could they possibly have been taken in? Could they themselves have become unwitting agents? Even that was not likely, for the proof lay beside Nina on the floor. One weapon spiked, ready for Bond's own use or misuse. He realised that his thoughts spun in circles, and that he really did not want to accept Michael Brooks' and Emerald Lacy's guilt, for their condemnation would be Nina's also, and his heart wanted Nina to be on the side of the angels. But she was not, and he had to accept that, unpalatable as it might be.

Then what of the silent Natasha? She was, she said, a member of *Chushi Pravosudia*, yet she gave them no answers and Pete had vouched for her. 'She's *with* me, if you understand,' he had said, or something of that nature. Had she also been doubled? If so, nobody was safe. He recalled someone else saying the only true way to freedom is through paranoia. Was he now drowning in his own doubts and uncertainties?

An old song came into his head. 'Blues in the Night'. He recalled some of the lyrics. 'A worrisome thing that leads you to sing the blues in the night.' Then another voice crept into his ear, Nina's. Nina murmuring to him, 'Trust nobody. Please trust none of them, not even Bory ...' she had whispered as they came out of Dom Knigi after buying *Crime and Punishment*. Bluff? Double-bluff? Truth? He fell into a shallow doze, wakening as Nina stirred. The darkness outside never altered, but their watches said it was time to start a new day.

* * *

In London, M was closeted with Bill Tanner,

examining the transcripts. They had Bond's map reference and had pinpointed the place. 'The Red Army Senior Officers' Centre,' Tanner mused. 'The place they built on the site of the old Orthodox monastery, St Kyril of Antioch, or some such.'

M nodded, grabbing at the other flimsies, the radio traffic of the Red Army, monitored from a hundred outposts. Certain types of transmission had increased, notably signals between the place where Bond was located and October Battalion, Spetsnaz, the equivalent of one of 22nd SAS squadrons, always held in readiness in Hereford. The Battalion consisted of some forty-five men. They were at constant alert, separated from other troops on a base near Leningrad.

M read the translated and decrypted signals carefully. 'Only a spit and a stride from Blessed St Kyril's,' he muttered. 'That is a Russian spit and a stride. Six or seven hundred miles. Looks like they mean business. Do we know who these people take their orders from?'

The Chief of Staff riffled through an annotated copy of the Russian High Command. 'Direct authority is Berzin,' he said, 'Gleb Yakovlevich Berzin, General. A hawk. Member of the old guard. A thorn in the side of the new Kremlin. But he commands the Spetsnaz Training Base near Kirovograd. That's the hell of a way from Leningrad.'

'Heard about jet aircraft, Chief of Staff?' M did not even pause as he read the signal. Then, 'I think it's probably time to speak with the PM.' He rose. 'It'll be up to the Prime Minister, of course, but I would imagine he'd want a quiet word on the hush-hush line with the President of the Soviet

251

Union. I'll take all copies of that traffic.'

They were not to know, even at this hour, that as they spoke, Boris Stepakov was still on his way to meet and pass on instructions to General Berzin. In advance of his arrival at the training base, the fuse had been lit.

★   ★   ★

Before Natasha came with Pete Natkowitz to conduct them all down to breakfast and the day's work, James Bond dressed more carefully than usual and took time to make sure Nina thought she was also prepared. The only other point Michael and Emerald had indicated was that something would happen quickly. Sooner rather than later. Whatever the truth about the *Huscarl*, he could not set the possibility to one side.

At the bottom of his backpack was a roll of wide duct tape and, standing naked in the bathroom with Nina, he carefully taped the useless P6 automatic pistol to her stomach and the extra magazines hard under her breasts. She winced, but silently assured him, with hands and eyes, that she could manage to move and keep the weapon well hidden under a heavy sweater.

When she had gone into the bedroom, Bond taped his automatic very low down on his stomach, the weapon at an angle so that he would be able to reach inside either his waistband or his fly and wrench the pistol out. Ripping the tape away would be painful, though not as painful as the idea of facing armed men with no means of protection.

He taped one of the spare magazines onto the small of his back. He then pulled on the long

252

thermal underwear, in case he was called upon to leave the relatively warm, comfortable interior of the hotel.

He put on thick jeans, a heavy rollneck and the favourite denim jacket reinforced with leather patches. The very fact that he chose to put it on this morning was an indication of how seriously he took the impending threat. The leather patches hid a multitude of small items which might help him in any escape or survival situation, and the concealed objects would be very hard to detect, even in a close body and clothing search.

He was going to be warm under the hot lights on the sound stage, but he would at least be ready. Just before leaving, Bond rechecked his parka, winding back the tape and replacing it in the notebook computer against the possibility of having to make a rush transmission. He put both the transmitter and notebook computer back into their hiding places and was ready to meet the day head on. These preparations he did in secret, so that Nina saw neither computer nor transmitter.

While they were making ready, Bond and Nina carried on a flow of small talk—the weather, the video, how working for *Chushi Pravosudia* had proved to be more interesting and rewarding than they had ever thought possible. Most of this chat was vacuous and on several occasions they almost ruined things by breaking into laughter at the banal sentences they were able to produce. It was, Bond thought, the Guy and Helen show, and his stomach turned over when he thought of how his Helen had most probably betrayed him.

As Natasha walked them down the corridor, she lowered her voice, muttering that she had heard

253

they would be working late into the night. 'They want to get the actual taping completed today,' she said. 'Looks like something's in the wind.'

Natkowitz made a puerile remark about it probably having something to do with the stew, and Natasha giggled. Bond frowned, realising this was a sign of increased stress. Pete Natkowitz's remark would normally have been met with either a sharp reprimand or groans.

After eating they made their way to the sound stage. The big wall made of the sliding metal doors was wide open though people were preparing for shooting. Clive stood near the camera talking to Yuskovich who looked ready to give the performance of his life.

'Guy,' Clive shouted, 'be an angel and do hurry up, please. We really must get this opera started or the day will just disappear. We're in the land that time forgot already.'

At a hint from Bond, Natkowitz excused himself, heading for the men's room with Bond following. They both glanced towards the third door through which they had been taken on the previous night. It now seemed like a surreal dream.

The men's room was empty, but the walls probably had ears. Bond grabbed at a bar of the rough soap supplied at the handbasins, broke a piece free and wrote quickly on the mirror, *Natasha? How sure?*

Natkowitz ran one of the taps and rubbed the soap from the glass. He then spoke in clipped, disjointed sentences, 'Is it a plane? Is it a bird? I do not know.' Then 'Never seen anyone like her. Amazing. She knows all the tricks, but I wouldn't trust her with money.'

It was enough for Bond. He gave Pete Natkowitz a half-minute of mime, to let him know the P6 automatic was probably useless.

'It is,' Natkowitz sang, tunelessly as he washed his hands, then broke into an equally discordant, 'There is nothing like a dame; there's not anything like a dame.'

Bond made some unrepeatable comments about his singing and the two emerged from the men's room. As they crossed the floor towards the sound stage, Natkowitz grinned his gentleman farmer grin and said casually, 'Been wanting to talk to you about the lady. A no-no if I ever saw one. Didn't work it out for at least six hours.'

They both realised that, as long as they kept the conversation suitably cryptic, nobody was likely to pick up on it. 'Would've been happier if you'd told me before, George old boy,' Bond replied.

'I didn't think you cared.'

They passed onto the sound stage, the sliding doors rolled shut and the previous night's labour and worry were almost forgotten in the long stint of work that followed.

They spent the morning doing reverses, the shots of people's reactions—shock, sadness, anger—concentrating on the three officers who made up the panel of the tribunal; then the prosecuting and defending officers, followed by Yuskovich whose hammy performance was modified by the truly sinister aura which surrounded him. Last of all, they did Penderek, who obeyed every instruction.

Bond, watching him in close-up through the large viewfinder, would have sworn that nobody could have detected the influence of drugs, but the man's reactions could only have been guaranteed by

255

chemical persuasion. Unless they had managed to talk him into being an unwitting victim.

After the lunch break they went back to it and by late afternoon they had done the summing-up speeches of both prosecuting and defending officers. They took a break around five, then went to work again, taping a long, carefully prepared speech by Yuskovich, who proved to be as temperamental as any starlet. Again and again they had to retake pieces of speech because he was not satisfied with his own delivery. Everyone, including Clive up in his control room, became edgy. 'You could cut the air with a piece of old rope,' Natkowitz whispered, but it went out through his mike into the control room, and Clive blew up, commanding everyone to keep quiet unless they had anything really important to say. 'I'll come down there personally and sort you all out if there's any more chitter-chatter.'

'Slap on the wrist,' Nina murmured, standing by Bond, working as his focus-puller.

Yuskovich's speech was a clever mixture of political harangue and humanitarian plea. He spoke of the Russian leadership as 'those who haven't the spine to bring this terrible matter out into the open. They promised a new order with freedom and fairness for all. It should now be obvious that the freedom did not include the minorities.' They had been afraid to act. Afraid because they had no intention of taking the Motherland into a new era. The current regime was bent solely on becoming another dictatorship. He went on, his voice calm and rarely raised, and all the more malign for that.

At last, it seemed they had got it right, but Clive, speaking through the headphones, told Bond that

256

the accused would be coming back. He had to prepare to do a short question and answer between Yuskovich and the supposed Vorontsov.

Later, Bond thought he should not have been surprised, but as the short exchange was being taped, he was shocked by the duplicity.

Standing directly in front of the dock, Yuskovich stared straight at the prisoner.

'You know who I am?' he asked.

'I know only that you are General Yevgeny Yuskovich. That's who I've been told you are.'

'Do you imagine you *should* know me from the past? From your childhood, perhaps?'

'I don't see how I should know you.' Penderek's Russian was suspiciously good. He even spoke with a Ukrainian accent.

'Your parents. They were Alexander Vorontsov and Reyna Vorontsov?'

'Correct.'

'And you were born and raised in the city of Kharkov, where your father was a doctor? It was a good family?'

'My father practised and taught anaesthesiology at the University Hospital, yes. My mother was a nurse. They were good people.'

'And your mother's maiden name—the name she was known by before she married your father?'

'Muzykin. Reyna Illyena Muzykin.'

'So. Do you recall any members of her family? Your maternal grandfather, grandmother, your mother's sisters?'

'Yes, very well. I remember my grandfather Muzykin, also my three aunts.'

'Did any of the aunts marry?'

'Yes, two were married.'

257

'You recall their married names?'

'One married a doctor called Rostovsky. The other took a husband by name Sidak. He was a soldier. An army officer.'

'Good. Did they have children? Did *you* have cousins?'

'Yes, my cousins Valdik and Konstantin. They were by my Aunt Valentina Rostovsky. My other aunt's husband was killed. They said it was an accident. In the thirties. I always wondered...'

'You do not recall any cousin named Yevgeny?'

'No, I had only two cousins.'

'And you had no relatives who bore the name Yuskovich?'

'That is your name.'

'And that is why I ask you. I shall ask again. Did you know of any relatives by name Yuskovich?'

'Never. No. None by that name.'

'Good.' He turned to the tribunal. 'I have put these questions to the accused because it has been suggested by unscrupulous persons who do not hold the future of our beloved Mother Russia as something sacred, that, in some way, I am related to the accused. I would like the accused's answers placed on the record so that, at no time in the future, can it be claimed I have any blood kinship with this wretched man.'

They broke immediately after this. The big doors were rolled back and Clive came on to the floor. He told them they only had one more long session to tape and it would amount to the accused's confession and plea for mercy. 'I really think we should try for a wrap tonight, dears. Go and get coffee, or whatever else you want. No wasting time or poodlefaking. We'll start in three-quarters of an

258

hour. Take forty-five, after that I want all the witnesses on the set. Understand? Every last one of them.'

'Mind if I get some air?' Bond asked.

'You can take a balloon ride, go sledding, whatever, love, as long as you're back in three-quarters of an hour.' The director turned on his heel. 'I'll brook no arguments,' he shouted over his shoulder.

'Should be back at Stratford,' Natkowitz yawned. 'Off with his head. So much for Clive.'

'You coming out?' Bond was already strolling towards the elevators.

'Too damned cold, and Guy, don't say anything stupid, like "I may be a long time", right?'

'Back within forty-five minutes.'

He went up to his room, grabbed at the parka and put it on as he rode the elevator down. His head felt thick and his eyes ached, the result of being up half the night. The bitter weather outside would soon put him right.

Ten minutes later the roof fell in when the October Battalion of Spetsnaz arrived, coming in from the air with clouds of thunder.

CHAPTER SEVENTEEN

THE DEATH OF 007

Everyone seemed to be standing around in the wide lobby leading to the sound stage. The metal doors were rolled back and a couple of Clive's assistants were putting finishing touches to the set. All the people who had played the part of witnesses had been coaxed into their make-up. They talked and laughed, drank coffee and smoked. Bond caught sight of Natasha standing with Michael and Emerald who appeared in their first guise as the very old Jewish couple. Natkowitz was fiddling with the sound equipment and Nina seemed to have disappeared.

Bond had gone into the men's room on his way to the exit in the main lobby before taking his brisk walk to clear his head. He was just emerging when it began.

They would have heard nothing had they already been taping, for once the doors were closed the stage was admirably soundproof. As it was, the roar of massive engines pulsed down, throbbing and making the whole building shake.

For a second it was as though everybody was engaged in the childhood game of 'statues'. A shocked stillness seemed to spread over the throng, laughing and talking one minute, stock-still, turned to stone the next, cigarettes, coffee and soft drinks poised. The liquids seemed solidified in a click of time.

Bond stepped back inside the empty men's room, unzipped his fly and dragged out the P6, thumbing the safety and zipping everything up again. He leant against the door to hear what was going on.

The stillness had passed and was replaced by confusion. Shouting, some screams, the noise of a herd of uncontrolled people moving in panic. Bond pulled on his thermal gloves and gripped the pistol more tightly.

From outside the building came the sudden distinct whoomp of exploding grenades followed by

260

shots, the burp of automatic fire and the thump-thump of single rounds. Then the sound of people running. Heavy footsteps racing towards the lobby.

Bond pushed the door open a few inches and saw Boris Stepakov in a camouflage jump suit followed by a tall, hard-faced officer and a group of soldiers, six or seven, he guessed. They were all in combat gear, carrying an assortment of weapons. Stepakov held one of the latest PRI automatics close to his hip. The others bristled with AKS-74 rifles, grenades, long-bladed knives sheathed high on their right shoulders. He even caught sight of an R-350 radio, the kind with encryption and burst-transmission ability. Only Stepakov and the tall officer had the hoods of their jump suits down, the men who followed were muffled so that only their eyes could be seen.

As they approached, the crowd of witnesses and technicians began to back away, clearing a path. To his right, Bond saw Michael Brooks edging towards the door leading to the closet and tunnel. He placed his back against it and worked the key with his hands behind him. Glancing to his left, Brooks' eyes met Bond's and he shifted his head, a signal for Bond to follow him as the door silently swung back.

Bond just looked at him, making no move to follow as the renegade spy slipped out of sight into the closet. Then he heard Stepakov's voice, loud, raised above the babble.

'Silence! Stay exactly where you are!'

He imagined the clownlike face turning, sweeping the crowd as they backed onto the sound stage. The talking had stopped leaving a stunned silence in its wake as though the crowd was making

261

way for Stepakov and his little group.

Bond wanted to push the door fully open, join Stepakov and watch the rout of the *Chushi Pravosudia*. But something, experience and intuition he supposed, held him back.

Again he caught movement to his right and through the crack of the open door, saw Emerald and Nina slip quietly into the closet. Nina had retrieved her pistol and held it, two-handed, low, the butt hard into her crotch as she backed through the doorway.

'General Yevgeny Yuskovich!' Stepakov's voice almost broke as he shouted the name, the pitch rising, caught on a dry spot in his larynx.

'*Marshal* Yuskovich.' Bond had listened to the voice declaiming for most of the day. Now it had taken on a new arrogance.

'Marshal by whose jurisdiction?' Stepakov sounded as though he had complete control of both himself and the situation.

'My own,' Yuskovich snapped. 'Marshal of the Red Army and soon secretary of the CCPSU, President of the Soviet Union.'

Stepakov laughed. 'Yevgeny, I fear you're no longer even a general. My friend, General Berzin here, has supported me in this operation on the direct instructions of the President of the Soviet Union. The building has been secured by the October Battalion of Spetsnaz. You should consider yourself under arrest together with any other troops you have suborned. We are to take you back to Moscow. Further resistance is...'

'Really? How interesting.' Yuskovich began to laugh, and another voice, Bond presumed it was the officer called Berzin, punctuated the laugh with a strange, chilling bark which sounded like a hyena.

'Oh, Bory, what a mistake you've made.' Then the crack of a command. 'Berzin, take that damned pistol from him, he could do a mischief with it.'

Bond drew in his breath as the sounds of a scuffle reached him.

'What?' He heard Boris explode. 'What the...'

'What indeed, Bory? I'm among friends. You, I fear, are alone. What about those two thugs he carts around with him?'

Berzin, Bond assumed it was he, made a sound like the ripping of cloth. 'Both of them,' he said. 'My men snatched them as they came off the helicopter. Bory, don't look so amazed. You know how these things work. You merely got yourself mixed up on the wrong side of the coup. You should have seen it coming. It's business, comrade. The business of Russia. The business of the Party and the future.'

'Yes,' Yuskovich again. 'You were an incredible subject, Boris. I've always said the way to deal with loyalty is through autosuggestion. You took the bait like a greedy fox instead of a shrewd one. I'd expected some doubts, but you gobbled up everything, even the stuff we fed to you through Lyko.'

'What the hell are you talking about?'

'The overthrow of the present regime. A return to normal.' There was a short pause before Yuskovich continued. 'We have a full regiment of Spetsnaz at our command. Who did you think carried out the *Chushi Pravosudia* executions, Bory? If you had thought it through, there was only one answer. Trained men who had the means to get anywhere, go anywhere, hit any target. Did you

263

never consider Lyko was planted on you?'

Some of the answers began to unravel in Bond's head. Some, but not all. He would have to move in a moment. Slowly he put pressure on the door, opening it wider as Yuskovich continued to speak.

'This trial, you knew we were taping this trial? Of course you did, you even took the lure suggested by Lyko and brought in people from the French and British intelligence services to help out. Where are the French and the British, by the way?'

Bond sucked in his breath and slid sideways through the door. The actors employed as witnesses, together with the technicians, were in a packed semicircle facing the sound stage. Bory Stepakov had his back to the crowd, as did the tall General Berzin. Yuskovich faced them, his lean ascetic face calm, the eyes fixed on Stepakov.

As Bond sidled out close to the wall, Yuskovich raised his head, his eyes scanning the crowd. Bond dropped to his knees, his pistol ready as the self-styled marshal repeated, 'Where are the French and the British? I have guards on the French, but the two British spies should be ...' His eyes remained on the crowd and he did not raise them to look beyond.

Bond moved slowly to his right, edging along the wall. He could reach the front of the hotel through the main lobby, and he would kill if he had to. Kill or be killed, it did not seem to matter a great deal any more.

He heard somebody reply, telling the marshal that one of the British crew was there, on the sound stage. He began to move faster, sliding along the wall, keeping his body low. Another few feet and he would be out of Yuskovich's sight.

As he reached comparative safety, he heard the chatter of the Spetsnaz R-350 radio, then another voice, unheard before, cut in. 'Comrade General Berzin, sir. Message in from the President. He insists we report if this facility has been secured. He also orders that we provide information on two British agents he knows are here.'

Yuskovich swore loudly, then rasped out, overriding Berzin, 'Report the facility secured and members of *Chushi Pravosudia* under armed arrest. As for the British, how in hell did he know they were here? Tell him we regret they were killed in an exchange of fire. Wait. Say they died bravely.'

* * *

M had been away for hours. When he returned, he looked grey and drawn. Bill Tanner, who was summoned to his office within minutes of his reappearance, had never seen the Old Man with such a pallor. It was as though he had suddenly aged a decade; his skin was drawn tightly against the facial bones, his hair seemed more grizzled and the look in his eyes was vacant, as if he had been injected with some drug which removed all life from his brain, leaving only a half-functional body.

M sat slumped behind the big glass-topped desk. When he spoke, Tanner was reminded of biblical stories of men rending their garments, pouring ashes on their heads and mourning for lost sons or daughters. His voice had an unearthly, terrible quality to it. The words seemed to be covered with gum, sticking in his larynx, almost refusing to come out.

Tanner felt the shock wave hit him as M slowly

recounted his news. 'I don't believe it,' he said, then repeated, 'I don't believe it. Are you sure, sir?'

'I was there. Presumably it has to be confirmed, but the news from the Kremlin seemed definite enough. It's the kind of thing you get in wartime. You know that. Worse when there's not even a Cold War. I've been through enough wars to know it's wrong to harbour hopes. He's dead, Bill. That's what the Spetsnaz general on the spot says. Anything to the contrary would be a bonus, though I expect nothing.'

M told him the Prime Minister was just as shocked by the news. He had read the transcripts taken to Number Ten by M. Then, as expected, he called the President of the Soviet Union, only to be told that he already had knowledge of the *Chushi Pravosudia*'s hiding place in the Red Army Senior Officers' Centre near the Finnish border. Troops would be on their way this night, and he would personally be in touch with the Prime Minister as soon as he had news.

'I started to get a bad feeling about it, Bill.' M stared at the glass top of his desk as though trying to summon up some vision which might mollify the news. 'Couldn't come back here. Phoned the duty officer. Said where I was if needed . . .'

'Not like you, sir.' Tanner knew that M had been toughened in the hardest school life offered. His byword was, 'Life goes on. Work *must* continue.'

The Old Man sighed. 'No, Bill—No, Chief of Staff. Not like me, but today's not been an ordinary day. The PM was very good. Came back to Number Ten specially. Took the President's call. Told me straightaway.' He gave another sigh and moved his shoulders like an aged dog shaking off rain. 'At least they got the bastards. They'll sweat 'em all right. It'll be interesting to hear what their real objective was. I've never been happy with this business about compromising the Kremlin with this stupid trial.'

He was silent, staring again, then he looked up, his grey eyes still vacant as though he could not comprehend the full import of the news. 'Better get Moneypenny in. It's only right that I tell her, she was damned fond of James.'

'Sir, if you like, I'll . . .'

'No. It's my job. I'll tell her James Bond is dead. You get in touch with the teams we've got monitoring along the Baltic and the ones on the Finnish border. I'm sure they can now be put to a better use.' He clamped his mouth shut and Tanner stood for a second as though unable to leave. 'Get out, Chief of Staff. Get out and send Moneypenny in. Damn it, she's been my PA for more years than either of us like to remember. I'll tell her that 007's gone.'

*   *   *

They had discovered James Bond's body, flat on his back, quite close to the wooden wall at the west of the building. There were three bullet holes in his chest and the face had been taken away by another burst of fire. But the clothes he was wearing were undoubtedly his—the khaki parka, thick jeans—denim jacket with leather patches and the rollneck. All were now soaked in blood from the ugly wounds which had torn his flesh and bone to pieces.

The search had gone on for over an hour. They

had the two French agents and the man who posed as George. Yuskovich had stamped around on the sound stage. Initially, when they realised the British spy was missing, he had even gone outside with General Berzin to watch the men's search for Bond, but as time passed he became more edgy, his nerves fraying. 'We'll have to get on. I want Vorontsov's confession in the can and this whole project wrapped up tonight,' he shouted at Clive.

'Well, if it's really that urgent, I'll operate the camera myself. I mean it's not my job, and the unions would play hell in England...'

'You are not in England now,' Yuskovich barked. 'Unions are for organising, not for disrupting essential Communist Party work. You handle the camera. Then get on with the editing. I want copies of this ready for global release sometime tomorrow.'

Clive gave an irritable shrug, muttering, 'All right, you great butch soldier, but I for one am going to have a nervous breakdown when this is over.'

Yuskovich strolled over to where Joel Penderek, posing as the infamous Josif Vorontsov, was sitting in the dock. 'Well, Joeli,' he gave the man a sideways look, 'how have you enjoyed your trip back to Mother Russia?'

'It's been interesting. I'd given up all hope of ever being used.'

'Yes.' The marshal gave a curt nod. 'Sleepers like you and Anna usually go past a point in their lives where they expect to be of value. I'm sorry your Anna is not here to see you perform this essential service to your country and the Party.'

'She would've been pleased.' The old man gave

268

him a melancholy look. 'What of your cousin? Your real cousin, Vorontsov?'

'You have to ask?'

'Not really. I presume he's dead.'

'Bory Stepakov really did have him tucked away in the other dacha. The French agents were very good. If we hadn't been watching carefully, I doubt if even our people would have spotted them. Stepakov will be a great loss. We could have used him, you know.'

'You're confirming his death? Vorontsov's, I mean.'

'Of course.' Yuskovich flapped his hand in an irritable gesture, like swatting away a troublesome insect. 'Dead and buried. Just as he had to be. It wouldn't have been wise for me to assume total power with *that* skeleton in my cupboard. You know the original, the real, *Chushi Pravosudia*, were going to press for a public trial. Lucky we had then all sewn up from their inception. But I have to give them credit for conceiving the plot. With my real cousin, and with better organisation, they just might have made a relevant statement. And if they had—well, the true cause would have been submerged for a decade at least. No, Joeli my friend, *now* is the time to finish with this idiotic *perestroika* and *glasnost*. It has to be crushed now. Completely. I pray that the Americans really make good their threat against Iraq. It's the only way we can obliterate them without the world becoming difficult.'

'And me?' Penderek asked.

'You?'

'You're going to kill me, of course?'

'Don't be foolish, Joeli. Why would we do that?'

269

'Because you won't leave anyone alive. You won't make the mistake of letting any of the players in this farce survive. You wouldn't sleep peacefully in old Joe's bed in the Kremlin if you knew there were people alive who could tell the true story, or at least provide a distinctive footnote to history.'

'Bah. These people. These actors. I'm having them taken away, yes. But they don't have to die. I'm not going to repeat Stalin's only mistake, his Great Terror. There will be no purges. These actors are small fry. Nobody will listen to them. Not in the Gulag anyway.' He gave a short, unpleasant laugh. 'Don't worry, Joeli. You'll live out the rest of your natural life with all the comforts I can provide. It'll be lonely, of course, in a guarded dacha on the Black Sea, but you'll be comfortable. Let's do your big scene, eh?' He strolled off towards Clive who was arguing with Pete Natkowitz about the set-up. Yuskovich's adjutant stood nearby.

'Major Verber,' Yuskovich murmured to him, 'will you see that the prisoner over there is very quietly disposed of as soon as we finish this. Do it quickly. No sadism. Just a fast, unexpected bullet. Then have him buried. I suggest you do that in the forest.'

The major nodded acknowledgement, and at that moment a young member of the Spetsnaz October Battalion came in with the news that Bond's body had been discovered. An officer had called him over, with his partner, then told him to inform the marshal personally. 'I left the officer with my partner to stand guard,' he told Yuskovich.

The self-styled marshal swore mightily. 'I wanted photographs of the British agents with ...' He stopped in time. 'Never mind. The whole idea of bringing in these men was to implicate Britain. Damn it. I'll have to settle for one. Not the pair of them.'

The officer had been with one of the squads which had guarded the Red Army Senior Officers' Centre from the start of the operation. He told the marshal he had almost tripped over the body during the search. 'Some fool must have killed him out of hand,' he said. 'I thought I heard some muffled shots from this area half-an-hour ago, and I assumed it was simply to keep up appearances. We exploded cordite and guncotton charges all over the place when the October Battalion came in. I personally saw to it that things looked, and sounded realistic.'

'You did well.' Yuskovich returned the officer's salute. 'You come from Moscow, yes?'

'Yes, comrade Marshal. Born and bred there. My parents are still in Moscow.'

'Yes, I'd recognise a Muscovite accent anywhere. Your name?'

'Batovrin, comrade Marshal. Sergei Yakovlevich, Lieutenant, Spetsnaz.'

'You're a smart man. I can do with smart officers. Report to my adjutant, Major Verber. Tell him I said you are now attached to my personal guard. Say that is my order. If you get any trouble, pass it on to me.'

'Thank you, comrade Marshal.' The lieutenant's chest visibly puffed out with pride. His somewhat affected waxed moustache seemed to bristle in the freezing air as he went off to report to the adjutant.

They carried the body inside and laid it out in one of the little staff offices near what had originally

271

been the reception area. After the taping was over, Nina and Natkowitz were brought in to identify the spy, James Bond.

They both nodded, not really looking at the shattered face. 'That was what he wore when I last saw him,' Nina said.

'It's him.' Natkowitz, who had seen his fair share of death, quickly turned away.

'Good,' was all the marshal had to say.

Nina Bibikova caught up with Yuskovich in the passage as he headed back towards the sound stage. Yuskovich was feeling pleased with himself. Old Joel Penderek had given the performance of his life for the penultimate ten minutes of the video. They had shot the sentencing phase late the previous evening.

'Comrade Marshal,' Nina caught hold of his sleeve, and he stood, still as a rock, glaring down at her hand until she removed it.

'Well?'

'Comrade Marshal, I've come to plead for my parents' lives.'

'Why?'

'Because they are old. Also because they are my parents. I have served you well, comrade Marshal. From the moment I was infiltrated into Stepakov's Banda I served you and the Party. I did everything you told me. There was a suggestion then that you might spare my mother and father.'

'They were long-term British penetration agents.' He glowered at her and returned the salutes of Major Verber and Lieutenant Batovrin who had approached. 'One moment,' he gestured to the two officers to stand aside, then turned back to Nina. 'As I say, British penetration agents. You informed

272

on them yourself. What did you expect once we knew they had not died in that automobile accident? You expected us to give them a pension and a dacha?'

'No, sir. I merely think they have acted well for this operation.'

'My dear girl, they did not know they were helping us. From what I saw, they bumbled around in the night like two blind people. We even had to give them clues. Lead them. What is it that British writer said, "There is nothing worse than an old spy in a hurry," eh? These were two old spies trying to break the sound barrier. Look, Nina, it is understandable for you to weep. Whatever they did wrong, they are still your parents. I see that, just as I know you have done well for us. You and the beautiful Natasha. Both of you kept the British comfortable and in a state of—what can I call it—cosy bewilderment? You also helped lead your aged parents a very merry dance, but you always understood it was a dance macabre. We even sacrificed people to them. Forget it now. You simply obeyed orders. You will be handsomely rewarded, I promise you that.'

Nina bowed her head. 'Very well, comrade Marshal. Might I know what you intend for them?'

Yuskovich made an explosive noise of petulance, puffing his cheeks out and expelling air through his pursed lips. 'Very well. They will be taken with the others. I have made arrangements for them to be processed at Perm 35. They will probably live there without undue hardship. They will die there.'

Perm 35 is one of the few remaining Stalin-era camps. It lies on the European side of the Urals, and, under the new President's lenient release of political prisoners, its population of three hundred has dwindled to some fifteen—hijackers, military deserters and one CIA spy.

★   ★   ★

They buried James Bond the next morning, wrapping his body in sheets before placing it in the hard cold ground. Spetsnaz soldiers had hacked their way through the earth to make the grave which was marked by a piece of wood, carved overnight by one of their number. It bore the legend:

> *Here lies the body of a gallant British officer, thought to be Captain James Bond. Royal Navy. Died for his own cause January 9th, 1991.*

Even Yuskovich attended the interment. He also allowed Natkowitz and Boris Stepakov to be present. A squad of four Spetsnaz fired a volley of shots over the grave, while another played the Last Post on an old bugle.

The surprise came from Stepakov who, when the last notes died away, stepped forward and spoke lines memorised from his beloved Shelley:

> It is a modest creed, and yet
> Pleasant if one considers it,
> To own that death itself must be,
> Like all the rest, a mockery.

Natkowitz could have sworn there were tears running down the clownish face as the KGB general walked from the graveside.

All the actors and technicians who had been gathered together by Yuskovich's fake *Chushi Pravosudia* were flown out in big Mi-12 Homer helicopters the next afternoon. They used three of the huge machines to shuttle the prisoners out to the nearest railhead. The monitors in Scandinavia reported that members of the arrested *Chushi Pravosudia* were being removed for trial.

On that same afternoon, Marshal Yuskovich watched the grainy black and white video, now fully assembled by Clive. When it was over, he instructed Clive and his assistants to work until late in the night, making three hundred copies of the video. One officer and two men were left to watch over them.

The officer was given a list of all television companies. The tapes were to be taken out by him and his two soldiers, and he was to be certain they were dispatched immediately by the quickest method to the companies on the list.

'And what of the director, Clive, and his men?' the officer asked.

'You are to dispatch them also.' Yuskovich drew his forefinger across his throat, then went in search of Major Verber and the rest of his personal force.

They reported that the two French agents, Boris Stepakov and the remaining Briton already waited aboard the last helicopter.

'Nina Bibikova?' he asked.

'She's there with five of the men. We've sedated the prisoners. They'll cause us no problems. A little something in their coffee.'

'You have heard from Baku?'

'It's quiet, sir,' Major Verber reported. 'Cold, but everything is in place. We can be there by

275

morning. The Scamps have been taken on board and we're ready to sail. There's even an icebreaker, just in case.'

'The Scamps *and* the Scapegoats?' Yuskovich snapped.

'All six of them. Everything, comrade General. The crews as well.'

'They are old weapons.' The marshal sounded as though he spoke fondly of children. 'Old, but still very effective. I have husbanded those Scamps and Scapegoats against just such a day as this.'

The Scamp is a Russian mobile launching system, now phased out. Its missile was the Scapegoat with a range of two thousand, five hundred miles. The Scapegoat nuclear warhead yields between one and two megatons. Six of these missiles, therefore, would be equal to almost three times the explosive power of all bombs dropped in World War II.

'Well, if all goes to plan, we'll have them in Iraq within three days. Right under the noses of the Americans, British, French: the entire lot.' Yuskovich nodded brusquely and led the way out to the waiting helicopter.

CHAPTER EIGHTEEN

SCAMPS AND SCAPEGOATS

The great port and city of Baku had been troubled by riots and demonstrations for over a year, like every other town and city in the Soviet Socialist Republic of Azerbaijan. All over the country, in the diverse regions which make up the Union of Soviet Socialist Republics, there had been an uneasiness which sparked unrest, disaffection, and the kind of ugly scenes which even five years ago would have been put down unmercifully.

In Azerbaijan the national feeling had run high. Mobs took to the streets in Baku and a dozen other centres. Everyone, it seemed, wanted to rule their own republic, frame their own laws, distribute their own food and raise their own armies. It was quite unworkable and this was the nightmare foreseen by the senior officers of the Soviet Army, Navy, and Air Force when the theories of restructuring had been set in motion. The nightmare came closer as each day passed.

In Baku the unrest whispered and bubbled through the old town, the port and the modern city. Perhaps because of it, nobody paid much attention to the three large fishing boats anchored offshore, alongside a naval T-43 Class ocean minesweeper, which bore on its side the white numbering 252. Certainly the citizens of Baku had no reason to fear a minesweeper, even though it sported a 45-mm gun both fore and aft.

Many naval craft were to be seen out on the Caspian Sea, but that was normal off Baku. There was a base, said to be used by the Soviet Naval Infantry, further up the coast, near Derbent, and those who plotted revolt and reform had taken it into account. At the moment, however, it looked as though the minesweeper was simply watching over its flock of three fishing boats. This was natural enough. Everyone liked the caviar from the sturgeon which provided almost six per cent of the annual fish harvest, which also included salmon, mullet, carp and a dozen other types of fish culled from the world's largest inland body of water. Fish, oil and the forests had made the Caspian Sea one of the richest natural plundering areas within the borders of the USSR. Though it was slowly being eroded, shrinking, overfished and polluted, the Caspian remained a major resource in the Soviet's beleaguered economy.

Marshal Yevgeny Andreavich Yuskovich thought with pleasure about the fishing boats and the minesweeper lying off Baku. He had dozed on the helicopter which took them to the nearest air support base. There they transferred to the aircraft which originally had been the personal transport of Boris Stepakov, the Antonov An-72 turbo jet with STOL capability.

Once they were airborne, Yuskovich immersed his mind in the dazzling accomplishments which had led him to his present situation. It was only a matter of time before he would reach the goal he had cherished for long years, to be master of the potentially greatest country in the world. He had always coveted power, now the power would be absolute.

He sat well forward on the aircraft. On the other side of the aisle, General Berzin closed his eyes and did not look his way. The marshal had made it clear he wanted to be left alone. Behind him were his personal guards—six Spetsnaz men with three officers, the redoubtable Major Verber, who would be promoted to general once the coup was complete, Verber's cousin, a major of the rocketry forces and the lieutenant he had plucked from the night, the Spetsnaz man, Batovrin, who sported the old style waxed moustache and had about him the look of a thoroughly efficient soldier. Yuskovich prided himself on his eye for the right people. In Batovrin, he was sure the choice was wise.

He thought the young Nina Bibikova had looked mournful as she boarded the aircraft, but that was only to be expected. It had taken guts to accomplish what she had done. Heady days lay before them and Yuskovich was sure he would find a large number of tasks to keep Bibikova busy. She would soon forget.

He smiled to himself. Nina had looked downcast, though not as disconsolate as the prisoners. They certainly had reason. Poor old Bory Stepakov must know by now that his life was not worth a kopek, while the two French agents, Rampart and Adoré, had to be confused and alarmed at the events which were now quite out of their control. A pity about the woman, Adoré, he considered. She looked very beautiful and it was always sad to do away with something that could provide such pleasure. Maybe, he thought, then quickly changed his mind. What had Tolstoy said? 'What a strange illusion it is to suppose that beauty is goodness.'

Then there was the Britisher who had turned out to be from the Mossad. Well, he would do. In fact, it would be a double irony. They would place him near the Scamps with their huge Scapegoat missiles and when the photograph was released after the devastation, he would be identified as a member of the British Secret Intelligence Service. The Mossad would remain silent, but Yuskovich would wager his entire future on denials from London. What a pity about the man Bond. If he had lived, his photograph would be there as well. They might have accomplished a double hit.

Yevgeny Andreavich Yuskovich positively basked in the glow of his own performance. Yes, there had been some luck, the right people at the right time, then the world-shattering events which had only contributed to the overall plan first conceived towards the end of 1989.

*   *   *

From the earliest days of the President's new order, there had been concern and anxiety among the senior members of the Soviet military establishment. Certainly the twin policies of openness and restructuring had an appeal. Indeed, some kind of reorganisation was necessary if only to court the West, both to defuse their anxieties and force them into humanitarian co-operation—in other words, to persuade them to contribute to the Soviet economy. But few, even the President himself, had expected the appalling backlash late in 1989 which, at a stroke, removed the buffer states of the Eastern Bloc, the backlash which tore down the Wall and removed the cushions of land which had been so carefully built up since the end of the Great Patriotic War.

All this had led to the chaos which the Union of Soviet Socialist Republics now faced. In October 1989 a caucus of senior Soviet officers had already chosen their new leader. They had put their personal reputations at risk and sealed with their signatures the secret document naming Yevgeny Yuskovich as the man in whom they trusted. They also swore allegiance to the general whom they privately referred to as marshal. He would have their complete support. Once they had begun the new long march back to the old order, they were committed. Having chosen Yuskovich, they considered it was his duty to set the fuses, bait the traps, overcome political chicanery and return them to the true way, the way of Lenin and the Communist Party. How, then, would he lead the Soviet military on to what they considered the paths of righteousness?

Yuskovich remembered the very moment when he had located the starting point of the journey. How strange it was that a group of idiot idealists had made a choice so close to his own past. The two pieces of information had come to him on the same day and through one person, though he did not comprehend it at the time.

He glanced back to see Nina Bibikova was sleeping. She had been the cornerstone. In September 1989, the telephone had rung in his office, and there was the commander of the GRU's Fifth Directorate telling him that he had a woman member of KGB who wanted to talk with him.

They had met—the GRU Commandant, Yuskovich and Nina Bibikova—in a specially prepared safe house almost within shouting distance of the Kremlin, and it was there that Bibikova unleashed her torrent of information. She was daughter to Misha Bibikov and his English wife, the strangely named Emerald, and she could not disguise her disgust. Her parents were known to have been one of the greatest assets of KGB's First Chief Directorate, two of the most highly placed moles, as Francis Bacon dubbed them back in the seventeenth century, ever run out of Moscow Centre. They had died tragically in a car wreck only nine months before his first meeting with their

281

daughter.

He recalled that almost his first words to the girl had been a speech of condolence, and he would never forget her outburst, nor his own sense of shock, when she revealed to him what she had already told the GRU. Her parents were doubles. They always had been and they were not dead. Indeed she had only recently discovered their true cause and their extraordinary resurrection.

All her life, Nina had believed her parents to have been heroes of the Supreme Soviet. She had even tried to emulate them by following in their footsteps. She had mourned them, like any other good daughter. Then, with unexpected suddenness, they had reappeared in her life. First, a note asking for a clandestine meeting at a charming villa on the Black Sea. She had been taking her vacation at Sochi with her friend, one of the few other women members of KGB.

She went to the villa and the trauma almost destroyed her. There they were, Misha and Emerald, as large as life. They felt, she was told, that she should know the truth, and they foolishly told her the whole story—the tale of how they had duped the Soviet Union for decades and that, at the end, they simply wanted to drop out of sight. Their deaths were staged and being the experienced people they were the Bibikovas had provided themselves with new identities. Now, in the early years of their old age, they were indulging themselves in their other great passion, the theatre. These two old spies were with a small theatre company based in Leningrad. With this troupe they travelled Russia performing the great classics. Never had they intended Nina to know the truth, but the company was playing in the Black Sea resort—*The Cherry Orchard*, as it happened—and they had seen her in a café.

The girl, Yuskovich considered, was amazing. She had kept her true emotions in check, had shown only joy in being reunited with her father and mother, had even told them that she despised the old regime and was hoping for better days under the emerging restructuring of Mother Russia. She had then kept the knowledge to herself, not sharing it with anyone until she went to the GRU.

Why the GRU? he had asked her, and she had replied in a sensible manner. She was with the most secret internal department of the KGB, so secret that her director only answered to the General Secretary and the KGB Chairman. She spoke, of course, of Stepakov's Banda—the counterterrorist department. Her ties to the KGB were tight. She did not desire to damage her own career by turning in her parents. 'You know how KGB can work,' she said. 'Sometimes the paranoia reaches back generations. I could lose my job. My life even.'

The next piece of information had come almost accidentally. He asked if she was satisfied with the kind of work she was doing? It was interesting, but, she told him, at the moment it was also stupid. Idiot's work. Then Nina Bibikova laid out their present target. She had called them a bunch of madmen. 'Personally, I'm convinced there are only a half-dozen of them. They have some wild plan to embarrass the Kremlin establishment.' These people called themselves the *Scales of Justice*—*Chushi Pravosudia* or *Moshch Pravosudia*—and the wild plan had been to focus public attention on the Kremlin's reluctance to show any real sympathy for Russian Jews. She said their argument was that the Kremlin was allowing many Jewish people out, but that was not enough. Never had the Soviet Union held a war crimes trial which accused a single Russian of anti-Semitic behaviour. She had laughed. 'They even seem to have a candidate. A Ukrainian called Josif Vorontsov who, they say, became a member of the Nazi SS and was partly responsible for Babi Yar and other horrors. It's absurd to try and embarrass the Kremlin with something like that.'

But Yuskovich was alerted. His stomach had turned over, the nearest he ever came to fear, when Vorontsov's name was mentioned. In any case, he did not really feel it was such a crazy idea. The Kremlin had been embarrassed by smaller things than a Russian war criminal.

He liked to think it was not just his desire to save his own skin that prompted him to recruit Nina Bibikova there and then. Later, he revealed much more to her, but her reaction was immediate. Yes, she would act as Yuskovich's agent within Stepakov's Banda. Yes, she would do whatever he asked. Later, when she was told the scope of the military coup to put Yuskovich in total power, she had leaped up and down with joy. On that night he remembered vividly how she had come to him without pretence. Her love-making had proved ferocious, and she had done all the things his wife had strictly barred from their bedroom. Some day, Nina could well become the Russian equivalent of what the Americans called the First Lady. Already he had plans to put his wife aside. It was easy for a man with power.

One thing finally led to another. They had

removed the original handful of *Chushi Pravosudia*, and in their place set up a whole network of notional agents, shadows, an entire cult of *Chushi Pravosudia* which did not even exist.

They had run the foolish Professor Vladimir Lyko within Stepakov's Banda. Eventually, when Lyko had served his purpose, his handler, a skilled Spetsnaz officer, was ordered to kill him, and before this they had snatched their old GRU sleeper, Penderek, from New Jersey.

Parallel to the *Scales of Justice* operation, they were also now committed to events outside the Soviet Union which appeared to be reshaping the world. America, with a strong backing from other countries and a United Nations' sanction, was preparing to lock horns with Iraq over the Kuwait question. It was time for the future leader of the Soviet Union to play his trump card.

Throughout the years he had been in command of Rocket Forces, Yuskovich had been a hoarder. While the SALT talks made slow progress, he had often disobeyed orders. In secret bunkers he retained weapons, even mass-destruction weapons. While certain missiles were phased out, Yuskovich made certain some of those he considered to be still viable were hidden and maintained by trusted people who knew how to keep their mouths closed.

The final plan was simple, yet so ingenious, that the future leader of all the Soviet Republics was dizzy at his own brilliance. The whole thing fitted together like a giant jigsaw puzzle which some divine being had placed in front of him to show that *he* was the chosen one.

The pinpricks of *Chushi Pravosudia*'s absurd daring, and their demands, simply goaded

285

everybody into the killing field. By setting up the taped trial, he had been able to bring essential elements to work. Nina's suggestions to Stepakov had brought about the snatching of his dark-horse cousin, Vorontsov. It had also put two French agents into his hands. The whole conception of *his* terrorists, *his Chushi Pravosudia*, had called for people from London to do the taping. Suggestion, via Nina, had prompted Stepakov to call upon the British Secret Intelligence Service to provide the camera crew and, even here, fate had taken a hand and brought him the godsent opportunity to add Nina to the British team.

Then there was the question of actors to play the roles of witnesses. Naturally, it was almost too easy for Nina to ensure that her mother and father came without a second thought to the Red Army Senior Officers' Centre where, with a little pushing here and there, they were allowed to find the secret tunnel all the General Staff had known about for years.

As it turned out, that had been a waste of time. The idea had been to make certain Nina's parents, and the two British agents, were corralled in the tunnel when Yuskovich's loyal Spetsnaz troops arrived to swell the garrison and make sure nobody was left to tell the tale of how the trial had been faked. There was no reason to doubt the impact of the tape when it was aired. The Kremlin *would* be placed in a position of extreme embarrassment and the Russian people would, possibly for the first time, become truly aware of the natural leadership of this ascetic looking, single-minded officer, Yevgeny Yuskovich.

Yet the final, and wonderful, card was yet to be

played. In the past weeks, six of his hoarded missiles, the big Scapegoats with their mobile Scamp launching systems, had been brought out of the bunkers where they had been stored but always ready.

At the Soviet Naval Infantry base near Derbent, skilled mechanics and builders had erected huge containers made from light alloys and lined with thick rubber hulls which incorporated flotation tanks. When the tanks were filled with water, the loaded containers would lie just below sea level. In expertly camouflaged hangars, they had designed and constructed these underwater monsters—three of them—each large enough to hold two Scapegoat missiles complete with their Scamp launching systems which had been fitted with tracks to make them usable in desert conditions.

Only last night, Major Verber had confirmed that the Scamps and Scapegoats were in place. This meant that these weapons of mass nuclear destruction had been taken, with great stealth, to Derbent where they had been loaded into the huge oblong containers. By now, those containers would be in the water, submerged, with their flotation tanks filled, while, on the top of each, the hull and upper structure of a large fishing boat had been affixed with explosive bolts. From sea level, and from the air, it would seem as though three fishing boats rode at anchor, guarded by the minesweeper that would be Yuskovich's command post. The Scamp and Scapegoat crews were housed in the useless hulls of the fishing boats, and in a couple of days, it would be accomplished.

Yuskovich would be there simply as an observer. His presence was, strictly speaking, not required.

But he was a leader, and to his mind, it was essential for him to be there.

As they approached Baku, he thought of the last phase. Certainly the American satellites might well pick up the oddity of the fishing boats, but that did not worry him. It would take them a long time to work out their sinister meaning. He had carefully laid the ground. The Iranians, so recently released from terrible combat against their neighbours, the Iraqis, were naturally in a difficult position. The bulk of the huge coalition force now spread across the deserts of Saudi Arabia was the Iranians' natural enemy. Until any fighting broke out, they were willing, for a consideration, to turn their eyes into the sun and go blind.

In the meantime, Yuskovich had sold the Iraqi leadership three of the old, but very serviceable, huge Mi-10 helicopter cranes—great stilted, ugly looking beasts which could lift vast weights and carry them for many miles and up to 10,000 feet above the ground.

The accommodation reached with Iran meant that the minesweeper could safely tow the three 'fishing boats' close inshore at the small coastal settlement of Bandar Anzali, where they would be blown from the top of the containers by the explosive bolts. The flotation chambers would be emptied and the containers nudged ashore. The Scamps, with their deadly Scapegoat cargoes, could then be hauled up by the Iraqi Mi-10s, taken high over the mountains and deposited in strategic readiness. Each of the flying cranes would make two trips, and it had been calculated that, should all go to plan, the off-loading might be completed in six hours or so.

Before these hideous weapons finally left on their journey, the final piece of the puzzle would be recorded for history. The French and British agents would be photographed assisting and supervising the hand-over of the missiles. They would smile and look pleased with themselves. Yuskovich had constructed the final trap, the last box within the nest of boxes. In the end, if it became necessary, they could prove that the treacherous French and British had been the real suppliers of nuclear weapons to the Iraqi leaders in Baghdad.

The whole thing should not take more than two days, three if there were handling problems. The containers would be towed out to sea again and sunk and the Iraqis would have the weapon for which they had spent so much time scheming and intriguing.

When the United Nations' deadline came on January 15th, if the Americans and their coalition forces did as they were expected, and attacked Iraq, the response would come in seconds. Six Scapegoat nuclear missiles would airburst over Saudi and the massed forces of the coalition would cease to exist. In a moment, in the wink of an eye, the entire enemy army would be turned into so much glass.

'What then can be done about immediate United States ICBM retaliation, the so-called second strike?' General Berzin had asked outside the Red Army Senior Officers' Centre when they had been searching for the agent Bond. Yuskovich had an answer for him, an answer which meant the crippling of the United States for decades to come. They would be decimated, unable to function for a very long time, and during that time Marshal Yevgeny Yuskovich would lead a new and recharged Union of Soviet Socialist Republics into the land promised years ago, early in the century, by Lenin himself.

* * *

The minesweeper with its painted white number 252 on the bows began to move. Beneath the Caspian Sea, the hawsers took up the strain and began to pull the three fishing boats in its wake. It looked like a mother leading her brood out to fresh waters, and in a sense that was exactly what it was.

Night was falling and it was dark on the sea by the time they got fully underway. The minesweeper had only a crew of seven on board, so plenty of room was available for Yuskovich and his entourage. Below in a secure hold aft, usually a storage compartment for depth charges, the four prisoners had been shackled and left with food and wine. The marshal did not want them to seem haggard or strained when it came to taking pictures, though he had been tempted to separate Stepakov from the others and place him in solitary confinement for the entire voyage.

Soon, Yuskovich thought, soon, his part of the operation would be over. He would return to Moscow and oversee the final days before taking absolute control.

* * *

Forty-eight hours later they were within sailing distance of Bandar-e Pahlavi. Yuskovich had been down to see the prisoners whom he described as 'unco-operative, but what can you expect? The sooner we get the symbols of Western decadence out of Russia, the better. I, for one, do not wish to be part of a society which produces Coca-Cola cans that dance when you clap your hands. For a country that's so advanced, America, and, by inference, *all* the Western countries, are backward.'

He ordered dinner early. 'By midnight we shall be starting to surface the first missiles. The signals have already been sent and the Iraqi Mi-10s should be here by two in the morning,' he told them. 'I suggest food and then a little rest. It will be a busy night for everyone.'

They ate large plates of *Shchi*, a spicy cabbage soup, which had been almost their staple diet since setting sail from Baku. After the meal, everyone did as the marshal had suggested, except Lieutenant Batovrin. 'I'll take a turn around the deck, sir, if I have permission.'

Yuskovich nodded. 'Go ahead, Sergei, but not for long. You also need rest.'

Lieutenant Batovrin went out on deck, the hood of his camouflage combat suit turned up against the cold air. He thought it smelled like snow. Someone had once told him that in this region during the winter you could get hailstones the size of tennis balls. People were killed by them every year.

He walked aft and went down the companionway to the compartment where the prisoners were being held.

The soldier on guard duty came to attention. 'At ease,' Batovrin told him. 'I'm going to see if I can talk these people into being more co-operative. If you want a smoke, you have my permission to go up on deck.'

'Thank you, comrade Lieutenant.' The man

smiled and Batovrin nodded. Sliding back the dead bolt, he opened the hatch and stepped inside.

Stepakov lay on his back drinking from a bottle of wine, one hand secured to a metal stanchion. The man they called Pete had his eyes closed and the Frenchman glowered. It looked as though he would like to tear his handcuffs from the rail to which they were attached and rip Batovrin's throat out.

The Frenchwoman, one wrist chained to another stanchion, looked up. She seemed to be taking it very well, for there was hardly a hair out of place. The marshal had said she insisted on being taken to the heads at least six times a day, and once there, spent much time in front of the mirror. Even though she had no cosmetics, they allowed her a comb for these excursions.

Lieutenant Batovrin threw back the hood on his combat suit, touched his waxed moustache, then chuckled.

'Well, what a sorry sight you are,' said James Bond. 'We're all going to have a long night's work, I fear. So rise and shine.'

CHAPTER NINETEEN

IN THE WOODSHED

On the night Boris Stepakov arrived at the Red Army Senior Officers' Centre with General Berzin and the Spetsnaz October Battalion, Bond had managed to make his way to the main lobby without being recognised.

There were two soldiers in the foyer, armed to

292

the nostrils, with grenades hanging dangerously, Rambolike, from the webbing over their combat suits. He thought briefly he should wipe them out but it would be a foolish piece of macho exhibitionism.

Bond looked them in the eye, his gaze running from head to foot, then from foot to head. He walked at speed, like a man with a mission. 'Glavnoye Razvedyvatel'noye Upravleniye,' he barked, telling them he was GRU. The tone of his voice was such that not even these trained Spetsnaz questioned him.

The transition to the cold outside almost winded him. Away in the distance among the trees, there was the occasional shot, hyphenated by a blast of guncotton. There was also a good deal of shouting. Berzin's troops had obviously been instructed to make it all sound warlike. They were doing well. So were the soldiers in steady employment under the tall, hawklike, ascetic Yuskovich. It sounded, he thought, like a good old-fashioned war film.

He had no idea where he could get the privacy he needed. Maybe he would find another entrance, go back inside, do what had to be done, then destroy the micro notebook computer and transmitter. After that, he might even give himself up. There were sillier alternatives, like being shot to pieces by the troops outside.

He stayed close to the wall for a full two minutes, letting his eyes adjust to the darkness. On the perimeter, figures moved under the small spotlights. They looked like battleground scavengers, and in his mind, he saw an ancient field littered with dead. There were horses and knights, bodies everywhere and women bending over the corpses. Men scuttled among the dead, removing weapons or anything of value. He remembered there had been a time in history when the gallant knights had decided to ban the crossbow as being too terrible an instrument of death, and he wondered what those gallant men would think of flamethrowers, machine guns, rockets or the AK-47.

The picture changed. Now he saw the trusted prisoners in the Nazi death camps rooting through the piles of luggage, then pillaging the bodies for the gold in their teeth, the SS men watching, smiling. If men like Yuskovich gained control in Russia, half of the world might sink back into those dark ages. Churchill had said something like that in World War II. Nothing really changed.

His thoughts overcame any cold or fear.

With one hand flat against the wall and the other gripping the pistol, he began to inch his way along, his feet placed flat, carefully, so that he neither slipped nor hit any projecting object. He hugged the wall in this fashion for about twelve feet, then froze as he heard noise from the main doors to his left. A long shaft of light broke through on to the ornamented porchway and a shadow printed itself in the frozen snow.

One voice was raised and angry, 'You fool! Idiot! It was the English. We're looking for him. I could have you shot!' Berzin, enraged, stamped out into the night.

'Gleb, the boy couldn't help it. The Britisher's clever as a snake.' The calm, soft voice of Yuskovich chilled more then Berzin's anger.

From the entrance porch, General Berzin shouted again. 'Sasha! Kolya! The damned English is out here somewhere. You see him? Kolya! Sasha!' It was as though he were calling a pair of gun dogs.

A voice floated back from the perimeter. 'He can't get out, comrade General. We'll pick him off.'

'In the name of Jesus, don't do that!' Yuskovich, even with his voice raised, sounded calm, like a whisper on the wind. 'We want him alive. It's essential.'

Why? Bond wondered, pressing himself harder against the wall, as if trying to become part of the building's fabric.

'We'll bring him back alive, comrade General. Don't concern yourself. There's no way he can get out. The place is sealed up like a virgin.'

Someone closer laughed.

'If they lose him, I'll have them all flogged. It was a hard day for Russia when they did away with the knout.'

Bond winced at Berzin's barbarity. The knout was the ultimate in flogging instruments, worse even than the old British cat-o'-nine-tails. He had seen one in some Scandinavian museum, Oslo he thought, a lash of leather thongs, twisted with sharp pieces of wire. For a second, his mind was filled with streaming blood.

'Calm yourself, Gleb. It will be. It will all happen.' Yuskovich began to talk, as though telling a story to a child who could not sleep. Bond heard it all—the Scamps and the Scapegoats, the submerged containers and the minesweeper, the arrangements in Baku and in Iran. The pick-up point, the Mi-10s and the final horror if the coalition forces so much as dropped one bomb within the Iraqi border. As he listened, he thought his bones would make icicles of his blood. He thought of a great wasteland with a

295

hurricane sweeping over it, and he knew the picture was of the world.

Then Berzin, petulant, asked, 'What, though, can be done about immediate United States ICBM retaliation? The so-called second strike?'

Yuskovich laughed in the darkness, as though Berzin had told him a joke. 'I shouldn't worry your head about that. The moment the Scapegoats go, we put another spoke in their wheels. Yes, of course, the timing could go wrong. Iraq might well have to absorb a nuclear strike. It might take us twenty-four hours, everything depends on the timing of their attack, if it comes. But I promise you, Gleb old friend, unless they cripple Europe and all the Russias in that time, Washington will be no more.' And he told the rest of it, with Bond stuck to the wall and the searching soldiers everywhere out in the darkness.

The two officers continued to talk for another five minutes, then, impatient, Yuskovich said that with or without Bond they would have to continue the taping. 'Tomorrow we must leave. We'll have to get on. I want Vorontsov's confession in the can and this whole project wrapped up tonight. I'll tell the man Clive, the silent one.' And the shaft of light cut out over the snow again.

Bond waited in the darkness, his mind obsessed with death. Once more he started to move, still nestling his back hard against the wall. If he had to kill or die out here in the bleakness, he would do everything possible to get some message through.

Towards the far end, he could now see the shape of a wall and roof, low, the roof sloping at an acute angle, the whole projecting from the building itself like an outhouse or bunker.

296

It took him nearly five minutes to reach the shape—a wooden wall slightly higher than himself where it met the main building, the slope dropping off sharply so that it would barely reach his neck at the outer limit.

It was fashioned from logs, and there was a door set into the wall at the highest end near where he stood. He tried the door and it gave slightly. Then he realised it was not locked but frozen into place. He put his shoulder against it and pushed, putting all his weight behind the shove. It gave a loud creak and he stood still, his heart thudding in his ears, concerned that the noise had carried to the searchers who seemed to be sweeping the outer edges of the perimeter. Eventually they would move inwards and he would be ringed and pegged down by them. Once more the desolate wind-swept wasteland came into his mind, and he pushed again. This time the door swung inwards.

It was a wood storage bunker. He could smell the bark and also tar, used to make the store watertight. Under the leather patch on his left shoulder he carried a small penlight. Unzipping the parka, he found the stitching and ripped through it, bringing out the tiny torch, holding it between his gloved thumb and first finger.

One fast sweep of the strong beam and it was clear that the woodshed had been sealed. No light could penetrate the tarpaulins which lined the interior. Softly, he closed the door and squatted on the floor, his back to the geometrically piled logs which took up about a third of the space.

He drew off his gloves and located the notebook computer and the transmitter. Once he had done the job and offered a prayer to whatever saint

297

guided communications, he would have no more use for them.

He held the penlight in his teeth, the tips of his fingers rapidly typing the signal, checking that the tape turned as he provided the input. He was totally absorbed in getting the bare facts into the message, though the conscious stream at the back of his mind showed pictures of microchips and the incredible miniaturisation which was part of today's word magic. They could make small computers like this with large memories and transmitters which would hurl messages on shortwave frequencies for miles, yet man could still try to bend other men to ruthless wills and destroy life in bizarre ways. It was as though the world, having gained so much, retained a lemminglike desire for self-immolation. As he completed the task, extracted the little tape, rewound it and slid it into the transmitter, his mind saw the brain of man and within it a small kernel of diseased cells, the seat of mankind's death wish.

Bond sat for a moment, waiting, deciding what else he might need, both to defend himself and render his own body useless to men like Yevgeny Yuskovich or Gleb Berzin. He was going to leave nothing to chance. The leather patches on shoulders, elbows and down half the back of the denim jacket contained a small hoard of items. He slid his arms from the parka, shivering as he took off the jacket and began to remove each of the items. Still holding the penlight in his teeth he ripped away at the stitching and thrust his fingers into the skilfully moulded hiding places, bringing out each new treasure and placing it on the floor. The collection grew and he put on the jacket again before moving the small items close to the far edge of the woodpile, slipping each addition between spaces in the logs where they could lie hidden for some time.

At last he put the parka on again and chose one thin, narrow plastic box. It contained three miniature hypos, one of which he took out and held gingerly. The pistol went into the zippered pocket, angled across the front of the parka, the notebook computer slid into the right front pocket. He switched off the penlight and felt his way towards the door, transmitter in his right hand, the hypo in his left.

If the worst happened, the juice inside the syringe would knock him cold for the best part of a day. When he had originally gone over the matter, the doctor said the effect would be instantaneous. 'One second you're there, the next you've gone. Out like a short course in death. You'll feel no pain.'

If he did inject himself, nobody would even be able to bring him to interrogation for twenty-four hours. In the scheme of things, it was probably not long enough, but sufficient unto the day. Slowly he pulled back the door.

They were still searching. His eyes, retaining the ghost burn of the penlight, swept the area from far left, at nine o'clock, and as they came to noon, he held his breath. Some ten feet from the edge of the woodshed a figure stood, his back towards Bond. The man turned slightly and there was the glow of a cigarette as he sucked smoke into his lungs. Holding his breath, Bond stretched out his arm and pressed the 'Send' button on the transmitter.

The shadow moved again, a dark patch against the night, the edges blurred by what small light filtered in from the perimeter fence. He appeared to be wearing the coverall combat suit with light webbing. Bond was sure the pistol was holstered on his right hip.

Very gently he put the transmitter on the ground and transferred the hypo from left hand to right.

The man called out, a clear voice, but laced with an officer's authority. 'Keep sweeping the far right. We should really have the floods on, but the marshal says no. Keep sweeping. We must eventually find him.'

By the time the last words of the sentence had left his lips, Bond was behind him. The officer was almost exactly his own height and build and the outrageousness of the plan had not yet clearly formed in his mind.

The cap came off the hypo without a sound, though the man must have smelled, or sensed him. At the final moment he began to turn, his right hand going for the holster, but it was too late. As he turned, the needle penetrated his neck and Bond squeezed the plunger. A heavy dose of Ketamine flowed freely into the man's carotid artery. He went down without a sound. Bond thought he should tell the doctor that it worked, when he got back. If he got back.

He caught the Russian officer under the armpits and slowly heaved the dead weight back towards the woodshed door.

Once he had him inside, Bond went out again and retrieved the transmitter. What he was about to do revolted him, but he had already weighed the risks. There were a number of officers and men scattered around. The October Battalion would be completely familiar with one another, but the troops who had already been guarding the Red Army Senior Officers' Centre would probably not be known to the new arrivals. It might just work and give him time, even a few hours, and there were still two more hypos in the container.

As the possibilities raced through his head, Bond set about destroying the transmitter and micro. The sooner he scattered the pieces the better it would be. When it was done, he gathered the remains into a small pile. Then he set about undressing the unconscious man. He was a Spetsnaz lieutenant with badges of rank sewn on to the breasts of his combat suit. Bond thought it was like undressing a drunk. The body flopped around, but the limbs were pliable and the job was done more quickly than he imagined.

He piled the officer's clothing and equipment carefully in the far corner, then began to undress himself. The whole business of exchanging clothes took around twenty minutes, including the transfer of the already hidden items Bond had removed from his denim jacket. He might need some of them now—the pick-locks, the three long tubes of RDX-based C-4 explosive, the most powerful in the world unless you got into things nuclear, the remaining two hypos, a small pillbox containing detonators, the coil of fuse wire—two types, the slow burning and the electronic—together with other useful pieces of hardware. He distributed them around his body. The P6 pistol and the magazines were jammed into the pockets of the parka. He had no use for them now, for the young lieutenant carried one of the latest PRI 5.45mm automatics with a fitted silencer, five spare magazines, a long killing knife and four high-explosive magnetic grenades. These last were dual-types which Bond had never seen before, but they were similar in appearance to the larger M560 'High Frag' grenades used by the Americans. The only difference seemed to be the magnetisation. He thought that if you stuck one of these onto heavy armour, it would blow a small hole through which its shrapnel would be sucked to spread itself around among the occupants, or it could be used as a simple anti-personnel grenade in the normal manner.

He clipped on the light webbing equipment, securing the grenades and spare magazine in the 'Alice' pouches built into the combat suit. He had taken off the officer's dog tags and deciphered them under the penlight. The poor fellow was called Sergei Yakovlevich Batovrin. If he got out of this, Bond had an idea that he might even write to the man's family. No, he stopped the thought. On the battlefield there is nothing that so limits a soldier as a streak of kindness. Military men put their lives squarely on the gaming tables. If it had been a straight confrontation, Bond would not have hesitated.

As well as the hood on his combat suit, the lieutenant had worn a round fur hat with earflaps. The red star and his rank were clipped to the front. Bond finally put the hat on and then turned to the matter which had concerned him most from the moment his mind had decided on this foolhardy action.

Field men dislike disguises and Bond was no different from his colleagues. The art of make-up and disguise in tradecraft went out with the eccentric Baden-Powell. If disguise was necessary then it was best done with a change of clothing, a pair of spectacles, a different walk, a limp, a mannerism or the reversible raincoat. Yet they had insisted on the small flat tin with the contact lenses to change eye colour and the set of false hair—three moustaches of different shapes and sizes, cunningly woven from the agent's natural hair and attached to a substance which, when pressed against skin, bonded the hair into place so tightly and seamlessly that you genuinely had to shave the hair from your lip and then apply a special solvent to remove any traces.

He did not like it, but it was necessary. There was no way he could walk back into the building without some form of disguise. The lid of the tin was made out of unbreakable mirror so he used the penlight and carefully rolled the moustache into place. He had chosen the flamboyant one with the long waxed ends for two reasons. If he had to use false facial hair then it was better to go over the top. Also, he had seen two Spetsnaz soldiers sporting moustaches which would have won prizes against those grown by fighter pilots in World War II.

Now, fully equipped, he went outside again, checking the distant shadows of the still searching men. He cast away the fragments of the transmitter and the micro, then went back to drag Lieutenant Batovrin on his last journey into the night.

The PRI 5.45mm automatic only made a faint popping sound, not commensurate with the destructive force of its bullets. Three tore great holes in the man's chest. Blood whipped out and his body twitched once. Two more destroyed the face.

He walked, in plain sight now, back towards the entrance porch. The sight of the body had shocked him more than anything else he had seen in the many dangerous and death-ridden lives he had lived.

Looking at Batovrin had been like gazing at his own murdered body.

*   *   *

They had almost finished packing away the equipment. Nigsy only had to bring in the encryption receiver, set to Bond's frequency. He had left it until last, just in case. Already the Lapp and Pansy Wright were astride the two Yamaha snow-scooters.

Nigsy was just reaching forward to unhook the receiver from the battery pack when he saw the needles flick and the tape whine.

'Come on, Nigs! For heaven's sake hurry up!' Pansy shouted from the scooter.

Meadows detached the battery and began to pack the equipment into one of the panniers. He took the tape out and slipped it into the pocket of his warm snowsuit. They would get a playback and decrypt in the Helsinki Embassy.

In the end, because of the weather and disruption to aircraft timetables, it was twenty-four hours before he reached the embassy.

There were further delays before the signal was passed on to the London office. After that it took M almost twenty-four hours to get hold of the Prime Minister who in turn had a little trouble raising the President of the USSR.

They spoke at length on the direct hotline between Downing Street and the Kremlin, just as the minesweeper was pulling its brood towards the

Iranian coast.

'For the want of a horse,' M growled. He thought they were too late and was already preparing to speak with his opposite number in Langley, Virginia.

CHAPTER TWENTY

THE SWIMMING CHAMPION

As he worked on their handcuffs with the pick-locks, Bond told them the score, the global danger and the odds. He did not mince matters. They were outnumbered, and the cargoes had almost reached their destination. Between these whispered briefings he raised his voice, talking loudly in Russian, saying that they would, with the exception of Boris Stepakov, be expected to do as they were told.

'The marshal says you are not co-operative, that you are being like stubborn children,' he almost shouted, turning his face towards the door.

Stephanie rubbed her wrist, massaging the circulation back. 'Please, James, don't shout. You're hurting my head.' She gave a sad little smile. 'You say ...' she began. Then Stepakov completed the question.

'You say these containers lie below the waterline?'

He told them, yes, and then described the clever way the hulls of fishing boats had been bolted above. 'They're having a pretty rough ride. The things are bobbing like corks in a bottle.'

305

'But if they were holed?' Stephanie glared at Stepakov as though he had behaved very badly at the dinner table.

Boris took no notice. 'And these things are attached to the minesweeper, this ship, by hawsers?'

Bond nodded, saying they were towing them in line astern.

Rampart asked what firepower was available on the ship.

'Providing we got lucky and took over?' Bond shrugged. He was working on Pete Natkowitz's manacles.

'But of course.'

'They've got a couple of 45-mms fore and aft in turrets. Also two 25-mms on each side. Midships, port and starboard. Anti-aircraft stuff.'

'Then, technically, we could blow them out of the water with the 45s.' Natkowitz nodded his thanks as his wrist came clear.

Bond reached inside the combat suit and took out one of the magnetic grenades. 'This would be better. In fact, I believe if we managed to get off in one of the inflatables—I've counted four—we might be able to rig up some way of timing these things. I let Yuskovich go on talking the other night. The containers are vulnerable, being made of a light alloy. The sides are flotation chambers, with some simple mechanism for blowing out the water when they get them inshore.' He hefted the grenade. 'Put this on the side of the last in the line and we'll probably upset the whole damned lot. The cargo's bloody heavy. When one goes they might all go. Down among the dead men.'

'Ah, yes,' Boris assumed a clown's look of

306

innocence. 'The cribbage effect.'

'Domino,' Stephanie sharply corrected.

Stepakov grinned and asked if he might see one of the grenades. Bond brought them all out and placed them on the deck.

'Yes, these have a little delay mechanism at the base, so.' He turned over one of the bombs, pointing to a knurled screw. 'You can set them for up to five minutes, at one minute increments. No more. No less.'

There was the sound of a boot scraping against the metal deck outside. Rampart was immediately on his feet, making for the side of the hatch. Bond motioned to him, indicating that he would go out.

It was the soldier, back on duty after his smoke. 'Are they suitably chastened, comrade Lieutenant?' He smiled to let him know he had heard what Bond had shouted loudly for his benefit.

'Not really. I know what I'd like to do with them.'

'Maybe you'll get the chance, sir.'

'Oh, the fun will go to the big boils ...' He stopped at the sound of another pair of boots coming down the companionway.

'My duty's up,' the soldier sighed, then greeted his replacement who saluted Bond.

'All well?' the new man asked.

'They have to be put in a better mood.' The guard winked at his comrade. 'The lieutenant, here, has been telling them bedtime stories about dragons with big boils.'

They both laughed.

'I'm coming back to give them more.' Bond looked at the new man. 'Expect me in a few minutes.' He nodded and went up the

307

companionway, stopping once he was out on the open deck, checking he could not be seen. Nobody else was about and the sentry just relieved began to come up the companionway, slowly as though tired, like soldiers the world over at the end of a boring guard duty.

Bond took him out with the long killing knife, similar in size and weight to the Sykes-Fairbairn he was used to. The point went into the man's neck as though it were penetrating butter. He did not even have time to shout. There was a great deal of blood.

When he had dragged the body behind the aft gun turret, Bond went down the companionway again. He smiled cheerily as the sentry came to attention, so the man did not even see the knife coming.

'There are weapons out there,' he told Rampart once he was through the hatchway. 'Pete, there's a body littering up the deck behind the aft turret. Be a good fellow and move it. Then pass out the goodies. I'm going on a recce. Just to see where everyone's got to. Then we'll have a go at launching one of the inflatables. It's dark enough. We might just be able to deal with the cargo. It's worth a try.'

Back on the mess deck which Yuskovich had commandeered for his staff, Verber was playing chess with his cousin.

'Couldn't sleep?' Bond asked, and Verber shook his head.

His cousin said the major never slept when there was about to be action.

'We won't get any action,' Bond said. 'We only have to watch them unload the weapons. Nobody's going to start shooting.'

Berzin's voice came from behind him, 'Not

308

unless you try something, Englishman.'

Bond spun around.

'Ah,' Berzin stood in the doorway, 'So it *is* the Englishman. I was concerned. The moustache fooled me.'

'What're you talking about?' Bond looked him straight in the eye. 'Comrade General, you are accusing me of something? I don't understand.' He spoke as though the Russian had made some disgusting slander concerning his mother.

Berzin locked eyes with him, his slim, leathery face held no expression. It was as though he had been bled of all sympathy, humanity and compassion. 'I just cannot place you, Batovrin. You worry me. Yes, I even think you might possibly be the dead Englishman. You believe in ghosts?'

'No, General Berzin. The only kind of spooks I understand are KGB and GRU.'

'Mmmmm.' Berzin's face did not alter and his eyes reflected not an ounce of feeling. 'I have seen most of the current Spetsnaz officers through the training school, some of them even at the airborne school at Ryazan. I knew a Batovrin. Younger than you, and he had no moustache. It's worried me since the marshal put you on to his staff. I know your name, but . . .'

Bond smiled. 'You're thinking of my young brother, Grigori, comrade General. I'm Sergei.' As he spoke, he edged towards the door. Out of the corner of his eye, he saw Verber and his cousin had stopped playing chess. They lounged back in their chairs, pretending to be mildly interested, but Bond could see the tautness of their muscles as they prepared to spring at a second's notice. There was a new tension in the air. He could almost smell it, as an animal smells fear on a human.

'Really, Batovrin? If it is so, you look nothing like your brother.'

'He takes after my father's side of the family.'

'Really?' Berzin repeated.

Bond laughed, 'Yes, really, comrade General.'

The strap was still in place on Berzin's holster, but now, at last, the eyes flickered. He was more certain of his ground. In a moment he would call Bond's bluff again; after that it would not take long. Rampart and Pete would be armed by now, but the odds were with Yuskovich's people.

'So, your brother takes after my very good friend Colonel General Petros Batovrin. And you favour my equally good friend, the Colonel General's wife, Anna Batovrin. Strange, they never mentioned that there was an elder son. And I was at the Frunze with Petros Batovrin.'

Bond turned sideways, hands on his hips, his right palm flat. He could reach the pistol quickly if necessary, but with three of them, there was little chance that he would get off the mess deck alive. 'Where is the comrade Marshal, sir? I think he should be here. I am a true and loyal member ...' It sounded lame, like words put into the mouth of an actor in some bad film. But he did not have to complete the sentence.

'Where do you think he is, Englishman? He's with his little whore. The lovely Nina. Or didn't you know, like every Spetsnaz officer, that the marshal and Nina were...'

Bond hardly heard the three pops. He smelled the cordite before the noise registered in his ears. Berzin's eyes widened and his arms went up, hands scrabbling for his back before he crumpled.

310

Bond was aware of Verber and his cousin moving. His hand went down to his own holstered pistol, but the adjutant and his doomed relative had simply been slung back against their chairs by the force of the bullets.

'Thought you might need help.' Natkowitz stood in the doorway. He did not look at all like a gentleman farmer now. He seemed at last to have lost the look of innocence and the foolish smile had disappeared. 'Damned good these PRIs,' he said. 'I think we should move. Bory was getting difficult. He wanted to be a hero.'

'Oh, Christ.' Bond was through the door, not even bothering about noise any more. If it came to a fire fight, they would have to take their chances. He followed Natkowitz along the deck, knowing they would have to use the gun in the aft turret. If they could hold off Yuskovich's men for long enough, they might just be able to blow the infernal floating cargoes out of the water.

When they got down to the hold, Rampart was on the deck nursing his neck, and Stephanie looked on the point of screaming.

'What the hell . . . ?' Bond began.

'Bory,' she said, looking wild. 'He's trying to swim it. Said it was *his* country and *his* duty. Said he was in the Dynamo Sports Club!'

Rampart cursed. For the first time since they had met, Bond thought he even looked half-human. 'He caught me by surprise. I'm sorry. The imbecile.' The Frenchman shook his head and squeezed his eyes.

'He'll never last in that water.' Bond started for the door. He knew the Dynamo Sports Club was KGB's crack field and swimming team.

311

'He just might.' Stephanie was helping Rampart to his feet. 'He said he'd been in KGB's swimming team, and he'd done the course of cold water survival. He said he was 1988 swimming champion. He went on about very cold water slowing the heart rate, and if you stuck with it, you could ward off hypothermia for a long...'

The explosion was followed by a lurch. The ship's deck seemed to move, and the klaxons began to howl almost immediately.

He heard Natkowitz revert briefly to his gentleman farmer mode, saying, 'That's torn it,' and by the time he reached the deck there were two searchlights trained on the water behind the ship. As he looked aft, Bond saw the rearmost fishing boat overturned in the sea with the container on its side, the whole contraption wallowing and starting to sink.

My god, he's done it, he thought. Then he felt the jerk and pull again, and realised his earlier prediction had been sound. The great weight of the rearmost pair of Scamps and Scapegoats was starting to pull at the next container. Already the bows of the second makeshift fishing boat were out of the water, disclosing the square bulk of the huge metal box beneath. If it continued, the total weight would draw the last container and then the minesweeper, down with it.

For a brief and stupid moment, Bond considered using some of the RDX he had brought from the cache in his denim jacket. It would cut through the hawser like a child breaking a thread of cotton. Then he realised that what had happened would be best in the end. Let the Scamps and Scapegoats act as anchors to drag the whole diabolical crew to the

312

bottom of the sea. It was almost poetic.

He turned to Natkowitz. 'There are a couple of inflatables on each side,' he shouted. 'I'm going to deal with the ones here. You rip up the pair on the port side.'

'Never mind,' Rampart was already running. 'I have a knife.'

As Bond reached the forward of the two inflatables, the middle container exploded. A yellow flash, outlined in orange, as the oblong box with its boat hull on top tilted over, turning turtle and already starting to slide into the dark water.

There was confusion on the deck and shouts coming from among both crew and Yuskovich's remaining troops as he ripped the thick rubber of one inflatable and turned his attention to the other. But Stephanie and Pete Natkowitz had it half over the side. He saw Pete tug at the lanyard and the black shape floated down, hissing as it filled with air.

Natkowitz grabbed Stephanie by the shoulders and hauled her up over the rail. 'Jump! Get down there!' he shouted at her, and she disappeared with a little squeal of fear. Natkowitz followed her a second later, and Bond, poised for the drop towards the inflatable, suddenly saw with horror that the searchlights from the bridge had both centred on one small circle of ocean.

There, in the middle of the silver puddle, Boris Stepakov swam with long, lazy strokes towards the nearest fishing boat, its submerged cargo container already coming out of the water as the other sinking Scamps and Scapegoats dragged at it.

It seemed as though the weapons were firing from a long way off and a lazy stream of tracer floated towards the little figure who was now so close to his final target. The water boiled around him and his body was lifted half out of the sea by the impact. But, in his last seconds, Stepakov continued to go through the motions of swimming and his right hand came up in a great arc, his left rising to meet it, then pulling away with the grenade's pin.

The next burst of fire threw him against the metal side of the container, and at that moment the third grenade exploded, tearing a long gash in the metal. Stepakov disappeared in the smoke, water and spray.

As Bond fell towards the water, he thought sadly that the man was certainly a swimming champion now. The icy flow rushed up to meet him, then Pete Natkowitz's hands were around his shoulders, hauling him into the boat. At the rear, Stephanie wrestled with the motor, and Natkowitz's face was turned upwards, his mouth open, shouting to Henri Rampart poised on the rail above.

The searchlights fluttered down, along the rail, chased by a clatter of bullets which ripped into the French major, knocking him along for six or seven feet before throwing him sideways. As he hit the water, the noise of helicopter engines seemed suddenly to blast from the sky. It was like the unexpected arrival of a violent thunderstorm on a clear day.

Stephanie had the inflatable's motor going, and they began slowly to draw away from the minesweeper's side. Other searchlights probed the ship now and Bond at first thought it must be the Iraqi Mi-10s arriving early.

Then he heard the Russian voice through a loud hailer from somewhere above. 'Heave to,

Two-Fifty-Two. Cease firing and we will take you off.' The voice repeated its message three times, but all it got for its pains was a stuttering snarl of fire from the starboard 25s.

Bond heard Pete yelling to Stephanie, telling her to open the throttles, and he felt the craft move and buck in the water. They were about sixty yards away when another helicopter came in from for'ard, hurling death from a pair of rocket launchers. The inflatable keeled over to one side, swung and bobbed back as the rockets hit and the ship seemed to burst like a great rose, a centrepiece of scarlet leaping from amidships. As it bloomed in vivid crimson, reds and then pink at the extremities, Bond could have sworn he saw the long shape of Marshal Yuskovich entwined with Nina Bibikova hurtling upwards in the very centre of the fire, as though new-born from chaos.

They felt the hot blast, and a rain of metal, wood and spray fell all around them. Then the first chopper was heading back, hovering over them, the detached Russian voice coming through the loud hailer. 'Is that the English? Good, is it the English and French?'

They waved weakly, not knowing what to expect. Then the voice called, 'Is Captain Bond with you? He has an important meeting in Moscow.'

CHAPTER TWENTY-ONE

MINSK FIVE

They were gathered in M's office. London was almost as cold as it had been in Russia. It was the afternoon of January 17th. Twenty-four hours earlier, the coalition forces, led by the United States, had launched their aerial bombardment on Iraq. They called it Desert Storm. Tornadoes, Harriers, F-15s, F-16s, A-6s, Wild Weasels, and Tomahawk Cruise missiles had blasted at targets throughout the country. There was no sense of glee or delight, simply the old numbness that comes when nations are forced to take action against another nation. Nobody would relish death on the new, untested, electronic battlefield.

Bond had returned after a longer than expected stay in Moscow, and now, with Bill Tanner operating the tapes, he had gone through a lengthy pre-debriefing with his old Chief. Throughout the afternoon, M had sat, pipe clamped between his teeth, listening, with some relief, to the minutiae of the operation. They had covered almost everything, including the last things—from the seizing of the trial videos, the finding of the four graves near the second dacha, the luckless Guy, George and Helen, plus the war criminal Vorontsov, to Boris Stepakov's posthumously awarded Hero of the Soviet Union.

'So you'll be getting Michael Brooks and Emerald back?' Bond made it sound half-question, half-statement.

316

M made a gesture which indicated it could go either way. Eventually he said, 'The idea of passing all those actors and people off as the true heart of *Chushi Pravosudia* might have worked.'

'It certainly would, had Yuskovich been successful. Who'd have known the difference, sir? They've hidden politicals for years, some without trial, even done away with them.'

'Back in the dark ages, yes.' M frowned.

'But you're getting Michael and Emerald back, sir?' This time it *was* a question. 'The Soviet President seemed...'

'Let's say we're negotiating. The Soviet President's certainly had the whole lot released. We're hopeful. Let's leave it at that.'

'Then I can go, sir?'

'Just one more thing, 007...'

'Yes?'

'What did Yuskovich have tucked away at the air base called Minsk Five?'

'Minsk Five, sir?'

'Come on, James. Your final signal was detailed enough. Caspian Sea, the cargo, how it was being carried, everything until you got to the bit about Minsk Five. Then you went vague on me. "Inform soonest and most urgent President USSR to search Minsk Five."'

'You know what Minsk Five is, sir?' An old-time drill sergeant would have called it dumb insolence.

M sighed. 'James, my dear boy, I'll read it after the full debriefing, so you might as well tell me now. I know it's a military air base.'

'It *has* been a long day, sir.'

'You should have thought of that before you asked for extra time in Moscow. I gather you then

317

went on to Paris. How *is* Mlle Adoré?'

Bond did not meet his eye. 'She needed a little comforting, sir. Henri Rampart was an old and valued friend.'

'I bet he was. Minsk Five, 007.'

This time Bond looked genuinely concerned. Since he had first heard it, outside the Red Army Senior Officers' Centre on the dark and cold night when he had 'killed' himself, Bond had tried not to think about the ramifications of Minsk Five. He sucked in air. 'It was Yuskovich's final gambit, sir. I could only put it to the Soviet President through you.'

'Well?'

'I know he had the place pretty well dry-cleaned, the President, I mean . . .'

'What was there to find?' M put on his patient voice.

'Possibly a Boeing 747, sir.'

'A special 747?'

'Pretty special. It was in British Airways livery. According to the late Yevgeny Yuskovich, they had also made modifications. Extra fuel tanks and a bomb bay containing a very high-yield nuclear device.'

'Go on.'

'This is what I heard, sir. The Soviet President did not confide in me. According to Yuskovich . . . What he said to Berzin, anyway . . . it sounds ludicrous, sir, but in this day and age nothing is too ludicrous. From what I heard, the intention was that, on the day after a strike was launched against Iraq, and following Iraq's response with the Scapegoats, they were going to decimate Washington.'

318

'How?'

'A mid-Atlantic intercept by fighters, refuelled en route, of course. Our usual BA flight to Washington. To start with, the BA flight would have all radio and radar jammed and the counterfeit 747 would transmit on their frequency, use their squalk numbers. The BA aircraft would then be blown out of the sky at long range. They would never see the fighters that did it. Their 747 would then become the BA flight. It could be done, sir. The aircraft would be off air for a couple of seconds, then back on again.'

M frowned. 'Yes, of course it could be done. The general public are getting their first taste of what can be done even as we speak.'

'When the flight came under Dulles control, it would go way off course. It would be all over before the Dulles ATC realised what was happening.'

'Right over the centre of Washington?' M sucked his pipe, and Bill Tanner drew in his breath.

'Washington, large chunks of Maryland and Virginia and other adjacent areas. I should imagine the bulk of America's politicians, generals, you name it, would have gone.'

'And you really believe he was going to have this done?'

'I have no reason to disbelieve it, sir.'

'The mad, mad ...' M stopped, shaking his head.

'No, sir, I don't think Yuskovich was mad.'

M rose and went over to the window. Below, the Park was almost empty. There was a long silence before he spoke. 'No, I suppose not. The man had a faith. He had served a system in which he had absolute belief. He saw it slipping away and he

319

already had great power. You're right, and I can only presume there're thousands like him. Believers. It doesn't simply disappear overnight. There most likely will be others. It has *not* gone away.'

Bond did not reply. He pulled a slim square jeweller's box from his pocket and laid it on the desk to which M had now returned.

'I think you should lock this away, sir. The Soviet President gave it to me. The very fact that it's still presented to people for services rendered should tell us something.'

M did not seem to have heard him. 'I'm certain the Soviets want to play by different rules, but it *is* hard to break the mould.' The old spy nodded to himself, then looked at the box.

'With permission, sir, I'd like to leave.' Bond stood up.

M nodded, smiled absently, and said a simple, 'Thank you, James. Drop in tomorrow, would you?'

Bond nodded, returning the smile.

When the door closed, M reached for the box and opened it. There lying on a bed of silk was an oval medal attached to a red ribbon bordered by thin white stripes. In the centre, surrounded by a gilt frame of grain, Lenin's face stared off to the left, moulded in platinum. The red enamel border was punctuated by the hammer and sickle, the red star, and the name ПЕНИН in Russian script. M had never seen one before, except in photographs, and then usually pinned to the breast of celebrated Soviets, but he recognised it immediately. One of the highest decorations the Soviets could award—the Order of Lenin.